HOT, HOT, HOT

Bunny steeled herself. Focus. *Focus.* "I need this job, Mr. McNulty. I'm a quick learner and I won't disappoint you. If there was someone who could point me in the right direction with the . . . event planning, I'm sure I could master the necessary skills."

Absolutely brilliant. Even she believed what she'd said.

Bunny watched as he flipped through her portfolio, his head bent low, expression serious and intent.

"Perhaps you'd like to review my references? There's a printed list in the pocket of the portfolio." She pointed toward the back of the leather case. McNulty slowly raised his dark eyes to meet hers.

Her heart gave a jolt. Hot, sultry fire burned in the man's gaze, yet he seemed totally unaware of its impact. A woman could lose herself in the depths of those eyes. And how.

BOOK YOUR PLACE ON OUR WEBSITE AND MAKE THE READING CONNECTION!

We've created a customized website just for our very special readers, where you can get the inside scoop on everything that's going on with Zebra, Pinnacle and Kensington books.

When you come online, you'll have the exciting opportunity to:

- View covers of upcoming books
- Read sample chapters
- Learn about our future publishing schedule (listed by publication month *and author*)
- Find out when your favorite authors will be visiting a city near you
- Search for and order backlist books from our online catalog
- Check out author bios and background information
- Send e-mail to your favorite authors
- Meet the Kensington staff online
- Join us in weekly chats with authors, readers and other guests
- Get writing guidelines
- AND MUCH MORE!

Visit our website at
http://www.kensingtonbooks.com

Get Bunny Love

Kathleen Long

ZEBRA BOOKS
Kensington Publishing Corp.
www.kensingtonbooks.com

ZEBRA BOOKS are published by

Kensington Publishing Corp.
850 Third Avenue
New York, NY 10022

All Kensington titles, imprints and distributed lines are available at special quantity discounts for bulk purchases for sales
promotion, premiums, fund-raising, educational or institu-
tional use.

Special book excerpts or customized printings can also be created to fit specific needs. For details, write or phone the office
of the Kensington Special Sales Manager: Kensington Publishing Corp., 850 Third Avenue, New York, NY 10022. Attn.
Special Sales Department. Phone: 1-800-221-2647.

First Printing: March 2005
10 9 8 7 6 5 4 3 2 1

Printed in the United States of America

For Dan,
the yin to my yang,
with all of my love.

For Emily Bernadette,
who taught me that nothing is impossible
if only we believe.

And last but not least, for Daddy,
who taught me to laugh and love.
This one's for you. I miss you.

Chapter 1

Nate McNulty slammed the phone onto the receiver, wondering exactly what constituted justifiable homicide.

Of all the controlling stunts his aunt had pulled, her latest took the cake. He squeezed his eyes shut, trying to calm the rapid pulse thrumming through his veins. He'd run this firm just fine since his uncle's death and intended to continue—whether Aunt Martha liked it or not. He shoved both hands through his hair and let out an exasperated breath.

How about temporary insanity? That was a popular plea these days, wasn't it?

Bert Parks, McNulty Events' vice president, stood in the doorway, lips twitching into a smirk. "New hairdo?"

Nate patted down his unruly locks, frowning. "I'm going to kill her."

"Who now?" Bert sank into the chair opposite Nate's desk.

"My darling aunt."

"Trouble in trust fund paradise?"

Frustration simmered in Nate's gut. "Very funny." He met Bert's pale gaze. "She wants to sell."

"Us?"

Nate nodded. "Says it's too much stress."

"Which part? Spending the money we earn or crashing every event we plan?"

"Both, apparently."

Nate swiveled toward his credenza and pulled a tumbler of scotch from the center cabinet. He splashed amber liquid into two glasses, then slid one toward Bert.

Bert's pale brow rose. "Drinking on the job? I'll get fired."

"Doubtful." Nate scowled. "Armand will love you."

"She's selling to Miller?"

Nate drained the scotch from his glass, choking on the fiery liquid as it slid down his throat. "The one and only," he grumbled. *Armand Miller.* He should have known. The man had been a thorn in Nate's side since prep school, even more so since his daddy set him up in the event planning business—as a direct rival to McNulty.

Heat infused Nate's cheeks. Miller running McNulty Events? Over Nate's dead body. He'd worked too hard for this firm. His father's firm. His uncle's firm. He was not about to let his aunt sell it out from under the family.

"Can we stop her?" Bert's normally bright features grew serious.

Disgust settled like a ball of clay in Nate's chest. "She'll reconsider if we land The Worthington Cup."

"The dog show?"

"The key to attracting Philadelphia society to the firm, in her vast event planning experience." Nate scowled, sarcasm dripping from his words.

"Dogs?" Bert's pale blue gaze narrowed, his expression incredulous.

"Seems Kitty Worthington's upset with Armand." Nate flipped open his electronic organizer and tapped the screen. "We've got a chance to steal the account."

A concerned look flashed across Bert's features, his eyebrows pulling together. "Isn't the show next month?"

"Little longer, but not much." Nate rubbed a hand across his face. *Damn Aunt Martha.* If he ignored her ultimatum, he and most of his staff would be out of jobs—or worse. They'd be working for Armand Miller. The smug, smiling event planner from hell.

"We'll be short-staffed." The furrow between Bert's eyebrows deepened.

"We'll hire." Nate dropped his organizer, blowing out a frustrated breath.

"Bowwow." Bert waggled his brows.

"My sentiments exactly."

Bunny Love smoothed the lapel of her winter-white suit. She squirmed against the oversized leather chair, attempting to find a comfortable position as she waited for her interview to begin.

Mr. McNulty's secretary had said he'd be with her in five minutes. Good. More time to mentally prepare. Or panic. Whichever came first.

She took a sip of the herbal tea the woman had kindly provided. It wasn't steeped properly, but the fruity aroma and warmth soothed her frayed nerves.

Bunny met with clients occasionally in her freelance graphic design business, but to be quite honest, most of her contacts were made online, or by phone or fax. Matter of fact, she hadn't had much human contact other than that of her neighbors for a very long time.

No matter. She needed this job. She was ready for the interview, and she planned to nail it.

She fussed again with her suit. White was good. Creative. Powerful. Lots of chi. Bunny was a big believer in chi. Cosmic energy. Life force. Whatever you wanted to call it, she practiced whatever it took to increase its flow.

She reached up to give her wild curls a test pat. Drat. They hadn't relaxed at all. Not good. This was the last time she'd let her neighbor, Tilly, set her hair in Velcro rollers. *Natural-looking fullness*, her foot.

And speaking of feet, Bunny struggled to wiggle her toes in the constricting high-heeled pumps that covered hers. She could wear the contraptions once in a blue moon—for weddings or funerals—but every day? She'd much rather sink her toes into the monstrous pink slippers that had earned her the nickname Bunny.

Oh well, it wasn't as if she had a choice. She could keep a roof over her head with a regular paycheck or freelance on the street.

Bunny let out a deep sigh. Her apartment building had been perfect before the owners decided to sell and the residents voted to go condo. Mortgage payments. Financing.

She shuddered. Even free spirits had to face the music sometime.

She stared at the décor of Mr. McNulty's office. Five minutes. How could anyone survive five seconds in the stifling space, let alone five minutes?

Gray walls. Gray carpeting. Heck, even the blotter on the beautiful mahogany desk was gray. The man must be seriously out of balance, if his office reflected his inner self.

Bunny clucked her tongue. Such an amateur mistake. Too much yin and not enough yang. Everyone knew you needed yang for creativity. Didn't they?

She stared at the equine prints on the wall and the lack of anything but the blotter on top of the massive desk. The room felt totally devoid of life force. She frowned. Maybe Mr. McNulty was beyond help.

She scanned the room again, her gaze settling on a row of framed photos atop the gray credenza. *A sign of life.*

She stepped close then shook her head. Orderly. Neat. *Too neat.* She peered into each framed face. Also orderly and neat. *Very* blue blood.

Bunny stepped back, narrowing her gaze. Was she nuts, or did each frame sit two inches from the next? Exactly. *Wow.* This guy needed a cosmic energy intervention and fast.

Should she? Dare she?

In a matter of seconds, she angled and rearranged the frames until they warmed the space. After all, a little feng shui never hurt anyone.

She sank back into the rich leather chair, fishing in her purse for her Pez dispenser. She tipped back Wonder Woman's head and a small, yellow candy appeared. Bunny popped the morsel into her mouth and smiled.

Deciding she'd better practice her pitch once more, she opened her portfolio to scan her design samples, mentally crossing her fingers. She'd have to use her best powers of persuasion to land a job with McNulty Events.

According to word on the street, Nathan McNulty was one tough nut to crack.

Nate straightened in his chair, plastering on his best I'm-the-event-planner-for-you expression. He'd managed to land a meeting with Kitty Worthington—the force behind The Worthington Cup. He couldn't help but wince, however, as the woman let a tiny white poodle lick her ear.

Kitty gave the dog a quick pat, then deposited the creature on top of the mahogany table. Nate's eyes grew wide. He'd have to get the whole meeting room disinfected by the time she and her poodle were done.

Something moved against his pant cuff and he glanced under the table. A second poodle snuffled his shoe. *Poodles*. He didn't know dogs came this *small*. The tiny fanged creature twisted and pulled at the expensive wool cuff of Nate's trouser leg. He resisted the urge to kick.

"Is Chardonnay bothering you?" Kitty asked. She clucked her tongue.

The offensive creature released its grip on Nate's pants, scampering toward its owner.

Nate pointed to the fur ball on top of the table, now

asleep, chin resting on crossed paws. "What do we call that one?"

"Why, this is Chablis." The woman smiled. "Isn't she lovely?"

"Lovely," Nate mumbled. The ball of fluff wasn't exactly what he considered proper table decoration. "Mrs. Worthington, perhaps Chablis would be more comfortable on the carpet?"

The elderly woman tipped her head, considering the slumbering canine. "She looks perfectly content, but thank you for your concern."

"Of course. Wouldn't want her to get a stiff neck."

"Oh she won't, dear." Kitty raised her gaze to look at Nate. "I'm sorry I can't stay long." She patted her close-cropped silver waves. "Salon appointment."

Nate tamped down a wince. Women. Why did they feel the need to share such details? "I see." He tapped his black Monte Blanc pen against his leather portfolio. "I appreciate you meeting on such short notice. I understand you may have an opportunity for our firm."

"Yes. As you know, The Worthington Cup is one of the oldest Kennel Club shows on the East Coast."

Nate brightened. "And certainly the most prestigious."

Kitty's expression turned hopeful.

"I understand plans have been underway, considering the show's just five weeks away."

"That's correct, but I've had a disagreement with our current event planner."

Nate nodded. So Aunt Martha had been right. Kitty Worthington was upset with Armand the Almighty and a Worthington Cup coup was within reach. As much as he hated to admit it, an event of this magnitude would make a solid name for the company and bring in top-paying referrals. Better still, a successful Cup would prove the firm belonged under family control—under Nate's control.

"I see," he said. "May I ask what type of disagreement you had with Mr. Miller?"

Kitty held her head high, nose pointed to the ceiling. "I requested purple draping for the staging area." She leveled a perplexed expression at Nate. "Armand told me purple was gauche. Can you believe he spoke to me in such a fashion?"

Nate slowly shook his head. Purple. What could one say about purple? Quickly. Think of something. *Anything.*

"Regal," he sputtered.

"What?" Kitty's eyes narrowed. She pursed her lips.

"I've always felt the color purple was a regal color. Suited for royalty, if you will."

Kitty beamed. "Why that's what I've always felt." She clasped a hand to her chest. Chablis woke momentarily, then rolled onto her back, paws in the air.

"Charming," Nate muttered.

Kitty patted the dog's stomach and slowly shook her head. "I knew it was a stroke of brilliance to come to your firm. Your Aunt Martha is a genius." She waggled a finger toward Nate. "I can tell you're a dog person."

Nate stood and walked to Kitty's side, extending his hand to seal the deal. "Perhaps we can meet again tomorrow to work out the details. If your schedule permits."

"Of course," Kitty said. "I'll be here first thing in the morning. The girls are having their portraits taken in the afternoon." She nodded to Chardonnay and Chablis.

Nate gave Kitty's hand a squeeze. "Let me assure you the McNulty team will deliver the most successful Worthington Cup the region has ever seen."

Moments later, out in the hall, he checked his pant cuff as he headed for his office. Fortunately, the offensive little fur ball hadn't damaged the fabric.

Dog person. He shuddered. He supposed there were worse things one could be called. Now that Kitty

Worthington had come on board, he had only to hire an extra planner.

He glanced down at his wristwatch, realizing he was ten minutes late for the interview. He *hated* to be late. Shaking his head, he searched his memory for the name of the interviewee. Ah, yes. Beatrice Love.

All of the firm's planners had been booked solid with repeat clients. He'd been too late to place an ad in this week's classifieds for a new coordinator, but previous listings for creative staff had produced Miss Love's resume. Her work history showed promise, boasting skills that lent themselves to event planning.

Certainly the woman could handle a dog show, even one as large as The Worthington Cup. After all, the major arrangements were in place. She only needed to be competent enough to finesse the details and keep things running smoothly. How difficult could it be?

Bunny's breath caught as Nathan McNulty entered the room. The man oozed raw, vital energy. *Literally.*

He shook her hand, and she gulped down a calming breath. If she had half a brain, she'd excuse herself now. This man and this firm were way out of her league. What had she been thinking?

Maybe she could ask her parents for money. She'd taken over their apartment when they'd retired to Florida, and even though they'd always predicted she wouldn't be able to afford the rent, she'd scraped by.

Bunny flinched. There was no way she'd give them the satisfaction of asking for help with a mortgage. She straightened determinedly. The time had come to land a real job and prove just how self-sufficient she was.

"Your resume speaks of varied experience," Nathan McNulty said as he sank into his chair. "I'd like to discuss the position of event coordinator with you."

Bunny fought to keep her jaw snapped shut. The

man had barely sat down before he'd spoken the words. Sureness sparked from his dark brown eyes. His strong, square jaw sat firm and masculine.

"I responded to your ad for a graphic designer," she stammered. "Not event planner."

The leather chair creaked as he settled against its back. "Your resume is impressive and I need an event coordinator. Immediately." He shrugged one broad shoulder. "Match made in heaven."

Her heart began a steady rapping against her ribs.

The elegant man drummed his fingers on the desktop. "You're organized, correct?"

Bunny's thoughts raced. A vision of her warm, creative apartment flashed through her mind. Perfect colors. Perfect accessories. Perfect aromas. "Yes." She gazed into his expectant eyes. "I'm very organized."

"And have you ever planned anything? Anything at all?"

She frantically searched her mind, spewing forth the first thing she managed to pry from her panicked brain. "My nephew's seventh birthday party."

"Big, complicated affair? Lots of planning?" One dark, handsome brow arched.

Bunny shook her head.

"Medium sized? Challenging?" The dark brows met in a hopeful peak.

She continued to shake her head, fighting to maintain her composure. Between the line of questioning and the heat emanating from the man's eyes, she was about to melt into a puddle on the gray carpet.

McNulty leaned forward, steepling his fingers. "What size was it?"

"Immediate family only, sir."

"And how many is that?"

"Six, Mr. McNulty."

"Six," he repeated. He drummed his fingers again then pursed his lips.

Bunny's breath caught in her throat. She tried to swallow but her parched mouth bore a sudden resemblance to the Sahara. The man exuded some serious cosmic energy. She mentally chastised herself. *Focus on the interview, Bunny. The interview.*

"I've brought my portfolio," she offered. "Would you like to review my work?" She pulled the leather case from where it leaned against her chair, sliding the folder of work across the desk. "As you'll see, these are samples of the collateral pieces I've done."

"But no event planning." McNulty's otherwise full lips pressed into a slim line. Bunny tried not to stare at the small dimple peeking out from one cheek. How could she notice a dimple at a time like this?

Nate met her gaze and sighed.

Bunny steeled herself. Focus. *Focus.* "I need this job, Mr. McNulty. I'm a quick learner and I won't disappoint you. If there was someone who could point me in the right direction with the . . . event planning, I'm sure I could master the necessary skills."

Absolutely brilliant. Even she believed what she'd said.

Bunny watched as he flipped through her portfolio, his head bent low, expression serious and intent.

"Perhaps you'd like to review my references? There's a printed list in the pocket of the portfolio." She pointed toward the back of the leather case. McNulty slowly raised his dark eyes to meet hers.

Her heart gave a jolt. Hot, sultry fire burned in the man's gaze, yet he seemed totally unaware of its impact. A woman could lose herself in the depths of those eyes. And how.

"I've already checked references based on your resume, Miss Love. They were all excellent."

"Beatrice," she said. "If you'd please."

"Very well, Beatrice." He closed the portfolio and slid it back to her side of the desktop. "How soon would you be able to start?"

"How soon would the job require me to start?"

"Tomorrow morning at eight."

"Tomorrow?" Bunny's mouth gaped open, but she quickly snapped it shut. How in the heck would she ever . . . "Tomorrow's perfect, sir."

"It's not necessary for you to call me sir." He stood and shook her hand. "Mr. McNulty is fine."

Bunny stifled a laugh. How could someone with such a gorgeous life force be so uptight?

"I'm assigning you to our newest event. I'll work along with you until you get the hang of things."

Her stomach flip-flopped at the thought. "I'd be honored, Mr. McNulty."

He turned to push his chair under his desk, but froze when his gaze landed on the rearranged photo frames.

Bunny swallowed down the lump in her throat. Uh oh. Maybe the feng shui could have waited.

McNulty shot a suspicious glance at her over his shoulder.

"Something wrong, sir?"

"Apparently someone rearranged my family photos." He methodically straightened the frames as he spoke, returning them to the exact positions they'd held previously. "Perhaps that someone didn't realize they were arranged as I prefer them. Nice and neat."

Bunny's heart resumed its steady drumming against her ribs. Oh, please. She couldn't have blown the job with her love of chi, could she? *Keep your mouth shut. Don't explain. Just keep* . . . "It creates positive chi, Mr. McNulty."

McNulty frowned, his gaze penetrating and deep. "Chi?"

"Positive energy." She straightened, struggling to sound confident. "The slightest change can shift or create energy in a space."

He ran a hand carelessly through his hair, leaving the silky chestnut strands standing on end. Uh oh. Hot, cosmic energy *and* rumpled. What a combination.

"My energy was fine as it was, Miss Love."

No kidding. Bunny nodded, reaching for a soothing sip of tea. Heat flared in places it had no business flaring. It wasn't possible to spontaneously combust, was it? She fumbled her cup, sending tea flying across the mahogany desk onto the spotless blotter.

"I'm so sorry." She grabbed her napkin, frantically mopping at the puddle. She looked up in time to meet the deep, dark depths of Nathan McNulty's gaze. *Gulp.*

"No harm done, Miss Love." His Adam's apple bobbed in his throat. He winced as though the spill caused him pain. "We all knock things over occasionally."

His musky aftershave tickled Bunny's nose, sending her thoughts tumbling right back to the possibility of spontaneous combustion.

She chased the idea out of her mind. Where was her balance? Her focus? She didn't have time for schoolgirl fantasies about Nathan McNulty. She had to make this job work and save her apartment.

Sheesh. She'd have to use every deep breathing trick in the book to pull off this one.

Nate fought the urge to slap his palm over the top of Beatrice Love's hand. Her frenzied mopping motion had sent her . . . well . . . her entire body into an alluring wiggle. Unfortunately, the vantage point from his side of the desk was doing nothing to help his body's warm response to the sight.

Instead it afforded a clear and enticing view of the soft swells of her breasts peeking from beneath her creamy jacket.

"Miss Love . . . er . . . Beatrice, the desk is quite dry." He waved his hand in her general direction. "Stop that wiping."

She raised her chin, exposing the inviting ivory

flesh of her throat. He swallowed. Hard. "You've done enough."

"But the wood—"

He closed his hand over hers. "Stop . . . now."

Her lips parted and her pale eyes widened, their exotic blue color hypnotizing him momentarily, like the crystal clear waters of a Caribbean Sea. Bright red splotches blossomed on her cheeks. Had his touch done that? His gaze dropped to their joined hands. His brain fired off the signal to let go, but his body refused to cooperate.

"Sir?" Beatrice's voice was nothing more than a whisper.

He met her startled look. How was it that her eyes had grown wider? And brighter? And bluer?

"Mr. McNulty?"

Nate released his grip, stepping away from the desk. "Sorry about that." *Hold it together, man. Control.*

The woman straightened, smoothing the front of her jacket and skirt. "No problem." She shook her reddish brown curls and spread her fingers in the air. "So, eight o'clock tomorrow?"

"Correct." Nate's husky voice sounded foreign to his ears.

Beatrice gathered her portfolio and fled, obviously flustered by their exchange. Nate tried to remember another time meeting a woman had affected him so, but couldn't come up with a single instance.

Between her positive chi mumbo jumbo and the brilliance of her eyes, Beatrice Love had bewitched his senses. Worse yet, starting tomorrow he'd be presenting her to the world as his newest event coordinator.

If there was one thing Nate prided himself on, however, it was control. The thought calmed him. *Control.* Certainly he'd be able to control his reactions to Beatrice Love. He was a McNulty, after all.

He poured a full glass of water from the pitcher on

his credenza, yet chugging down the ice-cold liquid did nothing to chill the heat racing through every inch of his body.

Not good. He shook his head. Not good at all.

Chapter 2

Bunny rushed into the hall, fighting the desire to un-button her jacket. *Whew.* All that mopping had left her blood boiling. Was it hot in this office, or what? Oh, who was she kidding?

Nathan McNulty's life force sizzled, whether he knew it or not. Bunny gazed down, shaking her head as she rounded the corner, running smack into Barbie. At least the woman looked like Barbie.

"Oh, my," the life-sized doll murmured.

"I'm terribly sorry. My fault," Bunny stammered. "I wasn't watching where I was going."

The woman waved a gloved hand dismissively. "It's all right," she chirped. "No harm done."

Bunny flinched from the shine of her smile. *And her clothing.* The woman was a vision in cotton candy pink. Pink shoes. Pink suit. Pink purse. The ensemble com-plemented the gray surroundings beautifully, Bunny mused. Matter of fact, the woman exuded pink right down to, or rather right up to, her headband. Silky blond hair fell from the velvet accessory to the woman's shoulders.

"Are you quite all right?" Barbie asked.

Bunny straightened her spine, wondering if all Mc-Nulty employees wore suits like the woman's. It looked to be Chanel. Even if Bunny could find one, she'd never be able to afford the price tag. Was she nuts?

She'd never pull off being an event planner. "I'm fine. You?"

"Just peachy."

Or pink. Bunny excused herself to continue her flight from the office. She had less than twenty-four hours to prepare for her first day at McNulty Events— under the guidance of Nathan McNulty. A shiver rippled up her spine.

What a girl wouldn't do to save her apartment.

Nate pulled out his handkerchief to wipe his forehead. When had the office grown so warm? Someone needed to correct the thermostat setting. He loosened his tie.

A soft feminine cough jarred him from his fixation on the soaring office temperature.

"Are you quite all right, darling?"

He spun to find Melanie Brittingham standing just inside his office door. Today's suit boasted a pale pink that corresponded perfectly with her handbag. Melanie's shoulder-length hair hung like a polished waterfall of honey—so unlike Miss Love's carefree curls.

"You're terribly flushed, Nathan. Are you ill?"

Ill? Bedazzled, perhaps, but not ill. He stepped around the desk, extending his arms. "No, I'm fine. Just a bit warm."

They planted soft kisses on each other's cheeks.

Melanie touched her gloved hand to his face. The supple leather brushed gently against his cheek.

"Are you sure I shouldn't call a doctor?"

A doctor. No. A shrink? Maybe.

He shook his head. "I'm fine. What time is our reservation?"

"Not until six," Melanie said. "But I was hoping we could stop at Berman's on our way to the club."

Berman's. Nate bit down on his lip. Jewelry? Had he missed an anniversary? Highly unlikely.

A slow smile tugged at the corner of Melanie's pink lips. "You look like a deer caught in the headlights, Nathan. I need to check on Mother's ring, nothing more. Although we should discuss an engagement ring for the holidays this year."

Nate sighed inwardly. A man could do worse than marry Melanie Brittingham. They'd been together for the past five years, and had been expected to be together for years before that. Their families had made that much clear.

She came from good stock, she was a bright young woman, and she could, on occasion, make Nate laugh. *But can I make him as hot as Miss Beatrice Love did?*

He coughed, tamping down the mutinous, whispering voice in his brain.

Melanie's pale blue gaze narrowed. "Do you have a cough as well? Perhaps we should cancel our dinner plans. I'll come to your apartment and make some soup."

Melanie? Cook? Now that *would* be enough to put him in the hospital. "No, no." He cupped her elbow in his palm, steering her toward the door. "I just need some fresh air. Aunt Martha's looking forward to seeing you."

He waved good night to his secretary as he slipped his arm around Melanie's waist. "I've got exciting news to share with you both."

Bunny snuggled into the beanbag chair in the corner of Matilda Stringer's living room, sipping her lime daiquiri. She watched Tilly dance excitedly across the room. "This is so wonderful. I can't believe you landed the job with McNulty on your first try." Tilly beamed with excitement.

Bunny smiled at the amazement etched across her friend's face, warming from the friendship and the daiquiri. Tilly had been the bright spot in Bunny's life since she'd moved into her parents' apartment. As the only two residents under the age of fifty, they had quickly learned the value of sticking together.

Tilly sank to the floor. Her raven hair hung well past her shoulders, cobalt streaks brushing softly against her pixie face. She plucked her own fruity cocktail from an end table and took a quick sip. "Maybe he likes you." Her eyes sparkled with amusement.

Bunny wrinkled her face, remembering the smoldering heat in Nathan McNulty's gaze. She let out a rush of breath. "Oh, please. I was the only warm body he could find for the job."

"I sense he's smitten." Tilly squinted, scrutinizing Bunny's features. "Are you blushing?"

Bunny lowered her gaze to hide the heat flooding her cheeks. "You, my friend, are certifiably insane."

"No. Peggy Sue from the hotline says I've got a gift." She tapped her temple. "I'm touched."

Bunny gulped her drink and smacked her friend's knee. "You're touched all right, but I don't think it's with psychic ability. Do you ever wonder whether it's a bad thing you know every psychic on the hotline by first name?"

Tilly shook her head, her eyes growing wide. "No. I'm right about this one. Nathan McNulty will fall in love with you. It's destiny." She winked dramatically. "You'll see."

A shiver rippled up Bunny's spine as she waved off her friend's suggestion. After all, an uptight suit like McNulty probably never had a romantic notion in his life, although serious heat had simmered in the depths of his mocha eyes.

She thought of the Barbie vision she'd encountered

after her interview, wondering what type of woman turned Nathan's head.

"You should have seen the woman I ran into after my interview." She shook her head. "Totally polished and refined. Now *she* belonged in that office. Me, I'm not so sure about."

Tilly scooted close to tap Bunny's knee. "Like what? Tell me."

Bunny described the cotton candy ensemble and the woman's flawless, smooth hair. "I'll never look like that."

Tilly wrinkled her nose. "Why would you want to look like that?"

"I need this job to keep a roof over my head." She met her friend's curious gaze then let out a dejected breath. "Maybe I need to look like that."

Tilly shrugged. "At least your parents will be happy."

"Great." Bunny rolled her eyes. "I'll finally be the corporate daughter they always dreamed of."

Her parents had never understood her creative side. How could they? They'd been too busy attending dinner dances at the club and planning golf outings. Her sister had somehow slid under the radar screen, marrying right out of college and producing the first grandchild. But Bunny? Bunny had never quite measured up to her parents' idea of success. If anything, her often unorthodox ideas had given them fits.

And forget about men. She had yet to bring home one that fit their picture of the ideal son-in-law. Heck. She had yet to bring home one that fit her own picture of the ideal son-in-law. Every man she'd dated had either scoffed at her creative thinking or wanted her to change. *Change.* Were they kidding?

Tilly held up one finger, jumping to her feet. "Be right back." She dashed from the room. "Close your eyes."

Bunny did as Tilly instructed and sat, eyes shut, waiting for her friend's return. She felt the brush of rough fabric against her hands and blinked her eyes open.

A violet suit lay draped across her knees. "What's this?" she whispered excitedly.

"A Chanel suit." Tilly shrugged, taking a long draw on her straw. "Well, I mean, I think it is."

"Where on earth did you get a Chanel suit?" Bunny stroked her fingers across the nubby wool, fingering the double row of beautifully polished buttons. Minute flecks of orange and green peeked from the fabric's weave. Gorgeous. The suit was simply breathtaking.

Tilly grinned. "I wore it in last year's production of *Auntie Mame*. They let us keep our costumes . . . sort of." She tipped her chin. "You'll knock 'em dead in that."

Tilly sank to her knees, and leaned toward Bunny. Bunny often wondered how so much vitality could be packed into such a tiny person, but Tilly pulled it off. She was nothing but raw energy, which might explain her inability to hold a job for more than one week. If not for her family's trust fund, she'd be no more able to afford living in the building than Bunny.

"I heard about the Condo Board and Thurston." Tilly's face pinched into a deep frown.

Thurston Monroe. Bunny's enthusiasm for her new job and the beautiful suit faded. "He hates me."

"A little feng shui never hurt anyone," Tilly offered in a falsely cheerful tone.

"He fractured his wrist." Bunny grimaced. "I think that hurt him a bit."

Tilly shook her head. "Six weeks in a cast and four months of rehab."

Bunny ran a hand over her face. "He'll never approve my application."

"He should have been looking where he was going."

Tilly was right. How could someone fall over a sofa, for crying out loud? And the rearrangement had created a major improvement in the lobby's energy. Anyone could see that. Except Monroe.

"They can't say no now that you'll be able to get financing, right?" Tilly's features brightened hopefully.

"Well"—Bunny gave one shoulder a quick shrug—"I haven't gotten the financing yet. I haven't even started the job."

"But it shouldn't be a problem." Tilly's concerned gaze narrowed.

Bunny fought to contain the flutters building in her own stomach. She squeezed her friend's hand. "He can still block me just because he thinks I'm unsuitable."

Tilly's jade green eyes narrowed to tiny slits. "He wouldn't dare. The rest of the board would never let him. They adore you."

"I hope so."

"I *know* so." Tilly moved in close, giving Bunny a reassuring hug. "Everything will be all right." She sat back and winked. "It's in the stars."

Nate hoisted his glass, raising his voice to be heard above the din of the popular restaurant. "I'm pleased to inform you McNulty Events has landed The Worthington Cup."

"Marvelous," Aunt Martha declared.

"Oh, Nathan." Melanie clapped her hands. "Fabulous."

A waiter bustled past, his serving tray piled high with steaming entrees, trailing the aroma of succulent beef.

Nate took a long sip of scotch. "We only have five weeks. Tight planning is crucial, but won't be a problem."

A mischievous grin spread across Aunt Martha's face as she set down her martini glass.

"Once again," Nate said, "you got your way."

She winked, forking a bite of cheesecake into her mouth. "This will make the firm. All those smaller clients are too much stress and not enough income.

This will be different. Besides, Kitty Worthington is a dear friend and a lovely woman."

"She's a bit . . . odd." He chose his words carefully.

"Nathan." His aunt's tone admonished, but her artificially blue gaze intensified. "Why do you say that?"

"For one thing, her poodles are named after white wine."

"Well, yes, there is that." Martha took another bite of cheesecake, swallowed and rolled her eyes. She dabbed a linen napkin to her lips and narrowed her eyes. "She's a dog person, Nathan. You'll need to understand dog people if you're going to make The Worthington Cup a success."

He closed his eyes and wished for sanity—in his family and his clients. "I'll do my best."

His aunt smiled the serene, practiced smile those with money learn to affect at a young age, tapping a burgundy acrylic nail against her chin. "This is the opportunity you need to catapult the firm to a new level. Don't blow it."

"Nathan, darling. I'm so proud." Melanie's words were soft but sincere.

Good old, predictable Melanie. He could always count on her to do or say the expected.

"Your parents would have been proud of you as well," Aunt Martha said, waving her fork in the air. "May they rest in peace."

Nate sat quietly for a moment, digesting her words. He lifted his glass to the woman who had raised him and his older brother after their parents' tragic deaths. "Here's to you. For sending Kitty Worthington my way."

"Just remember our discussion from the other day," she reminded him.

"Don't worry." Nate's gut clenched. She always knew which button to push, and when. "How could I forget?" He met his aunt's cool expression and smiled. If she thought he'd let her get away with selling the firm, she had another thing coming.

"What discussion?" Melanie asked, her eyes bright and perky.

"Nothing you need to be concerned with." Aunt Martha dismissed her question. "What we do need to discuss is your engagement."

Nate coughed on his mouthful of scotch, tears welling in his eyes as the liquid scorched the back of his throat. He jerked his handkerchief from his jacket and held it over his nose and mouth.

"Engagement?" he croaked.

"Yes." Aunt Martha wore a puzzled expression. "Melanie tells me you've discussed an announcement."

"We did discuss it"—Melanie's pale blue eyes grew wide, her expression meek—"but we hadn't set definite plans, Martha."

"Then it's time you do." Aunt Martha turned to Nate.

"Well, yes, but there's no need to rush—"

"You've been seeing each other for years," his aunt interrupted. "There are appearances to be considered."

Melanie leaned toward Nate, her slender fingers pressing lightly against his hand. "She's right. What will people think if we don't announce our intentions soon?"

His mind raced. There had been others before Melanie, but their involvement had lasted the longest. Probably because they had known each other since prep school and because what they shared was . . . comfortable. Straightforward. Refined.

He looked from Aunt Martha's expectant face to Melanie's. They were both right, of course. Polite society expected a decision, and McNultys respected the dictates of polite society.

He nodded. "Fair enough."

"It's settled then." Aunt Martha raised her glass. "To Nathan, Melanie, and a lifetime of joy and happiness."

Nate plastered on a smile as the three clinked glasses. Was it his imagination, or had Melanie gone pale? He truly cared for her, but did he love her? Would he know true love if it hit him over the head? Perhaps this thing called love was nothing more than a myth propagated by legions of romance novelists.

"Nathan McNulty."

His aunt's sharp tone cut through his rambling thoughts. "Yes?"

"I'm speaking to you."

"Yes, I'm well aware of that." Quite frankly, he hadn't heard a thing.

"You haven't answered my question."

He narrowed his eyes. "About the engagement?"

"No." Aunt Martha let out a small sigh. "About your staffing. Are you prepared to handle an event like the Cup? You know, if you'd give up the firm and accept the position at Brittingham Insurance with Melanie's father, you'd never have to worry about staffing again."

Nate bristled. "You want me to sell insurance?"

Her expression grew serious. "Insurance is safe."

Nate had been hearing the safe lecture as long as he could remember. "You can't blame a motorcycle accident on the family business."

"Your father and mother were rebelling against stress."

Nate paused, not wanting to revisit the tired topic. Someday he'd prove his aunt wrong, but for now he decided to refocus their discussion to The Worthington Cup. "I hired a new coordinator late this afternoon. She starts tomorrow."

His aunt pressed her palms together. "I'd love to meet her. How about lunch Wednesday? You'll clear your schedule?"

"Absolutely." Nate ignored the dread pooling in his stomach. Hopefully Miss Love had learned her lesson where chi, or whatever it was she had called it, was concerned. "Her name is Beatrice Love and she comes highly recommended."

Aunt Martha's eyes narrowed. "I'm not familiar with that name. Is she new to Philadelphia?"

"No"—Nate shook his head—"just a well-kept secret."

"Is that the young woman I saw leaving your office?" Melanie asked.

Nate choked again mid-sip. "You met Miss Love?"

"Petite? White suit?" Melanie wrinkled her nose. "Not terribly graceful, though."

Nate pictured Beatrice Love's wild hair, bright smile, and soft, warm touch. Sudden heat spread to his fingertips and toes, forcing him to recount the number of drinks he'd consumed.

"Yes, that sounds like her." He loosened his tie for the second time that day. What was wrong with the thermostats in this city? "I can assure you, Aunt Martha, Beatrice Love comes highly recommended and extremely qualified. We've got nothing to worry about."

He tossed back the last of his scotch and gestured to a passing waiter, all the while battling to keep Beatrice Love's vivid blue eyes and soft vanilla scent out of his brain.

No, he reassured himself. Nothing to worry about at all.

Later that night, Bunny spread out the Chanel for the next morning, her nerve endings quivering with excitement at the prospect of the new job. Fear for her apartment continued to simmer in her belly, even though Tilly had done her best to convince her otherwise.

She gathered a few of her beloved items from her work area, snuggling them safely into a small box. Glancing around her soothing apartment, she realized working in an office would be a horrible shock to her system. Especially spending each day within the gray confines of McNulty Events. Bunny plucked two more knickknacks from her desk, adding them to the growing collection.

She might be forced to join the ranks of corporate America, but she most certainly would not do so without her tricks for ensuring positive energy flow. She sank onto her heels, surveying her props and the lovely violet suit.

Suddenly her mind flashed on the image of Nathan McNulty's smoldering gaze. Awareness rippled through her and she reached for one last item from her desk.

Icy hot breath mints.

After all, she'd hate to make a bad impression on her first day.

Chapter 3

Strains of Barry Manilow filtered into Bunny's dream. Nathan McNulty wore a brightly colored island print shirt and called Bunny to join him in a quick salsa. Desire pooled hot and heavy in all the right places. She willed her feet to go to him, but couldn't.

The tune grew louder and she blinked her eyes open. Even awake, the song continued. She squinted at the digital clock. Five fifteen. A shiver of anticipation rippled through her.

She slipped from bed, the hardwood floor cold beneath her bare feet as she crossed cautiously toward the bedroom door. Maybe this was one of those dreams within a dream. The kind where you thought you were awake, but you really weren't.

Bunny opened the door and peered toward the living room. She blinked. Even through her sleep-blurred vision the identity of the short woman dusting furniture as Manilow crooned *Copacabana* was unmistakable. Alexandra Love. *My mother.*

Bunny clicked the door shut and thunked her forehead against the bright green wood. She gripped a chunk of her forearm between her thumb and index finger and pinched. *Ouch.* She cracked open the door, peering toward the living room once more. *Still there.* What was her mother doing in Philadelphia? Worse. In her apartment?

She stepped into the middle of the hall, slowly shuffling toward the frenzied activity in the living room. "Alexandra?" Heaven forbid she should call the woman by anything but her name. That had been a rule as long as Bunny could remember. Alexandra had age issues and, although she enjoyed her role as mother to Bunny and her sister, Vicki, she didn't want the constant reminder the name *Mother* carried with it.

"Good morning, sweetheart." Alexandra pulled her into a hug then held her at arm's length. "Did I wake you?"

Bunny scowled. "You're playing Barry Manilow at five o'clock in the morning. What do you think?"

Her mother frowned. "Stop making that face, dear. What if it freezes like that?"

Bunny tried to remember her breathing exercises. Surely there must be one for surprise parental appearances while you slept helplessly in the next room. "Where's Dad?"

Bunny's mother clucked her tongue and returned to her dusting. "I left him."

Bunny's heart fell to her toes. "Left him?"

"In Naples. A woman can only color code the canned goods for so many years before she snaps, dear. I figured I'd come here to find myself." She gave Bunny a conspiratorial wink. "Just us girls."

Oh, goody. The surprise got better and better. Bunny held up a finger. "Be right back."

She beat a path for the bathroom, slamming the door closed behind her. Okay. Maybe this was one of those really tenacious dreams within a dream where, no matter how hard you tried to wake up, you couldn't. Bunny twisted on the cold water, waiting until the flow turned her fingers ice cold. She leaned over the sink and splashed her face until her teeth chattered. If she wasn't awake now, she never would be.

She opened the door and squinted once more down

the hall. Beads of water ran down her cheeks and dripped from her chin. *Drat. Still there.*

"How about some coffee, dear?" her mother chirped. "Or do you still drink that dreadful tea?"

Bunny swiped the moisture from her face with her bare hands, resigned to her fate. She padded down the hall, sinking her feet into the safe security of her bunny slippers before following her mother into the kitchen. "Tea," she answered meekly as she watched her mother fill the kettle and set it on the stove. "Did you tell Daddy you were leaving?"

Alexandra jutted out her chin. "I left a note."

"How did you get here?" Disbelief fluttered through Bunny's stomach, a thread of hope still remaining that she'd wake up any minute.

"I drove all night."

"In the Caddy?"

Her mother nodded then waggled a finger at Bunny. "I can't believe you haven't changed the locks since we gave you the apartment. There's no telling what kind of lunatic might have a copy of that key, dear."

No kidding. "Aren't you tired?"

"Convenience store coffee and gummy bears." Her mother gave a quick shake of her expertly highlighted curls. "Amazingly energizing combination."

"You don't say," Bunny grunted as she reached for her English breakfast tea. If nothing else, once her mother's sugar levels crashed, she'd be asleep for hours, if not days. At least that was something to look forward to.

Two hours later, her mother was sound asleep in the second bedroom and Bunny was busy trying to squeeze her feet into a pair of chunky pumps. She gazed longingly at her bunny slippers, sitting deserted beneath her hand-painted desk.

"Sorry, babies," she whispered. "I'm afraid my days of working in bunny slippers are gone."

Purse over shoulder, box of tricks tucked securely beneath her arm, and chin held high, she headed into the hall to press the elevator button. Her confidence turned to panic with one quick glance at her watch. Seven forty-five. How in the heck had that happened? She'd never make it on time.

One of the reasons she'd gone after the job at McNulty was the proximity of the office to her apartment—make that condo—though making the trek in fifteen minutes was pushing it.

The crisp autumn air greeted her with a chill as she stepped onto the sidewalk. She pulled the throat of her suit jacket tight around her neck, drew in a deep breath and coughed. City air. She smiled. Nothing quite like it.

When she went to sleep last night, her biggest concern had been her first day of work. Now, a fifty-five-year-old woman determined to find herself had taken over her apartment. Great. She shrugged. Why should life be boring? Wasn't she the first to encourage people to embrace chaos?

Bunny checked her watch again. Ten minutes. She broke into a jog, elbowing her way through the crush of morning pedestrians. She pushed through the revolving doors and dashed into the reception area of McNulty Events at seven fifty-nine precisely.

A slim, thirty-something man stood waiting, glaring at her as she entered the space. He held his arms crossed and his lips pursed. "Miss Love, I presume?"

Bunny nodded.

He pointed to a huge wall clock and clucked his tongue. "You're late. Let's not make it a habit."

"But I—" Bunny glanced at the clock and blinked. Five after eight. How could that be? "I don't understand."

"What? The concept of time?"

Hot embarrassment fired in her cheeks. She shook her head. "No," she stated emphatically. "I assure you I understand the concept of time, but my watch must be slightly behind your clock." She tipped her chin. "It won't happen again."

He arched one pale brow. "Very well. You've got a full schedule today. Mr. McNulty asked that I show you to your office."

Bunny supported her box on one hip and followed the gentleman down a long narrow hallway. She hadn't seen this section of the office yesterday, but it was gray, nonetheless. She shuddered but pasted on a smile. She could do this. She could. She had no choice.

Her guide stopped before the doorway to a gray cubicle, gesturing inside. "Your office."

"Gray," Bunny murmured out loud before she could stop herself.

"Pewter." The gentleman swung his arm in a grand gesture. "Your desk, filing cabinet, and workstation."

Bunny winced. She hadn't realized office chairs and resin desks were available in gray. Now she knew they were. Sadly. "Thank you." She set her box of personal belongings on the desk then turned to the gentleman, extending her hand. "I'm afraid we got off to a rocky start. Beatrice Love. Pleasure to meet you."

He gave her hand a firm pump. A slight smile toyed with his severe features. "Bert Parks. No jokes, please."

Bunny grinned. "Listen, you're talking to someone nicknamed Bunny. I'd never make a joke about your name."

A full smile flickered across his lips, but he quickly straightened his features as if catching himself. He nodded toward Bunny's desk. "May I ask what you've got in the box?"

"Sure." She plucked an item from inside, proudly holding up a bright yellow slinky adorned with a large smiley face. "For when I'm lacking creativity."

She next pulled a small basketball net from the box, fastening the hoop to the rim of her gray trash can. "For those moments requiring brainstorming." She smiled. "Or for trashing bad ideas."

Bert's eyes grew wide. A smirk tugged at one corner of his thin lips.

Bunny forged ahead. "This is my favorite." She pulled out a stuffed hamster sporting a karate costume. "If you squeeze his paw he dances and sings *Kung Fu Fighting*." She shook her head. "Really quite fun, but I think it would be a bit loud for first thing in the morning."

"Undoubtedly." He slowly shook his head, his expression pained. "Is there more?"

"Oh, yes. There's—"

"Get rid of it," he snapped.

Bunny's heart caught. "Get rid of what? The hamster?"

"All of it." Bert shook his head, pressing his lips together. "Mr. McNulty discourages frivolity in the office. We're here to work." He waved a hand at her box. "I'd suggest you hide that. I'll let him know you've arrived."

Bunny watched as he made his way down the hall. She returned each item to the box, sliding the apparently offensive collection far beneath the gray desk. She sank into her gray chair, fumbling in her purse.

Tears welled in her eyes, but she blinked them back. Even the rules were gray. She cradled her Wonder Woman Pez dispenser in the palm of her hand, letting loose an exasperated breath. She frowned at the plastic superhero and whispered, "Looks like we're not in Kansas anymore."

Bert laughed quietly, shaking his head as he made his way toward Nate's office. "Nathan McNulty, what have you done?" he whispered to himself. "Hired a live wire, that's for sure."

"Is she here?" Nate stood as Bert stepped into his office.

"She's here, all right."

"Settled in?" Nate's brows arched.

"Completely." Bert stifled a snicker. He *had* been a little hard on her, but it had been so much fun.

Nate narrowed his eyes. "How did she seem?"

"Enthusiastic," Bert quipped.

"Enthusiastic is good." Nate's brown gaze grew hopeful.

"Well then, Miss Love is *very* good."

A surprised look flickered across Nate's face, but he quickly recovered. "Did you give her specifics on the Cup?"

"No." Bert crossed his arms and leaned against a large bookcase. "I thought I'd leave that to you."

"I have a good feeling about Miss Love." Nate paused next to Bert as he crossed to the door. "I think it's good to bring a fresh perspective into the firm."

Bert pictured Bunny Love's bright blue eyes, lively smile, and box of surprises. Definitely a fresh perspective. "Has she shared her nickname with you?"

Nate's dark brows met in a puzzled peak. "Nickname?"

"Apparently they call her Bunny."

"Bunny?" Nate took a step backward. "Well, that's . . . very country club." He nodded confidently. "*Very* country club."

Bert watched Nate step into the hall, headed straight toward Bunny Love's cubicle. He rubbed his chin, grinning. Watching these two work together would be more entertaining than ringside seats for the World Wrestling Federation.

He propped one elbow on the doorjamb, hung his head and laughed. He had known Nate for most of his life. Over the years, his friend had become so determined to live up to McNulty family expectations he'd grown half dead.

Bert had known Bunny for five minutes, yet he was fairly certain of one thing. If anyone could bring Nate McNulty back to life, it just might be Bunny Love.

Nate paused for a moment, taking in the sight of Beatrice Love. The woman sat slumped in her chair talking silently to a small red object in the palm of her hand. That couldn't be good.

Anxiety flickered in his chest and he momentarily wondered if his rash hiring of Miss Love had been a mistake. He stepped into the cubicle, clearing his throat.

Beatrice's head snapped in his direction. She tossed whatever she'd been holding beneath her desk and sprang to her feet.

"Mr. McNulty." She closed the space between them, offering her hand. "Good morning, sir. Pleasure to see you again."

Her stunning presence affected Nate more than it had the previous afternoon. A classic pale purple suit accentuated her slight, yet curvy, figure. A double row of buttons gleamed alluringly down the front of the jacket. She'd styled her reddish hair smooth today, tucking the strands neatly behind her ears. All she needed was a pair of tortoise-shell reading glasses to complete the whole sexy librarian look.

He gave her hand a quick shake, drinking in the bright blue depths of her eyes. *Something remarkable exists there,* he thought suddenly. *Energy. Vitality. Life.* A pool of warmth spread through his midsection, forcing him to inhale a deep, steadying breath.

"Sir?"

Nate shook himself from the trance. "Yes, Bunny . . . er . . . Beatrice. Good morning."

A bright red blush fired in her cheeks. "I see Mr. Parks shared my nickname with you."

"I apologize. That was a slip of the tongue on my part, and Bert shouldn't have told me."

A grin spread across her delicate features, tiny laugh lines crinkling the corners of her brilliant eyes. "It's fine." Her nose wrinkled as she spoke. "I prefer it to Beatrice, actually."

Nate shook his head. "It won't happen again." He jerked his thumb toward the hall. "Our client is waiting. This is a major account, so I'll expect you to present yourself as an expert. Understood?"

"Absolutely." Beatrice turned back to her desk. "Let me grab my pad."

Nate watched as she knelt beside her chair, pulling a box from beneath the desk and plucking a leather notebook from its contents.

"What do you have there?"

She quickly pushed the box out of sight, looking up at him. Her turquoise gaze locked on his. Nate's stomach caught and twisted. *So alive,* he thought. *So incredibly alive.*

"This?" Beatrice shook her head, pulling herself upright. "Just some . . . knickknacks I won't be needing."

"Knickknacks?"

"Yes." She stepped to his side. "They're nothing really. I had them in my office at home and thought they'd liven things up here." A furrow formed between her brows. "Mr. Parks pointed out my mistake. They'll be gone tonight."

"Very well," he said. "Ready to meet our client?"

Beatrice's eyes grew wide. "Yes, sir."

"Brace yourself," Nate mumbled as he led the way down the hall.

"Pardon me, Mr. McNulty?"

He could hear Beatrice scrambling to match his long strides. "Nothing. I didn't say a thing."

* * *

Bunny frowned at Nathan's back. She'd heard something, but the man seemed far too polished and smooth to mumble. He seemed perfect, actually. From the back of his hair, to the cut of his suit, to the fit of his pants. The man was, well, perfect.

Every nerve ending in Bunny's body kicked into overdrive. *Focus,* she silently chastised herself. *Focus.*

She cast a quick glance at her clunky shoes, managing only to stub her toe on the gray carpet, stumbling headlong toward Nathan's perfect back. She righted herself seconds before her nose would have connected with his perfect behind, then concentrated on calming her breathing.

"You're going to meet Kitty Worthington." Nathan stopped just short of a pair of closed doors. "Mrs. Worthington is a local powerhouse. Her family has sponsored The Worthington Cup for years." He arched a dark brow. "Are you familiar with it?"

Bunny shook her head. "I'm afraid not. Is it a boat race?"

Nathan's perfect features winced. "No. A dog show. A very old, very prestigious, very *important* dog show."

"And McNulty Events is handling the details?"

"Precisely." Nathan reached for the doorknob. "More specifically, you and I are handling the details. Together."

Bunny swallowed down the lump in her throat. "Yes, sir."

"We have a lot of work to do quickly." His expression grew serious and intense. "Mrs. Worthington must not know you're a novice. Follow my lead, and we'll be fine."

"I'll do my best, Mr. McNulty." Bunny fought the tremble that threatened to shake her shoulders. "How soon is the event? Six months? Nine months?"

Nathan leveled a gaze at her that sent shockwaves to her toes. "Five weeks."

"Weeks?" she squeaked.

He nodded. "We're going in. Brace yourself."

That's what she thought she'd heard him say before. She swallowed again. Hard.

Her heartbeat thumped in her ears. Five weeks. Event planning. Dogs. *Holy cow.* Where were her bunny slippers when she needed them most?

They were no sooner in the door than a white blur rushed Bunny's feet. She yipped and grabbed for Nathan's arm. He grasped her elbow to hold her steady, sending shockwaves of awareness outward from his touch. She could have sworn she heard him mumble again.

"Beatrice, meet Chablis."

The tiny lump of fur wiggled and squirmed at her ankles.

Bunny's face warmed with embarrassment at her initial reaction. "Oh, my," she cooed. "She's beautiful." She dropped to her knees, letting the dog lick her face.

"And this is Kitty Worthington," Nathan continued, clearing his throat. "The force behind The Worthington Cup."

Bunny scrambled to her feet, smoothing her suit front.

Kitty Worthington looked as though she'd stepped off the page of a safari adventure brochure. Her sage jacket and skirt accentuated the green in her hazel eyes, but were better suited for a stint in the outback than a meeting to discuss a dog show. Short, crisp silver waves framed the woman's patrician features.

Oh well, Bunny thought. She'd be the last one to criticize the woman's fashion sense. If anything, Mrs. Worthington should be commended for cultivating a unique look. Bunny glanced down at the violet suit she'd borrowed. At least Kitty Worthington hadn't become a slave to fashion in order to blend in.

Bunny extended her hand and smiled. "It's a pleasure to meet you."

Kitty gave Bunny's fingers a quick squeeze. A warm smile spread across her face as she nodded. "I can tell you're the perfect choice to coordinate The Worthington Cup, Miss Love. Look how genuinely Chablis took to you." She waggled her finger. "My Chablis is a flawless judge of character."

At her words Bunny gazed down at the little dog. The ball of fluff sat staring up at her, tiny rump wiggling, miniature paw swatting at Bunny's pumps.

"She's adorable. Is she a Toy?"

"Teacup," Kitty answered.

"Charming," Nathan muttered.

Bunny shot him an inquisitive look.

He straightened and gestured toward the conference table. "Where's Chardonnay?"

"Chardonnay?" Bunny asked.

"At the groomer's." Kitty clucked her tongue. "She had an unfortunate accident in the garden. Decided she liked the feel of mulch against her fur." The woman pressed her lips into a tight line and shook her head. "Ghastly."

Bunny stifled a giggle and turned to Nathan. For the briefest of moments, she could have sworn he bit his lip. Well, what did you know? Perhaps the stiff wasn't so stiff after all.

"Well." Nathan took Kitty's arm, steering her toward a chair. "I'm very sorry to hear that. Beatrice is disappointed she didn't have an opportunity to meet her. Isn't that right, Miss Love?"

Bunny nodded and followed.

"What we'd like to accomplish this morning," Nathan continued, "is to bring you up to date on how we plan to make this Worthington Cup the best ever."

Kitty's eyes brightened. She looked expectantly at Nathan as she slipped into a leather chair.

He nodded in Bunny's direction. "Miss Love's

credentials are stellar. With her expertise, we're assured of an unforgettable Cup."

Kitty swiveled in her seat to look at Bunny. "Tell me what you've got planned, dear."

"Perhaps it would be best if I ran over the list," Nathan interrupted.

Kitty held up one hand, eyeing Bunny. "I can tell she's a natural talent, Nathan. Let her speak."

Incredulity flickered across Nathan's face. Bunny wondered how in the world she was going to bluff her way through this one. Would it be completely inappropriate to run screaming from the room?

"Well," she stammered. "There are a variety of things that are crucial at this point."

Nathan leaned his chin against one fist, turning his face toward her. His lips moved.

"Pardon?" Bunny asked.

"I didn't say anything, dear," Kitty replied.

Nathan rolled his eyes and mouthed the word "No." Bunny blinked. Ah. Whisper down the lane.

He moved his mouth emphatically. Bunny squinted, concentrating on each position of his lips. A warm flush raced up her neck. She couldn't help but wonder if the sensation was due to her predicament or the object of her focus.

Suddenly, she understood the first word. "Media. We need to be thinking about media," she said excitedly.

Nathan nodded, mouthing a second word.

"And hotel," Bunny continued. "You know," she ad-libbed, "there are many details to consider when preparing for our four-footed friends."

Hey, this wasn't so difficult after all.

Kitty nodded in agreement as Nathan mouthed a third word.

"Communications." Bunny gave a knowing head tip to Kitty. "This aspect is vital in an event of this size."

She narrowed her gaze at Nathan, unable to decipher

what he was now saying. His eyes widened and he repeated the phrase.

"Night . . . planning," she stammered. What in the heck was that?

Nathan winced, squeezing his eyes shut.

"Night planning?" Kitty frowned. "I don't understand, dear. Are you referring to the evening receptions?"

"Yes." Bunny brightened. "Night planning."

Nathan shook his head, mouthing the word "No" repeatedly.

"The opening cocktail party?" Kitty's gaze widened. "That would be the first night to be planned, correct?"

"A cocktail party for the dogs?" Bunny couldn't imagine it, but she supposed it could work.

Nathan slashed a finger across his throat, using caution to keep the motion out of Kitty's line of sight.

Why was he so agitated?

"A cocktail party for the dogs." Kitty clapped her hands with delight. "What a marvelous idea. Oh, I can tell you have a gift for this."

Nathan shook his head and spoke. "I hardly think a cocktail party for the dogs is necessary." He shot a glare at Bunny. "Perhaps Miss Love got a little carried away with her enthusiasm for the project."

Kitty pushed back from the table, straightening her safari suit jacket. "Nathan, you are to be congratulated on adding Miss Love to the firm." She nodded her head appraisingly. "Sheer brilliance. A cocktail party for the Cup participants."

Bunny flinched at the frustration etched across Nathan's face. She had a sneaking suspicion her event coordinator charade was off to a shaky start.

"Would you keep an eye on Chablis while I visit the ladies' room?" Kitty asked.

"Of course," Nathan replied.

Bunny stared at her lap as Kitty left the room.

"Well." Nathan's tone was anything but approving.

There was only one thing to do. Make a preemptive strike. "Yes." She met his gaze. "It did go well." She gestured toward the door. "Mrs. Worthington is thrilled with our plans."

He blinked. "I'll grant you that. But I specifically said site planning. How could you misinterpret that to say night planning?" His cheeks flushed to a soft pink.

She tipped her chin defiantly. "You should learn to enunciate more clearly."

Nathan let out a deep breath and plowed a hand through his chestnut locks. "Now we're expected to host a cocktail party for one *thousand* pampered pooches and their owners."

Bunny straightened in her seat. "Think of the potential, Mr. McNulty. This firm will be seen as cutting edge. Everyone will be buzzing about McNulty Events."

Nathan squeezed his eyes shut again, pausing for a beat. "You may have a point." He shot her a frustrated look. "Time will tell, Miss Love."

The conference room door opened and Kitty reentered. "I'm confident I've made the right decision in switching the Cup to your firm."

Nathan rose. "You won't be disappointed."

The woman turned her warm smile toward Bunny. "It was an absolute delight to meet you, Beatrice. I know the Cup is in good hands." She glanced down to her feet then quickly around the room. Her features twisted into a panicked expression. "Where's Chablis?"

The next few moments passed in a frenzied look under chairs and behind credenzas. They came up empty-handed.

Bunny's gaze locked onto the conference room doors. A sliver of the gray hallway carpet shone where they sat ever so slightly ajar.

She cleared her throat. "I think Chablis may have slipped out." She nodded toward the hall.

Kitty gasped, and Nathan waved one hand in the air. "Let's remain calm. She couldn't have gone far."

He pulled the doors open wide. Sounds of mayhem filtered down the hall. Voices laughed, whooped, and . . . sang.

"What the—" Nathan scowled.

Bunny tipped her head, trying to make sense of the commotion. Suddenly one voice among the many became clear. *Kung Fu Fighting*. Her stuffed hamster. She swallowed down the lump in her throat and pushed past Nathan.

"I know where she is, sir."

They excused themselves, pulling the conference room doors closed behind them.

Bunny raced to her cubicle. A group of McNulty employees stood gathered around the work space's entrance. Several laughed uncontrollably and a few dabbed at tears beneath their eyes.

Bert Parks stood with his fingertips pressed to his lips, a glint in his eyes. "Bunny." He grinned as she stopped next to him, staring into the gray space. "Seems to be some sort of commotion in your office."

"Cubicle," she murmured.

The singing hamster had been tossed against one of the cubicle's walls. Tufts of fake fur lay scattered on the surrounding carpet. It must have been a massacre.

"Oh my," Bunny said softly. She stepped into the small space just as a blur of white charged from beneath the desk. The poodle's tiny jaw clamped down on the hamster's paw. The singing began anew.

Everybody was Kung Fu fighting!

The hamster danced and spun, bald patches gleaming where Chablis' attack had left its mark. The poodle yapped and charged, retreated, yapped and charged again.

Bunny dove into the melee, wrestling the hamster to a standstill. Chablis nipped at her ankles in between bursts of shrill barking. Bunny fumbled the hamster's battery cover open, and a pair of double-As fell onto the gray carpet. The cubicle grew silent. Deathly silent. Chablis finally sat, her tiny head cocked to one side.

The heat of countless eyes burned into the back of Bunny's head, and her insides twisted. She sucked in a steadying breath.

"Chablis, darling." Kitty Worthington's voice was light with relief. The tiny dog scampered out of Bunny's line of vision. "Mumsy was so worried."

Bunny squeezed her eyes shut. She and her darned box of tricks.

"Beatrice."

Nathan's voice dripped icicles. So much for creating positive energy.

Bunny steadied herself, turning to meet his gaze. He held his strong chin high and his brown eyes narrow with disdain. The anxiety in Bunny's chest threatened to strangle her.

Nathan gestured to her with a grand sweep of his arm. "Everyone. Meet Beatrice Love. Our newest event planner."

Chapter 4

One half hour later, Bunny sat next to Nathan in the backseat of a yellow cab. Her stomach churned, flipping with embarrassment and dread. "I want to apologize one more time—"

"Not necessary," Nathan interrupted. "Your first apology was sufficient—let alone your sixth. I do have one question, though."

"Yes?"

"Why the hamster?"

"Creativity, sir."

He let out a sigh. "You've got to stop calling me sir, and what on earth does a fake hamster have to do with creativity?"

"Cosmic energy, sir. I mean, Mr. McNulty." She fought not to squirm in the seat.

"Cosmic what?" He turned to face her. His rich mocha stare yanked at something deep inside her belly, and her mouth went dry. This could be trouble. She couldn't afford an attraction to her boss on top of her unforgettable debut today.

"Cosmic energy," she repeated.

He narrowed his eyes, looking at her as though she were certifiably insane.

"The force of life." Bunny shrugged slightly. "Surely you've heard of it. Haven't you?"

"If it's been covered in the *Wall Street Journal*, I've heard of it."

"Well, sometimes I get stuck creatively and a little distraction gets me unstuck."

Nathan nodded. "I see." He turned to face her. The late morning sun cast shadows across the pure male planes of his face, sending a shiver down her spine. "Are there any other creative surprises in your office you'd like to tell me about? And is getting 'stuck' something you experience frequently?"

Warmth fired in Bunny's cheeks. "No, sir."

"Very well." He turned away from her, glancing out of the cab window to judge their location. "We should be there in a moment." He returned his focus, serious and intent, to Bunny. "I know you've been thrown into The Worthington Cup rather abruptly. Other than the canine cocktail party and the hamster incident, are you comfortable with things so far?"

"Yes." She nodded.

"Please remember how vital it is to appear expert in all you do. I have the utmost confidence in you." His momentary wince belied his words. "Concerns? Questions? Comments?"

Bunny tipped her head, wondering just how much honesty he was looking for. "May I be truthful?"

He frowned, then arched a brow. "Yes."

"It's very gray, Mr. McNulty."

"Gray?" A furrow formed between his eyes.

"Yes." She nodded slowly, squinting. "Very gray."

"What . . . exactly . . . is gray, Miss Love?"

Nate watched Beatrice's vibrant blue gaze narrow. What on earth was she talking about now?

"Everything at McNulty Events," she answered. "The carpet, the hall, the cubicles."

"Offices," he corrected.

"It's seriously lacking creative stimulation."

"Creative stimulation?" What did the color of the carpet have to do with stimulation? His fears were correct. She was insane.

The cab pulled to a stop in front of the entrance to the Philadelphia Convention Center.

"You worry about The Worthington Cup. I'll worry about the carpet."

"But color plays a crucial role in the balance and feel of a space," she replied.

Nate pulled his wallet from his pocket and handed the driver a twenty-dollar bill. "This is somehow important to you?"

"To everyone, Mr. McNulty." Her emphasis on the words reinforced her sincerity.

He met her twinkling gaze and warmth seeped through him. There was something about Miss Beatrice Love he couldn't quite put his finger on.

"Why don't you call me Nathan?" he said. "It's easier than Mr. McNulty."

Beatrice's features lit with surprise, then a breathtaking smile spread across her face. Something inside him hummed to life. Though unfamiliar, the sensation felt oddly exciting.

"I'll call you Nathan, if you'll call me Bunny."

"Bunny." The word rolled effortlessly off his tongue. "I meant to ask you earlier if that was a country club nickname."

A mischievous glint fired in her eyes. "Yes," she said quickly. "Pure country club."

"Then, Bunny it is."

She opened the door to slide out, stopping momentarily to lean toward the front seat. "Thank you," she chirped to the driver. "Have a great day."

The cabbie smiled as though he hadn't heard those words in a very long time. Nate paused for a beat before he climbed from the cab. Perhaps something could be said for cosmic energy after all.

Tilly Stringer braced herself for impact, then slammed into the corner of the imposing building's wall. She glared angrily at the Rollerblades on her feet. Why did people in commercials make these look enjoyable? She shifted her insulated pouch to one hip and gingerly navigated the revolving doors.

A perfectly coiffed young woman looked up from the receptionist's desk. She frowned when she spotted Tilly. "May I help you?" She wrinkled her nose, eyeing Tilly's delivery bag. "Do you need me to sign for something?"

"Not unless you ordered a medium half-mushroom pie."

"Pie?"

"Pizza."

"I don't think so." The woman's nose tipped skyward.

Tilly stepped daintily across the marble foyer, struggling to keep her balance atop her skates. "I actually needed to speak with Bunny Love for a moment, please."

"Bunny Love?" The receptionist's frown grew more intense.

Tilly considered giving her the frozen face warning, but decided against it. "Beatrice Love," she explained. "Today is her first day. I think her boss is named Nathan."

"Everyone here has a boss named Nathan," the receptionist sighed. "He runs the company."

Tilly clucked her tongue. "Gotcha." She glanced around the foyer, spotting the time on the wall clock. "Listen, I gotta skate. Is there any way I can get a message to Bunny . . . er . . . Beatrice? It's a matter of life and death."

"Whose death?" A clipped male voice spoke from

behind her. Tilly whirled around, losing her balance and grasping for the granite counter.

The blond gentleman caught her, steadying her by one elbow. A smile flickered across his face as he repeated his question. *"Whose* death?"

"Bunny Love," Tilly whispered. The most beautiful shade of sapphire she'd ever seen ringed his cornflower blue eyes. She swallowed. Hard.

"Bunny's life is in danger?" Laugh lines crinkled the corners of his eyes.

Tilly's mouth turned to cotton. This was unheard of. The man was a suit. In the truest sense of the word. She gazed down the length of his charcoal pinstripes and sucked in a sharp breath at the sight of burgundy tassled loafers. The unmistakable pull of excitement tightened in her belly. These were the sexiest loafers she'd ever seen, and she was fairly certain the sensation had everything to do with the man wearing them and not the shoes themselves. "Nice shoes," she murmured.

He gazed down at her Rollerblades and arched a blond brow. "Nice skates. Out exercising?"

Tilly shook her head. "I'm working."

"In your skates?" His pale gaze narrowed on her.

"I'm a mobile waiter."

"A what?"

"Mobile waiter."

He nodded toward her uniform cap. "Why the Domino's hat?"

"I deliver pizzas."

"Interesting." He smirked.

Tilly nodded, searching her brain for any sign of a coherent thought. "You meet the most fascinating people."

The man smiled. "And they, in turn, meet you."

He released her elbow and extended his hand. "Bert Parks."

Tilly shook his hand. "Matilda Stringer."

"Friend of Beatrice's?"

She nodded. "We live across the hall from each other."

"Well," Bert said. "I'm afraid she's out at a meeting with her boss. I'll tell her you stopped by."

"Would you be so kind as to give her a message for me?"

Bert eyed her closely, wrinkling his brow. "Your hair is blue."

Tilly shrugged. "So?" She pointed at Bert's precisely clipped cut. "Your hair is blond."

"Yes." He reached out to touch a strand of her hair. "But blond is natural. Blue is not."

"Well." Tilly's heart tapped a rapid beat against her ribs as he dropped his hand and stepped backward. "Don't tell that to a blueberry."

A slow grin spread across his face. "I suppose you have a point there. You mentioned a message for Beatrice."

"Yes." Tilly glanced again at the clock. Her heart caught. She had eight minutes to deliver the pizza or cover the bill. Again. She positioned her pouch in the crook of her arm and pushed off of the counter. "Please tell Bunny the Condo Board meeting was changed to six o'clock sharp. She can't be late."

She glanced over her shoulder in time to catch Bert's grin.

"Any other messages you'd like me to deliver? Errands to run, perhaps?"

"Quick wit, Bert. I like that."

Tilly skated to an abrupt stop as she hit the edge of the revolving door. "Has anyone ever told you you've got a perfect aura?"

Bert's blue eyes sparkled with amusement. "Aura? Perfect?" He gave a quick shake of his head. "No."

Tilly tapped the peak of her cap. "A perfect rainbow. Balanced and healthy." She winked, pushing against the heavy glass of the door. "Call me if you ever need a pizza."

As she clattered down the sidewalk dodging lunchtime pedestrians, Tilly frantically hoped he'd do just that.

Bunny and Nate waited just inside the entrance to the convention center. He glanced at his watch, tamping down his impatience. Leave it to Armand Miller to keep them waiting.

The rapid slap of hard heels against the expansive marble hall jolted Nate from his thoughts. He turned in time to watch Armand effortlessly flip down the collar of his herringbone jacket. He slipped off a pair of sleek black sunglasses, tucking them neatly into his breast pocket. A split second later a stunning smile adorned the man's face.

Nate couldn't help but wonder how many times Miller had practiced the moves in a mirror. He returned Armand's smile with a calculated glare. "You're late. As usual."

Armand's smile broadened. Nate hadn't thought it possible. "I got tied up on the phone with a very important client. You probably can't relate. I hear business is slow."

"You hear wrong." Even though Nate's blood simmered, he savored the victory he and Armand both knew he owned. "Take The Worthington Cup for example."

Armand laughed. "I'm not terribly broken up about losing the account."

"You can't be serious." Nate stopped short.

Armand's focus changed, zeroing in on Bunny. "And who is this heavenly creature you've brought with you?"

Nate did a mental eye roll. Bunny would never fall for that line of bull. As he watched, a pale blush bloomed in her cheeks. Unbelievable.

"Bunny Love," she said, shaking Armand's hand. "It's a pleasure to meet you."

"The pleasure"—Armand dragged his words out dramatically—"is all mine."

Nate fought the urge to yank their hands apart. This was all he needed—to have Armand Miller charming his newest coordinator.

"Miss Love will be overseeing The Worthington Cup." Nate gestured down the hall toward the main area of convention and exhibit space. "We do have other business to attend to today. Do you think we might get on with this?"

"Of course." Armand gave Bunny one last head-to-toe appraisal, then stepped out ahead of the trio toward the convention center's exhibit hall. "I've notified the floor manager that you'd be here. She's expecting us."

"Very well," Nate said curtly.

He tipped his head toward Armand's quickly departing backside. Bunny took his cue, following the event planner from hell across the expansive corridor.

Nate couldn't wait until this little tour was over.

Bunny knew she was blushing, and try as she might, she found herself completely unable to stop. Quite frankly, in a battle between the rapid beat of her heart and the somersaults in her stomach, the blush was the least of her worries.

She'd never before received a compliment from such a devastatingly gorgeous sample of the male species. She was pathetic. Tilly was right. She needed to get out more often.

Just the sight of Armand's ice blue eyes as they raked their way down her body had been enough to turn her into a quivering heap of female flesh. Whew. She fought the urge to shudder. She could still feel the hot trails his gaze had left behind.

She mentally chastised herself. Never one to swoon at the sight of a handsome male, the last forty-eight hours had drawn some interesting reactions from her body. Maybe her hormones were out of balance. Herbs might help, she thought. She'd do some research when she got home.

She watched Armand Miller's not-so-subtle swagger and hesitated for one step. Better yet, maybe there was a more *natural* solution for what ailed her.

"Problem?" Nathan's hand cupped her elbow, urging her along.

The contact sent a jolt of molten lava right to her core.

She sighed deeply. She needed to get out *way* more often.

Twenty minutes later, the three had completed the tour and stood near the exit doors. Bunny tucked her notebook under her arm. She'd never known she could scribble as quickly as she had. Armand had recited the list of the arrangements to date in rapid-fire fashion. It had been all she could do to keep up.

"Well." Armand slipped a business card from his breast pocket and pressed it into Bunny's hand. "Please call me should you need . . . anything."

She met his fiery-hot blue gaze and swallowed. Somehow she managed to mouth the words "Thank you," and she was fairly certain she had said them out loud.

"That won't be necessary," Nathan interrupted. "We'd never bother you about an account that's no longer yours."

"I never was one to say no to a beautiful woman." Armand bowed dramatically.

"Or a tumbler of scotch," Nathan mumbled.

Bunny shot a disbelieving glance in Nathan's direction.

"I'm sorry," Armand said slowly. "Was there something you wished to share with me?" He thinned his lips.

"I said there's not much to botch," Nathan replied. "You've laid out the groundwork beautifully. I'm sure Bunny will have no need of your number."

"Be that as it may"—Armand closed Bunny's fingers around the card—"I'd sleep better at night knowing she has it." He gave her hand a quick squeeze then turned to leave. "Ciao," he called out as he left the building.

Bunny rubbed her hands together to erase the chill caused by the absence of Armand's fingers. She and Nathan stood wordlessly for several long seconds. When the silence grew uncomfortable, she turned to meet his gaze. His brown eyes stared, locked on hers.

"I was only being friendly."

"That"—his glare flashed with anger—"was evident."

Great. She watched as he tossed one last glance toward Armand. A second emotion flickered across Nathan McNulty's face, and it was not anger.

He glanced back to Bunny. "We've got to get back to the office. You have everything you need?"

"Yes."

"And from Mr. Miller?" One dark brow rose above the other. "Will you be needing anything more from him?"

There it was again. Butterflies flitted inside Bunny's abdomen. Nathan McNulty was jealous of Armand Miller.

"For now." She tipped her head as if deep in thought. "But I do have his number if I think of anything."

"About that—" Nathan began.

"Look." She pointed toward the exit doors, interrupting Nate before he could finish his thought. "There's a cab."

She hurried toward the door hoping Nathan would leave his warning unsaid. For the time being, she rather enjoyed having the attention of Armand Miller, even if the man had a high opinion of himself.

She'd rather have the attention of Nathan McNulty, but suspected Mr. Prim and Proper would never let himself fraternize with the likes of Bunny Love.

Chapter 5

Bunny stared at the wall. Blank. Gray. How did these people stand it? She scanned the top of the gleaming credenza. Nothing. Not even a fingerprint.

Closing her eyes, she drew in a deep breath, trying to pick up an energy vibe from the conference room. *Zip.* She sighed. She craved zing and all she got was zilch.

Someone entered the room and she blinked her eyes open.

Bert pulled out a leather chair and settled himself at the head of the long, mahogany conference table. "Your friend Matilda is quite interesting."

Bunny tore her contemplative stare from the energy-lacking space, focusing her frown on Bert. Her mind raced. "You met Tilly?"

"She stopped by to give you a message. The Condo Board meeting's been changed to six o'clock tonight."

"Thanks," Bunny said softly. Six o'clock. She had hoped to get home in time to center and calm herself, though as long as Alexandra was in residence, there'd be nothing calm about home. The meeting change would mean she'd have to dash straight from work into Thurston Monroe's lion's den.

She glanced down at the violet suit. Maybe her new, refined image would dazzle the feng-shui-loathing grouch.

Bert continued to ramble about Tilly. Bunny paused her obsessive thoughts long enough to examine the brightness of his expression. Well, what did you know? It seemed Tilly Stringer had cast her spell on the unsuspecting suit.

"Did she read your aura?"

"Yes." Bert frowned. "How did you know that?"

"She fancies herself gifted." Bunny opened her notebook and clicked out the point of her pen. "So? What did she see?"

He raised his chin, puffing out his chest. "A perfect rainbow. Balanced and healthy."

Bunny stifled a laugh. *Wow. Tilly must be smitten right back at Bert.* "Most impressive."

Bert composed himself, shuffling his notes. "Yes, well, no matter." He cleared his throat. "You and I have a campaign angle to develop."

Five minutes later, the deafening tick of the brass wall clock filled Bunny's otherwise empty brain.

"Anything?" Bert asked.

She stopped tapping her pen against the blank sheet of paper long enough to cast a worried glance in his direction. "I've never done a full media campaign before." She shook her head. "I've got stage fright."

"Nonsense." Bert leaned forward on the mahogany table, lowering his gaze to meet hers. "Apply your design skills." He patted the tabletop. "Be creative. What angle would boost coverage and attendance for The Worthington Cup?"

Bunny swallowed, trying to concentrate. Nothing. She hadn't one single idea. What in the heck was wrong with her? Brainstorming had always been her forte.

She glanced around the gray room, down at the gray carpets and across to Bert's gray pinstripes. "It's too gray here," she said. "There's no energy in this room."

"Pewter," Bert murmured.

"Pardon?"

"You keep calling it gray." He clucked his tongue. "The color is pewter."

Bunny bit her lip then forced a smile. "Sorry."

"Well." Bert stood, pacing the length of the room and back. "I can't come up with a thing, either."

"We need to create energy."

He pivoted on one heel, shooting a disbelieving frown in her direction.

Bunny straightened. "We need something to ease our focus on the problem. Something to free our creative juices."

Bert sank into a chair and rubbed his chin. "Do you still have the batteries for the hamster?"

Bunny felt her tension ease. "No. I thought it best to dispose of the evidence."

He shook his head. "Pity. That was a diversion of epic proportion." His brow furrowed. "Refresh my memory. What other tricks did you have in that box of yours?"

Bunny thought for a moment then grinned. "How do you feel about basketball?"

A slow smile spread across Bert's face. "I was once feared for my bank shot."

Bunny straightened. "I'll be right back."

A few moments later, she reentered the conference room. She pulled a trash can from behind the credenza and snapped the plastic hoop onto its rim.

"What do we do now?" Bert looked at her expectantly.

"We brainstorm." Bunny slipped into her seat, giving a quick shrug.

"I know that, but how does the basketball hoop help?"

"Distraction." She grinned.

"Distraction?"

"Here." She ripped off a sheet of notebook paper and slid it across the table to Bert. "Crumple it up and shoot."

She watched as Bert's pale brow arched. She warmed in response. In the little time she'd known this man, she'd had a glimpse into the real Bert Parks. The softie.

Bert made a dramatic display of crumpling the paper. "Do I shoot standing or sitting?"

"Up to you." She waved one hand. "Be creative with it."

"Okay." Bert nodded. He twisted to shoot the wad of paper from behind his back. It nipped the edge of the rim and bounced to the carpet.

"Try again." Bunny scrambled to retrieve the paper. She tossed it back to Bert. "This time, throw out a slogan."

Bert squinted, carefully aiming his shot. "The Cup for All Canines," he called out. His shot caught the lip of the rim and fell into the basket. He let out a whoop and grinned.

"Nice shot. Lousy tag line," Bunny teased.

Bert extended his hands, wiggling his fingers. "Give me another one." Bunny slid a second piece of paper across the table. Bert crumbled the sheet and aimed. "Your turn."

"This is not your father's dog show," Bunny blurted out.

Bert let the shot fly. The paper hit the floor more than a foot from the basket.

"That was sad," he said.

"So was your shot."

"You think it's so easy?" Bert asked. "You try."

Bunny crumpled a sheet and took aim. The shot fell perfectly into the hoop.

"You've practiced."

She shrugged. "True."

"What's your slogan idea?"

"Dog shows. They're not just for poodles anymore."

Bert snorted and the pair laughed until tears filled their eyes.

They continued to brainstorm until a list of twenty slogans sat scribbled across their notes. They had settled on a revolutionary idea when Nate's deep voice sounded outside the door.

"Damn," Bert whispered.

The doorknob rattled. Bunny dove for the trash can and hoop, sweeping both beneath the conference table. She dropped into her seat just as Nate entered the room.

"What have we here?" he asked suspiciously.

"Brainstorming," Bert answered.

Nate turned his dark brown gaze in Bunny's direction. Anxiety flickered in her chest. As attractive as this man was, he was still the ticket to her job security. And that job security was the ticket to keeping a roof over her head.

Nate frowned. "Sounded like laughter."

A dimple winked from his cheek and Bunny's anxiety morphed into butterflies. Between the heat that surged through her whenever Nate was near and the sensations Armand Miller had inspired earlier in the day, she was exhausted.

Her response to Nate intrigued her. Unlike Armand, Nate made no effort to evoke a reaction. He didn't flirt. He didn't compliment. He did nothing out of the ordinary. Whereas Armand used every line and move in the book to impress Bunny, Nate did nothing.

She scrutinized the strong line of his jaw. Her gaze traveled to where his brown hair stood haphazardly on end. As if on cue, he reached up, smoothing down the wayward strands.

Nathan McNulty simply was. And that was more than intriguing. It was mesmerizing.

"Did you hear me?" His smile had turned into a bone-rattling glare and Bunny's stomach flip-flopped.

Zing. She snapped to attention. Electricity sparked from his rich brown eyes. "I'm sorry?"

"I asked about the campaign slogan. What did you come up with?"

"We have a list of possibilities," Bunny stammered. "But they aren't fully developed."

Bert opened his mouth to speak, but Nate held up a hand to cut him off.

"Miss Love. I realize you are a new employee who has not benefited from a proper orientation period. Our job is to ensure our clients' satisfaction. We do that by delivering well-run events. Well planned. Well organized. Well orchestrated." He ticked off the points one by one on his fingers. "Have you developed an acceptable concept or not? It's a simple question."

Bunny cringed at his firm tone. The man was seriously stifled. A drop-dead-gorgeous life force trapped in a suit—a *gray* suit.

"Well," Bert spoke quickly, "it's not set in stone, but we were thinking of a reality-show theme."

"Reality show?" Incredulity flashed in Nate's eyes.

"Hear me out," Bert said. "We'll add an interactive voting component to the Best in Show judging." He waved his hand to quiet Nate before he could interrupt again. "The public will watch and vote, adding a People's Choice category to the competition." He pointed to Bunny. "Our tag line?"

She straightened in her chair, shivering as Nate's chocolate eyes locked with hers. "The Worthington Cup—The People's Choice for Excellence."

Nate stood silent for several long seconds, finally releasing a slow breath. "It has potential." He turned to Bert, ignoring Bunny. "I'll count on you to finesse the idea. We need to remember Miss Love lacks experience."

Bunny felt relief that Bert was in on the event planner charade, but Nate's words cut to her core, just the same. As she gathered her notebook to leave, she realized he'd hired her to fill a spot. Plain and simple. No matter how hard she tried, he'd probably never see her as more than an underqualified designer hired in a moment of desperation.

* * *

After Nate concluded his final lecture on decorum, Bunny hurried back to her cubicle. Mere feet from her goal she came face-to-face with the Barbie doll in pink. Only today's shade was a pale melon.

Bunny plastered on her best smile and extended her hand. "I should have introduced myself yesterday. I'm Bunny Love."

"Bunny?" the woman asked. "I thought Nathan said your name was Beatrice." Barbie's pale features puckered into a confused expression.

"It is." Bunny gave a quick shrug. "Most people call me Bunny."

The Barbie smiled. "It's very country club chic."

Bunny swallowed down her laugh. "So I've been told."

"I'm Melanie Brittingham."

"Pleased to meet you." Not practiced at office chitchat, Bunny blurted out the first conversation starter that popped into her mind. "Have you worked here long?"

Melanie laughed, a bright smile lighting her beautiful features. She shook her head. "I don't *work* here. I'm meeting Nathan for dinner. We need to discuss our engagement."

The words fell between them like a ton of bricks. A pang of jealousy rippled through Bunny, and she mentally chided herself. She'd known the man with the sizzling cosmic energy for little more than twenty-four hours, yet her heart ached because he was engaged? Absurd.

"Congratulations. I had no idea." She hoped she appeared more cheerful than she felt. She scanned Melanie's left hand, but the ring finger was bare.

As if sensing her glance, Melanie placed her hands on her hips, fingers out of Bunny's view. "It's not official yet," she whispered. "We'll be announcing our good news sometime over the holiday season."

Melanie glanced at her watch. "I've got to go. He's a stickler for punctuality." She moved past Bunny, but stopped to turn back. "I hope you enjoy working with Nathan. I hear he's a wonderful boss."

Bunny nodded, focusing on the opening of her cubicle. *I hope you enjoy working with Nathan.* Somehow, she had enjoyed it a whole lot more before she found out he was as good as engaged.

Oh well, she guessed it was too much to ask to find a great job and a great guy all in the same week.

Nate fought the urge to yank off his jacket. The vibrancy of Beatrice Love's blue eyes had sent his internal temperature soaring.

Bert grinned devilishly. "She's packed with energy, isn't she?" He nodded toward Nate. "You seem especially receptive to her charge."

Nate straightened the notepad on his blotter. "I'm practically engaged."

"I never said you weren't. But there's nothing wrong with noticing a vibrant female." He laughed. "Did you notice the way her buttons—"

"Yes," Nate hissed. "But I have better things to worry about."

"Pity." Bert shook his head. "Hate to see a man who can't appreciate a good set of buttons."

Annoyance rolled in Nate's gut. "I'm going to lose this firm if we don't nail this event."

Bert stood, features pinched.

"Now what?" Nate asked.

"You forget how long I've known you. I can see the attraction in your face whenever she's around you."

Nate tamped down his quickening pulse. Was he that transparent? "I don't know what you're talking about."

Bert waved his hands in defeat then crossed the room. He stopped, his features serious and a bit sad. "If you don't know what I'm talking about, you're more dead inside than I thought."

His nerves raw from his exposure to Bunny, Nate focused his frustration on Bert. "I've had enough lectures for one day."

"Really?" Bert's pale gaze narrowed. "I could say the same thing."

"Bert." Nate took a step toward his vice president. "You and I may be friends, but within these walls, you are my employee. I'll expect you to remember that."

Bert's features fell slack. "I'll keep that in mind."

Nate sat quietly after the door clicked shut. He closed his eyes and ran his hands through his hair. Bert was right, as usual. The atmosphere sizzled whenever Bunny was near, but McNultys had willpower. And Nate McNulty was no different.

He had a job to do, a business to run, and a socialite to marry. He wasn't about to let a self-proclaimed positive chi expert turn his world upside down.

Even if she did have the most electric blue eyes he'd ever seen.

Bunny shifted in her chair, staring at her blank notebook pad. Creativity had never been a problem for her before. She glanced about the small, gray space. Of course, she'd never been in such a stifling environment.

The day had been a whirlwind of meetings, and she hadn't had a chance to settle in. Not that she'd get a chance to if she continued to annoy Nathan McNulty. She tapped the toe of her pump against the box of personal items beneath the desk. Pity. She'd feel much more at home if only she could decorate her cubicle. Make that *office*.

She tried to wiggle her toes, but succeeded only in reminding herself how much her feet ached from too many hours in the confining shoes. She lowered her face to her palms, sighing deeply. What she wouldn't give for her bunny slippers and a cup of hot chamomile tea.

"His bark is worse than his bite." Bert's voice rang out close and soft.

She spun to face him, shaking her head. "I blew it today."

He pursed his lips. "You're good for this firm. We could use some shaking up."

She frowned disbelievingly.

"About your box of tricks." Bert winked. "They're fine under your desk. They've proven quite useful thus far." He pulled the basketball hoop from behind his back. "We left this in the conference room. Wouldn't want it to disappear."

She took the plastic rim from his hands and tucked it into the box. When she turned back to face him, she rolled her eyes. "This day has been a disaster."

"Not at all." He glanced at his watch. "You'd better hurry up before you're late to your meeting. And, Bunny?"

"Yes?"

A genuine smile warmed his face. "Welcome to Mc-Nulty Events. I'm glad you're here."

Chapter 6

Bunny fought the urge to squirm. She sat alone, separate from the other residents who'd gathered in the Wellington Arms's lounge for the Condo Board meeting. The room felt stuffier than usual, and she couldn't help but think what a simple rearrangement of the furniture could accomplish.

The six members of the Condo Board panel sat at the front of the room with Thurston Monroe leading the charge. Not one strand of the man's slick, silver hair fell out of place. His tweed jacket, paisley ascot and gavel completed his perfect, upper-class ensemble.

While Bunny waited for Monroe to call her name, she eyed the bright, red object clinging to the side of her pump. A crushed candy-coated chocolate. Another subtle reminder of Alexandra's surprise invasion. Honestly, if not for sugar and caffeine, the woman would shrivel up and die.

Greeting cards. Bunny winced, trying to flick off the sticky candy by batting one shoe against the other. Her mother had come back to Philadelphia to write greeting card verses. This from a woman who had devoted her life to maintaining the perfect home for the perfect husband in the perfect lifestyle.

Why couldn't she have gone to California to take out her midlife crisis on Vicki? She and her boring family probably would have welcomed the excitement. *Yawn.*

The only creative energy Bunny's sister had ever experienced had been the birth of her son. Now that kid showed much chaotic promise.

"Miss Love."

Bunny snapped to attention. Monroe's tone sounded even crankier than usual.

"Were you planning on joining us anytime soon?" he continued. "Or were you going to bang your feet together all night?"

Heat flushed Bunny's cheeks and she quickly straightened, doing her best to appear polished and responsible.

A few minutes later, she felt as though the interrogation had been going on for hours.

"What about your income level for financing?" Thurston asked. "I don't see how a freelance . . . whatever it is you are . . . can gain approval."

"Actually, I'm employed full time now." Bunny held her chin high and straightened her spine. "I'm proud to say I'm the newest event coordinator at McNulty Events."

Thurston's gray brows met in a peak. "Martha's firm?"

Bunny did a mental eye roll. What did these wealthy people have? A private club?

"Yes." She offered her best I-will-be-the-best-condo-owner-you've-ever-seen smile.

"Impressive." Thurston nodded while making a notation on a lined pad of paper. "The firm is quite selective."

Yes, Bunny cheered silently. Willie Simpson winked quickly. This was good. Very good.

"Of course there was that unfortunate incident with the lobby furniture." Thurston's voice dropped to a low grumble.

Bunny winced. *So close.* She'd been seconds away from an approval. She just knew it.

"Well." Bunny paused for a moment, concentrating on controlling the defensive tone of her voice. Sheesh. How long was Monroe going to hold this grudge?

"Other than the accident involving your wrist, for which I am so, so sorry, I felt the residents were receptive to the improved flow of the space."

Bunny smiled at Willie Simpson who bobbed her snow-white head in agreement. Thurston shot the woman a glare. She froze, offering a nervous smile to Thurston and a shrug to Bunny.

"Be that as it may," Thurston continued, "I'm not sure it's in the best interest of the Wellington Arms for you to take up permanent residence."

An audible gasp rose from those gathered.

Bunny's heart tattooed against her rib cage. "But Mr. Monroe, I never meant any harm. I've never tried to do anything but be helpful to the residents here." She blinked back tears. She was *not* going to appear weak. Not now. "I love the Wellington Arms. I can't imagine living anywhere else."

"Did you know, Ms. Love, that I am incapable of a one-handed backhand?" He leaned forward. "I was the league champ. *Champ*. Do you realize what your little stunt put me through? Six weeks in a cast and months of painful physical therapy."

"Should have been looking where he was going," Tilly's voice muttered from the small group behind Bunny.

"What was that, Ms. Stringer?" Fury boiled in Thurston's steel gray gaze.

"She didn't say a thing, sir," Bunny interjected. "I wish there was something I could do to make it up to you. But, please, I'm asking you—the panel—to approve my application."

"Is your financing ready?" Thurston's silver brows met in a bushy peak. Bunny cringed.

"I should have final approval within days."

"What's holding it up?"

"Nothing, really," she stammered. "I was only able to apply this week, once I started my employment."

She nodded her head, hoping she appeared financially solvent. "It's a standard waiting period. There won't be a problem."

Thurston sneered and rapped his fingers on the tabletop. "I should hope not." He turned to the other members of the Condo Board. "Any other questions for Ms. Love?"

"Yes." Margaret Jamison held up a frail hand, pointing toward Bunny's suit. "Isn't that the suit that disappeared from the Wellington Theater wardrobe closet?"

A choked snort came from the crowd. Bunny had no doubt the sound had emanated from Tilly's throat.

"Why, I don't believe so." Bunny lovingly brushed the front of the jacket. "This was a gift from a dear friend." She gave Margaret her warmest smile.

Thurston eyed Margaret closely. The elderly woman shrugged then nodded. "All right." Thurston rapped his gavel against the desktop podium. "This board hereby grants you approval, conditioned upon final financing arrangements." He opened a small personal planner. "We expect your settlement to be complete by November first. Understood?"

"Understood." Bunny stood to leave. "Thank you."

November first. The day after The Worthington Cup concluded. Her pulse roared in her ears and anxiety played havoc with her belly. Her entire future rode on her ability to successfully plan a dog show. *A dog show.* If that wasn't cosmic irony, she didn't know what was.

She'd almost made it to the door when Thurston cleared his throat. "I'll be watching you, Miss Love. Very, very carefully."

Great. She mentally rolled her eyes. *Join the club.*

"I'll be watching you," Tilly mimicked as they headed for the elevator.

"Shh," Bunny warned. "With my luck he's probably got the whole place bugged."

"I did hear he rigged an alarm to that sofa." Tilly winked. "Slightest rearrangement sets it off."

"Very funny." Bunny punched the up button.

"You happy?"

Bunny shot her friend a glare. "That I get to keep a roof over my head? Or that I'll be forced to live with Thurston Monroe watching every move I make?"

Tilly patted her shoulder. "He'll get over it. You'll see."

"How could you let me wear a suit you *stole* from the wardrobe closet?"

Tilly rolled her eyes. "Hey, I thought they said we could keep our outfits."

"I'd strangle you if you weren't my best friend."

Tilly winked. "You'd never strangle me. I'm too cute."

Bunny made a face, but Tilly was right. She'd be lost without her support and friendship. "Want to run to Daffy's with me before they close?"

"Can't." Tilly frowned. "It's online chat night for the Psychic Hotline."

The elevator doors slid open and the two stepped inside. Bunny leaned heavily against the polished brass wall. "I need suits." She leaned to rub one heel. "And some different shoes. These pumps are killing me."

Upstairs, Tilly followed Bunny into her apartment, then perched on the arm of an oversized stuffed chair. "Where's Alexandra?"

"How'd you know she was here?" Bunny eyed her friend curiously, kicking off the dreadful pumps.

"Please." Tilly rolled her eyes. "All I heard all day was the vacuum or Barry Manilow."

Bunny winced. "Sorry."

Tilly widened her eyes, as if waiting for an explanation.

"She left my dad." Bunny opened a kitchen cabinet, gesturing toward the immaculately organized plastic storage containers. "She's taking it out on me."

Tilly's nose crinkled as she stepped close. "I didn't know those things were meant to be stacked."

"It gets worse." Bunny reached for the newest addition to her once sacred kitchen space. The sleek, black coffeemaker stuck out like a sore thumb next to the delicate herb garden.

"Omigosh." Tilly shuddered at the sight of the machine, taking a melodramatic step backward. "This is worse than I thought."

"You can joke." Bunny yanked a hand towel from the rack and flipped it over the machine to hide most of the plastic and glass. "But this is serious." She patted the top of the appliance. "This means Alexandra's staying for a while."

She headed for the bedroom, Tilly close on her heels.

"You two get along all right, though, don't you?"

"When she's not trying to control my life? Sure." Bunny slipped off the suit jacket and carefully hung it on a padded hanger. Stepping out of the skirt, she reached for her softest pair of blue jeans, then plucked her favorite tie-dyed T-shirt from a dresser drawer.

"That's better." Tilly beamed. She waggled a finger at Bunny's head. "That smooth hair's freaking me out. You know the messy look is in. If you have to wear suits, at least you could keep the messy hair."

Bunny self-consciously touched her hand to her head. She felt like an alien with the slick look, but apparently Nate McNulty had thought otherwise. The heat in his eyes had been unmistakable when he'd first seen her that morning. Ah well, now that she knew he and Melanie were an item, it all made sense. A man like Nathan McNulty *would* go for someone wearing Chanel and polished, smooth hair. It's what society types did.

"Are you coming with me or not?" Bunny nervously glanced at the wall clock. "They'll be closed in an hour."

Tilly hopped down from the chair. "Can't. Gotta

chat." She shook her head. "I think my chakras would shrivel up and die if they witnessed you buying suits."

Bunny nodded toward the limp outfit on the hanger. "I'll get it cleaned before I return it to the theater."

"You can't return it now. They think it's yours. Besides," Tilly said softly, "it complements the new you."

Bunny winced at her friend's words. "I need the new me."

"I liked the old you just fine." Tilly frowned, then brightened suddenly. "Hey, I met one of your coworkers today."

"I heard."

Tilly's jade gaze widened. "Yum."

"Yum?" Bunny's mouth gaped in disbelief. "Tilly, he's a nice guy, but not your type."

"I wouldn't be so sure. If you can become a suit, I can lust after one." She pulled open the front door, hesitating at the threshold. "It's going to take some time for me to get used to the whole Bunny-Love-goes-corporate idea."

After Tilly left, Bunny stared at the closed door for several long seconds. "You and me both," she whispered. "You and me both."

Nate took a long sip of his scotch, savoring the burn of the liquor as it slid down his throat. Cigar smoke filled the Union League lounge. His dinner with Melanie had ended early, so he'd thought it best to take care of other business while it was fresh on his mind.

"To what do I owe the honor of my summons?" Jeremy's voice startled Nate. His golden-haired brother slid into the opposite chair. The leather creaked and Jeremy's eyes widened expectantly. "I can't wait to hear what account necessitated asking for help."

"The Worthington Cup." Nate swirled another

mouthful of scotch, enjoying the warmth seeping through his extremities.

"The dogs?" Jeremy's smile curled into a bemused grin. "How'd you get roped into that one?"

"Aunt Martha." Nate downed the last of his drink and gestured toward the waiter. "What are you drinking?"

Jeremy leaned back against his seat, crossing ankle to knee. "I'll have the same."

"Two scotches." Nate scrutinized his older brother. Jeremy's pale blue sweater draped open at his neck where he had left the buttons undone. His blue jeans were crisp and creased, but blue jeans nonetheless. Relaxed. At ease.

"Why does she want The Worthington Cup?" Concern flickered in Jeremy's dark blue eyes.

"Why does she want anything?" Nate formed quotation marks with his fingers. "Safety and security." He ran a hand through his hair and let out a frustrated breath. "She wants the firm on solid footing and me married to Melanie."

The waiter set two tumblers of scotch on the table. Nate drank down half of his as Jeremy looked on.

"You drunk?" Jeremy asked.

"McNultys don't get drunk."

"It wouldn't hurt you to live a little." Jeremy gave a quick shrug. "No one asked you to be so good."

"Didn't they?"

Jeremy shook his head.

"I'm not having this conversation tonight," Nate said. "You wouldn't know the first thing about living up to expectations."

"I set my own expectations." Jeremy's tone grew stiff. "You should try it sometime."

"So you think." Nate polished off his remaining scotch, then laced his fingers behind his head. "Can you design an interactive Web site?"

"For McNulty Events?" A smug grin spread across

Jeremy's movie star features. "Welcome to the future, little brother."

Wiseass, Nathan thought. "It's for the Cup."

"The dogs need a Web site?"

A deep furrow formed between Jeremy's perfect pale brows. His was a face women swooned over. Lord, his brother was right. He had had too much to drink.

Nate focused on keeping his words from slurring. "I want interactive voting from the television audience. Is it feasible?"

Jeremy stared at Nate incredulously. "Completely." He pressed his lips together. "Your idea?"

"I was part of the team that developed the concept." Not a total lie. "You don't think I'm capable of creative thought?"

"You're perfectly capable," Jeremy replied. "I'm impressed you allowed yourself the luxury, quite frankly. I didn't think creative thought fit your version of the McNulty mold."

"Well, it does." Nate tossed several bills onto the table and stood. "Can you be at the office tomorrow morning? I'd like you to meet the coordinator handling the event."

"I'll be there first thing. What's his name?"

"*Her* name is Bunny. Bunny Love."

Jeremy's brows met in a puzzled peak.

"Don't ask," Nate snarled as he turned to leave. "Just be there by nine."

"Wild horses couldn't keep me away."

Jeremy's words echoed in Nate's mind as he hailed a taxi. *Wild horses.* Hopefully his brother wouldn't share his sentiments with Miss Love. The last thing Nate needed was anyone giving her additional ideas.

Bunny browsed the racks of Daffy's designer suit section without excitement. These outfits weren't her. Too stiff. Too structured. Too . . . well . . . suits. She ran her fingertips down a rough burgundy crepe sheath and sighed. She didn't belong on this floor. Hell. She didn't belong in this *world*.

She ruffled her hair, stopping to look at herself in a full-length mirror. Tilly was right. The straight hair was freaky. Corporate. But freaky.

She blew out a frustrated breath, turning back toward the discount rack. She'd pick three basic suits and buy them. They'd mix. They'd match. They'd be boring. Piece of cake.

While quickly scanning the rack for promising colors, her gaze settled first on a turquoise silk. The color was perfect—key for self-expression and creativity—exactly what she needed for her role at McNulty Events.

She next plucked a bright orange sheath and long jacket from the rack. She held the outfit at arm's length and nodded. Not bad. Orange was great for creativity, security and sexuality. She stifled a laugh. What a combination.

One more. If she could find one more suit and a pair of comfortable shoes, she'd head home.

A monotone woman on the overhead public address system announced fifteen minutes until closing. Drat. She needed to move quickly.

A rich emerald sleeve peeked from between the black and grays of a second rack. Bunny tugged the suit free and grinned. It was actually quite charming. A short flared skirt with a long, fitted jacket. Oversized antiqued brass buttons gleamed down the jacket's center.

Bunny glanced at the price tag and winced. This corporate stuff wasn't cheap.

She tossed the suits over her arm and headed for the dressing rooms. A burst of feminine laughter drew her attention and Bunny looked toward the source, stopping dead in her tracks.

A striking blonde circled and twirled before the

triple mirrors. Her hair twisted smoothly into a large clip and a tight, sequined sheath of cobalt blue hugged her curves.

Bunny was about to turn away, when the woman spun toward her, twisting to admire the low cut of the garment's back. Bunny recognized her instantly—the life-sized Barbie doll.

Melanie Brittingham. Little Miss Pink Chanel wouldn't be caught dead in a sexy number like that. Would she?

The woman planted her hands on her hips, struck a pose, then twirled once more. She disappeared into the dressing room, leaving Bunny to stare at the spot where she'd stood.

Bunny blinked. She glanced at the suits over her arm, snapping herself from the trance. If she wanted to have anything to wear tomorrow, she'd better get a move on.

She peered beneath each closed door as she made her way toward an empty dressing room stall, but saw no sign of the woman in blue. She must have been seeing things.

A few moments later, she frowned at her reflection in the mirror. The turquoise suit fit beautifully, but was so not her style. She squinted. Was that her energy field she saw shriveling up?

She stared lovingly at her tie-dyed T-shirt and jeans draped across the dressing room bench. They were her style. She ran a hand through her hair, doing her best to mess up the smooth strands. And *that* was her style. Not smooth. Not corporate. Not McNulty Events.

After she returned the turquoise and orange suits to their places on the rack, only the emerald suit remained slung over the crook of her arm. She quickly moved to the clearance section and pulled a floral dress from where it hung. A soft ruffle wound its way down the wrapped front and traced the edge of the skirt's hem. Perfect.

Bunny dashed for the shoe department, pausing

long enough to glance in a full-length mirror. She gave her hair a good shake and smiled.

Tilly had been right. She'd always marched to the beat of a different drummer, encouraging creative freedom. Why stop now?

Chapter 7

The next morning Bunny shook her damp hair into its usual state of disarray and let it air dry while she moved through her morning yoga routine. After downing the last of her green tea, she pulled the burgundy floral dress from its hanger. The delicate fabric brushed softly against her skin as she slipped it over her head.

She pulled on her new, black patent-leather slingbacks, glossed on a rich, ruby lipstick, and stopped for a quick final check in the bathroom mirror. Her hair curled and waved uncontrollably, natural highlights kissing the tips of each peak and valley. *Better,* she thought. *Much, much better.*

Her mother hadn't stirred from the other bedroom. Bunny paused outside the door to listen. *Silence.* At least she slept like a log once she went down. Alexandra had been out late with her greeting card design instructor doing God knew what. Based on the gleam of the kitchen floor, the woman had been mainlining espresso. Either that or there had been some seriously pent-up frustrations to work out.

Bunny glanced at her answering machine. Not a peep from her father. The king of denial. Why confront the problem when eventually her mother would soften and go home, once again shoving down a little piece of her own rebellion?

This was exactly why Bunny avoided serious relationships. They always ended up with one person doing all of the conceding and the other getting off scot-free. Talk about emotional torture. Marriage was not for her. Not now. Not ever.

She grabbed her briefcase from beside her desk, casting a long, yearning look at her bunny slippers. What if she had a creative emergency? What good would she be without them? She plucked them from the floor and tucked them inside her briefcase. The floppy ears were a bit difficult to conceal, but she managed. Barely.

The green shoots of her lucky bamboo stalks caught her attention next. She hesitated. Nathan wouldn't complain about a small plant, would he? Bunny gently tucked the ceramic container into the crook of her arm, grabbed her keys and headed to work.

An hour later, she sat at her desk doing her best to ignore her throbbing toes. The delicate shoes had seemed heavenly in the store, but certainly felt anything but after the walk to work. She'd have to break out the bunny slippers soon if she wanted to keep her ability to walk intact.

"Beatrice." Nate's rich voice rumbled into her cubicle. His tall, masculine figure followed, coming to a halt as soon as he set eyes on her. A look of surprise washed over his face, sending anxiety fluttering through Bunny's stomach.

"Something wrong?" she asked coolly, pushing the lucky bamboo shoots out of sight behind her computer monitor.

"You're not—" He plowed a hand through his dark brown locks, leaving them disheveled. "You're not wearing a suit."

"No." Bunny stood from her chair to smooth the front of her dress, admiring how the ruffled hem brushed the tops of her knees.

A flush fired in Nate's cheeks, and his Adam's apple

worked in his throat. "Those are ruffles." His voice had grown thick and robotic.

"Yes." She held her chin defiantly high. "You don't have a dress code here at McNulty Events, do you?"

He met her determined stance with a leveled glare, a fraction of heat slipping from his mocha gaze. "No." His dark brows arched. "But we do insist on professionalism. I'm not sure how appropriate that"—he nodded his head toward Bunny—"dress is for the office."

Frustration fired in Bunny's midsection. She thought of her mother, probably back in the apartment right now bingeing on cheap, chocolate candy because she'd woken up one day and realized how stifled her life had become. There was a lesson for Bunny there—to defend her individuality while she could. If she didn't act now, she'd suffocate in this gray place.

"I am a creative, professional woman, Mr. McNulty."

His brown eyes popped a bit wider. Bunny stepped closer.

"And I will respect your need for gray"—she waved one arm in a wild gesture—"everywhere in this firm. But I need you to respect my need for positive chi. That's more than fair."

Nate took a step backward. "I never intended to stifle you or your chi." Wild thoughts raced through his head. The woman was the sexiest lunatic he'd ever seen. He admired the soft curves of the ruffled dress. *Curves.* At least her suits had hidden some of *those.*

Warm heat surged up his neck and face. This was precisely why women in offices should wear suits. It prevented men in offices from noticing things like curves.

Bunny took another menacing step toward him—not that anyone with her disheveled hair, creamy skin, and brilliant eyes could ever be considered truly menacing. "I will not disappoint you as far as The Worthington Cup is concerned," she said, eyes flashing. "But I insist you allow me to express my unique self."

The Worthington Cup. The sole reason Miss Bunny Love stood before him, posing as his star event coordinator.

"I've given this a lot of thought," she continued, "and I feel quite strongly that——"

"Very well, Beatrice." Nate held up a hand to interrupt her diatribe. "I'll respect your need for positive chi, if you'll focus on the task at hand."

Her vibrant blue gaze widened. "You agreed to call me Bunny."

"That was yesterday."

Surprise and sadness flickered through her features. Nate's stomach tightened. He opened his mouth to apologize for his tone, but quickly rethought the move. He had to maintain the upper hand here. After all, he was the boss.

"As I explained yesterday, this is a place of business, Miss Love. Let's keep that in mind." He turned to leave her work space. "Right now, you're needed in a meeting. I've decided to pursue the idea of interactive voting. There's a Web design expert waiting in the conference room."

He turned to find her gathering her notepad and pen from her desk. The hem of her skirt inched up her leg, exposing a generous slice of creamy thigh. He swallowed.

When he forced his gaze back to her face, his eyes locked with hers. A soft pink blossomed in her cheeks and she smiled.

"I'll be right there."

"Fine." Nate turned and sped from the cubicle.

As soon as this meeting was over, he'd have to give some serious thought to establishing a formal dress code.

* * *

Bunny sat riveted by the power struggle between Nate and his brother, Jeremy. Judging by the smirk on Bert's lips, he found the give-and-take more than entertaining.

Jeremy appeared to be everything Nate was not. Relaxed. Open to new ideas. *Human.* She mentally chastised herself. That wasn't fair. Nate was human. At least he displayed human tendencies every now and then, like when she'd caught him checking out her legs back at her cubicle.

At this particular moment, they all watched his brother sketch a Web site flowchart on the recessed presentation panel.

"Bunny?" Jeremy's voice broke through her thoughts. "What do you think of the site plan?"

This was her chance, she realized. She had designed countless sites for clients and had mastered the use of color and layout to maximize impact. "I think it's excellent," she replied confidently. "I wonder if I could make a few suggestions?" She jumped to her feet, gathering an assortment of markers in her grip. "May I?"

"Well, I—" Nate's words were interrupted by Jeremy.

"Be my guest." Jeremy stepped aside.

Bunny tossed Nate a victorious grin as she set about sketching a design idea for the site. She used a variety of bright colors and shapes to frame a sample Web page, drawing in banners and buttons with quick sketches of various dog breeds.

"There." She took a step back to admire her work. "See anything you like?"

Yes, Nate thought. He most definitely saw something he liked and it wasn't the image on the board. Relief washed through him as Bunny took another step backward. All that sketching had turned his thermostat up a notch—or ten. He slipped out of his suit jacket.

What in the hell was wrong with him? He was about

to become engaged to Melanie, for crying out loud. And Melanie was far more suitable for a McNulty than Miss Bunny Love. But Melanie had *never* made his blood boil.

Bunny's brilliant eyes narrowed on him. "Are you all right? You look feverish."

"I think he's just a bit warm," Bert muttered. "He's had a recent tendency toward hot flashes."

Nate shot Bert a threatening glare. Bert lowered his face, but his quaking shoulders belied his amusement.

Bunny's eyebrows arched. "You're not ill, are you?"

"No," Nate replied, tossing his jacket over the chair back. "I believe your vision could work, Bunny . . . er . . . Beatrice."

He warmed at the smile that spread across her face. Her idea was quite good, actually. There was something to be said for positive chi after all, not that he'd admit that to her.

"Bunny." Jeremy interrupted their exchange. "Perhaps you and I could meet later to dig into the site design."

"Not necessary," Nate interjected.

Bert leaned a fist against his mouth to hide his obvious amusement.

"I think it's a good idea," Jeremy said slowly. "Do you have plans for lunch today?"

Anger began to simmer in Nate's belly as he watched his brother's gaze absorb Bunny's presence. "She's having lunch with me," Nate snarled. "And Aunt Martha," he quickly added. "For the record, Miss Love has the entire Worthington Cup to organize, not merely the Web site."

Bert's fingers were now pressed to his lips. "If we're through here, I'm going to slip out," he said, stepping toward the door. "Interesting concepts," he added as he fled.

Nate could have sworn he heard a tight burst of laughter once the conference room doors clicked shut.

"Well," Jeremy said. "Perhaps another time, Bunny." He gathered his notes, turning his attention to Nate. "In the meantime, I'll work up sketches, cost estimates, and a production timeline for you, baby brother."

Nate flinched. "Thanks."

Jeremy shook Bunny's hand, holding it just a moment too long. "I look forward to working closely with you."

Not too closely, Nate thought possessively, silently urging his brother to leave. He and Bunny stood in uncomfortable silence for several long seconds once they were alone.

Nate broke the ice. "Nice ideas."

"Yes, your brother seems quite good at what he does."

"I meant *your* ideas, Bunny."

The familiar blush fired in her pale cheeks. "Thanks." She returned the markers to the board and closed the cabinet doors. "I'd better get some work done before our lunch."

Nate nodded, watching the colorful ruffles flutter about her knees as she stepped across the room. He glanced at his watch. If he worked quickly, he could draft that dress code before lunch.

Bunny had been back at her desk for several minutes when she decided she couldn't take it for another moment. Her feet throbbed with pain. She kicked off the sling-backs and glanced over her shoulder to the entrance of her cubicle. Clear.

Reaching beneath her desk, she tugged her box of goodies from its hiding place. She'd stashed the slippers safely inside earlier this morning. In one deft move she plucked them from the box and slid them onto her sore feet.

Bunny wiggled her toes, letting the soft, plush cushion of the fur caress her tired arches and insteps. She leaned back against her chair and stretched out her legs. Ecstasy. If there were a dress code at McNulty Events, *these* should be number one on the list of required items.

Bunny inhaled a cleansing breath as she pulled out her notes from the meeting.

"Let's go." Nate's voice boomed from behind her. "I've called down for a cab."

Bunny jumped so hard she slammed her knee on the underside of her desk. "Sh—" She muffled her swear as she glanced at her watch. "You're twenty minutes early."

"Punctuality is key in this business. Let's go."

She shuffled her feet farther under the desk, twisting to meet Nate's impatient gaze. "I'll meet you in the lobby."

"Nonsense. Whatever you're doing can wait."

Bunny smiled brightly as she fumbled to kick one slipper off with the other. Try as she might, she couldn't wiggle her feet free.

Nate's eyebrows drew together. "Problem?"

She quickly shook her head. "I'll meet you. I need to go to the ladies' room."

His lips pressed into a thin line and he nodded toward her feet. "What are you doing? Stand up and let's get going. You're wasting time."

A shiver of dread whispered through Bunny. So much for maintaining a low profile with her box of tricks. She took a deep breath, straightened and stepped toward Nate.

His features pinched into a pained expression and he pointed toward her feet. "Want to explain those?"

"My feet hurt. I didn't think anyone would mind if I slipped these on for a moment." Lord, she was babbling. "No one saw me. I promise."

"I saw you, Miss Love." He frowned. "What the hell are they supposed to be? Some sort of rodent?"

Bunny gazed down at the worn pink ears and the faded black noses. "Bunny slippers," she whispered.

Nate's eyelid twitched and he pressed a finger to hold it steady. "I don't think I heard you properly."

She cleared her throat. "Bunny slippers."

His chest heaved and he visibly worked to steady himself. "I was afraid that's what you said." He waved one hand toward the hall. "I'm going to step out there to wait for you. You have precisely twenty seconds to meet me there wearing proper footwear. Understood?"

"Yes."

Nate disappeared through the opening. Bunny dove for her shoes, tossing the slippers into the box and shoving it beneath the desk. Grabbing her notebook, she dashed for the hall.

Nate stood leaning against the wall, eyes closed, hair rumpled into an unruly mess. His eyelids fluttered open as she neared. "Ready?"

Bunny pointed toward his head. "You might want to fix your hair."

"And you might want to permanently lose those slippers."

Bunny followed Nate's perfect back down the gray hall, anxiety swirling in the pit of her stomach. She knew *she* wasn't perfect, but at least she didn't try to hide it.

Nate McNulty might appear to be a tidy package, but the rumpled hair and the twitch gave him away. Although he tried his hardest to present a smooth, unflappable image, he couldn't fool Bunny. No way. Beneath that cold, collected exterior lurked some serious positive energy—undeniable and stifled.

An idea tickled the back of her brain and she smiled devilishly to herself. What *would* it take to set his energy free?

He stood several steps ahead, glaring at her. A furrow formed between his dark brows, his mocha eyes smoldering with impatience. "We're late, Beatrice."

She hurried to catch up, doing her best to ignore the wave of heat his eyes sent through her body. *Yes.* All signs pointed to a major stash of cosmic energy pent up inside Nate McNulty.

But did Bunny have the skills to set him free? She'd never know unless she tried. And she'd never been one to back down from a challenge.

After all, helping Nate discover his energy was the least she could do for the man who had helped save her apartment.

Chapter 8

Nate held open the heavy glass door. Bunny brushed past, inhaling as much of his warm scent as she could without appearing obvious. Tantalizing smells from the interior of the restaurant quickly overrode her senses. Spices. Herbs. Cappuccino. Her nose struggled to sort one aroma from another.

An extremely polished woman waved from a far table.

"There she is," Nate muttered.

He pressed his palm against the small of Bunny's back, sending a ripple of awareness up her spine.

"For God's sake," he whispered, "act like an expert in event planning."

"But I—"

"Just do it." His curt tone silenced her.

The striking woman stood and extended a hand to Bunny as they neared. Her close-cropped auburn waves expertly framed her flawless face. Bunny had heard the phrase *dripping with diamonds*, but until this particular moment, hadn't fully understood what it meant. She did now. Every available inch Martha McNulty had to offer was jeweled.

"I've been looking forward to meeting you, Miss Love." She gave Bunny's hand a firm shake and gestured to the open seat next to her. "Nate tells me we're lucky to have found you."

Bunny tamped down her amusement. She wondered

if he'd say that now that he'd seen her in action. "Thank you, Mrs. McNulty. I'm thrilled to be part of such an exemplary firm."

"Please, call me Martha."

"Thank you, Martha."

"I'm curious about one thing." The elder woman sipped a glass of sparkling water. "I've been in this business a long time." She gave Bunny a scrutinizing look. "Your name is not familiar to me. Why is that?"

"Well, I—"

"Miss Love is a well-kept secret," Nate interrupted. "She employs a more holistic approach to planning than we've explored previously." He nodded confidently at his aunt. "I have no doubt she'll have a positive effect at McNulty."

Bunny watched the woman's eyes narrow. "Holistic?"

"Positive chi," Nate replied. "Isn't that right, Bunny . . . Beatrice?"

"Bunny?" Martha's eyes popped from narrow to wide.

"Family name," Nate answered.

Any anger Bunny harbored for Nate since yesterday's lecture evaporated at the sight of him touting positive chi. She watched sympathetically as his face flushed. "Warm in here?" He cast a hopeful glance at Bunny.

"Terribly." She nodded. "Not good at all for your chakras."

Anxiety flickered through his rich brown gaze and his eyelid twitched.

"Chakras?" he and his aunt asked simultaneously.

"Spiritual energy centers." Bunny tapped his arm. "Perhaps you should slip off your jacket. I'd hate to see you become any more blocked than you already are."

Martha made a tsking noise with her tongue. "A gentleman always wears his jacket at meals. Never mind your discomfort."

She turned her attention to Bunny. "I'm a bit confused

as to what any of this has to do with event planning."
Scorn tinged her words.

"Without positive energy," Bunny explained, "creativity is stifled. By utilizing different tools, we can increase the flow of chi, thereby improving the effectiveness of our planning efforts at McNulty. This is possible through color, through feng shui, through—"

"And how will this chi impact the bottom line?"

"Happier clients. Repeat clients. Bigger bottom line." Bunny straightened, meeting Martha's question head-on.

"Hmph." Martha scrutinized Nate. "You agree, obviously."

His Adam's apple worked in his throat. He raised one hand toward his head, but caught himself at the last moment. He quickly lowered his arm. "Completely."

Martha tapped a well-manicured nail to her chin. "I knew a John Love in school. Married some horridly chipper cheerleader. Can't remember her name."

"Alexandra," Bunny answered softly.

Martha snapped her fingers. "Alexandra Conroy. Always spouting off poetry."

Poetry? Alexandra? Maybe her mother's greeting card adventure hadn't come out of left field after all.

"Are you related?" Martha's words dripped with superiority.

"My parents." Bunny traced the lip of her plate with her finger.

"We've developed a cutting-edge program for the Cup," Nate interjected.

Bunny shot him a weak smile, grateful for his effort to divert the conversation from her chipper, cheerleading mother.

"Such as?" Martha's words were curt, completely refocused on the task at hand.

Bunny decided she did not want to get on the wrong

side of this woman. "We've added an interactive Web site and expanded the preview night cocktail party."

"To the public?" Martha's features pinched.

"No." Nate cleared his throat. "To the contestants."

Martha took a dramatic sip of her water, returned the glass to the table, and crossed her arms in her lap. "Surely you aren't referring to the dogs?"

"Revolutionary, isn't it?" Bunny chirped.

Nate shot her a warning look, and she snapped her mouth shut.

"Dogs drink from toilets." Martha's expression grew pained. She let out an exasperated breath. "Why on earth would they require a cocktail party?"

"Kitty Worthington loves the idea." Nate's lips curved into a hopeful smile.

"She would. She's a dog person, Nathan."

Martha waved to get the waiter's attention. "I've got a massage at two," she announced. "You've got to keep on top of them here."

Bunny nodded. The control issue most definitely was an innate McNulty trait.

"Dogs and cocktails." Martha spoke the words slowly as if she were trying them on for size. "Well, if nothing else, it should guarantee coverage in the society pages." Her eyes narrowed, carefully studying Bunny. "Which firm were you with prior to joining McNulty?"

"I was self-employed." Bunny's voice tightened.

"Why join a firm? Weren't you successful?"

The woman shot straight from the hip. That much was certain. "You obviously appreciate honesty."

Martha rocked back in her seat, arching one perfectly plucked brow. "Yes, I do."

"I've been forced to take a mortgage on my apartment, now a condo, and my previous freelance income wasn't sufficient."

Bunny watched the woman's eyes grow wide and realized she'd provided far too much insight into her personal life.

Martha gave Bunny a measured look.

Bunny's heart worked in her throat. She opened her mouth to speak, but Martha waved her jeweled hand dismissively. "So what if you did this for the money. That's a perfectly acceptable reason and one for which you need not apologize. I find your candor refreshing."

Relief washed through Bunny. "Thank you."

The remainder of their lunch passed uneventfully. Bunny successfully held her own against Martha's no-nonsense manner, and the topic of her parents never resurfaced.

Martha McNulty didn't care for the way Nathan's gaze followed each expressive flip of Miss Love's hands. Not that the girl wasn't without charm. Far from it, but she would never do for a McNulty. God, she had to arrange financing to afford a *condominium*. What kind of upbringing had she had?

This was Alexandra Conroy's daughter, after all. She was obviously as energetic as her mother had been. Hell, her mother had been a lunatic—like a cheerleader on speed. Rumor was she'd calmed down after marriage, but the apple couldn't fall far from the tree.

Martha carefully measured Miss Love's bright expression. Not far at all, apparently. Be that as it may, as long as any inherited familial energy was channeled into planning The Worthington Cup and away from Nathan, they'd get along fine.

Nathan was to marry Melanie Brittingham, and their marriage would seal his position in Philadelphia society. Their union would be the perfect blending of two of the region's finest families.

Security. Martha had sacrificed her own dreams to raise Nate, and she wasn't about to watch some free-spirited, ruffle-wearing young woman distract him from the plans she'd made.

Melanie's father had already offered Nate a position in the family's firm. All that stood in the way was her nephew's loyalty to his father's event planning business and an engagement ring. She was capable of handling both.

Perhaps her promise to Nate regarding The Worthington Cup had been premature. She should have sold the firm when she had the chance. Of course, Miller's offer still stood.

A bright smile illuminated Nathan's face in response to Miss Love's laugh.

Dread tickled Martha's insides. This situation needed handling quickly. She would not sit back and watch history repeat itself. Nathan's mother had been his father's undoing. She had no intention of letting the boy make the same mistake.

"Aunt Martha?"

She pulled her attention from her scheming.

"Jeremy agreed to handle the interactive site for us."

"Did he?" Martha asked.

Interest flickered across Bunny's pert features.

Suddenly, Martha's brain wrapped around a potential solution to at least part of the problem. "He never ceases to amaze me," she quipped.

Nate sat back against the uncomfortable chair. What did they mold these seats from? Rocks? And now he had to listen to his aunt's standard chorus of "Jeremy the Wonder Boy." Wonder boy, his ass.

"Bunny would be a charming companion for Jeremy at the Autumn Harvest dinner dance, don't you agree, Nathan?"

Nate shook himself from his mental rant. "Who? What?" Anxiety wound its way through his gut.

Aunt Martha sneered. "You know, Nathan, Miss Love might be correct. Perhaps your chakras need cleaning, as well as your ears."

Heat flared under the collar of his shirt and he longed to toss a glass of ice water down his neck.

"I asked you who your brother is taking to this week's dinner dance."

Nathan shook his head. "I have no idea. I'm not privy to his social calendar."

"I thought Bunny might enjoy the event." Martha peered at Bunny who sat like a wide-eyed doe caught in the headlights of an oncoming truck.

Nate stared. This wasn't happening.

"What about Jeremy, Nate?" Aunt Martha asked. "He broke it off with that Suzy creature, didn't he?"

"He didn't mention a thing about it when he was at the office this morning." Nate swallowed hard, reaching for his water glass before realizing he'd already drained it.

"I'll ask him," his aunt said cheerfully. She stood from the table, tucking her purse beneath her arm. "It's settled then. I'll see you this weekend, Bunny."

Nathan's eye twitched and he pressed a finger to his lid. Bunny. Jeremy. Dinner dance. Not good. Not good at all.

"You and your aunt seem very close." Bunny glanced out the window as the cab pulled into traffic.

"She raised me," Nate answered.

Bunny refocused her attention on Nate, noticing the muscle of his jaw working in his cheek.

"Jeremy and I lost our parents when we were very young. Aunt Martha took us in. She did her best to raise us in proper McNulty family tradition."

Bunny's heart twisted. "I'm sorry."

"Don't be." He smiled tightly. "I've had a great life."

Her curiosity got the best of her. "Why did you present me as you did?"

"What do you mean?"

Bunny rolled her eyes. "Please. Why did you talk about positive chi when you obviously don't believe in it?"

"If she believes you're bringing something fresh to the firm, there's a chance she won't sell."

"I see." Bunny clasped her hands together to steady them. "She wants to sell the firm?" *So much for job security.*

"I intend to stop her." Nate's intent stare sent hot skewers of electricity straight to Bunny's toes. "You've got raw talent, Bunny. I believe we can make the Cup better than any event this region's seen. If we do that, even Aunt Martha will agree to hold on to the company."

"Why didn't you hire a more experienced planner?"

His expression softened. "You want the truth?"

She braced herself. "Yes."

"Because there wasn't time, and you struck me as someone who could learn quickly. And you will."

Bunny tried to tell herself his matter-of-fact statement didn't hurt. But it did.

"I'm sorry my aunt was a little rough on your mother."

She shrugged. "No harm done."

"Did you follow in the family footsteps?" Nate's voice took on a lighter, teasing tone, sending warmth swirling to Bunny's center.

"Cheerleading?"

He nodded, his expression expectant.

"No." Bunny shook her head. "My job was to stand on the sideline." She stared out the window, cringing at the old memories. "When they threw me the ball, I had thirty seconds to dry it off and throw it back."

She glanced back to meet Nate's gaze, unsure of whether she saw sympathy or amusement in the dark brown depths.

"You don't have to attend the dinner dance, by the

way." He glanced away from her. "My aunt was being polite."

Bunny's heart hit the pit of her stomach. "You don't want me there?"

"I assumed you wouldn't want to go." Nate's voice tightened.

"Do you really think I'm that far beneath you?" Her sudden words surprised even herself.

Nate's head snapped to attention, his mocha eyes riveted to hers. "I never said that."

"But you think it." Bunny forced a slight smile. "It's on your face whenever you look at me. You hired me because you had no other choice. I accept that."

"Bunny." He reached out to touch her hand, but pulled back as quickly as he had extended his fingers. "Most people in my social circle aren't like you at all."

"What?" She forced a soft laugh. "Eccentric, like Kitty Worthington?"

His gaze softened and Bunny felt the pull of attraction all the way to her toes. Lord help her, she was falling for a suit who could never be hers.

Nate shook his head. "You're unique." He smiled. "Isn't that what you want me to recognize? Your unique self?"

Heat flared in her cheeks. *If only.* She hadn't yet met a man who'd recognized her unique self. Those she'd dated had only wanted to squash her creative ideas. Not that she wouldn't mind testing Nate's sincerity. "I did say that."

"I'll do my best to respect your individuality, if you do your best to respect the rules of the firm. Give us all some time to accept your positive chi. Deal?"

"Know what I think?" Nervous excitement rippled through her. She knew she should keep her mouth shut, but that had never been one of her strengths.

Nate shook his head. "No, what?"

"I think your cosmic energy would shock you."

The cab pulled up in front of the entrance to the Loews Hotel. "We're at your stop." Nate reached out to squeeze her hand.

Awareness radiated from his touch through every one of Bunny's nerve endings. His eyes widened and she wondered if he sensed the undeniable chemistry between them.

"I must say one thing in my defense." His dark brows bunched together.

"What's that?"

"McNultys do not have blocked chakras."

Genuine laughter spilled from Bunny's lips. "You have no idea of what a chakra is, do you?"

"None." A deep red blush fired in Nate's cheeks.

Desire seeped to the tips of Bunny's fingers. She knew this man was off-limits, but she couldn't deny the depth of feeling evoked by something so simple as his smile.

"Go," Nate urged. "You'll be late."

Bunny stepped out of the cab, leaning back toward Nate. "If you ever want those chakras unblocked, just let me know."

Nathan ripped off his jacket before the cab pulled back into traffic. Heat poured from his body. He could think of several things Bunny Love could unblock, but they weren't called chakras.

He leaned against the vinyl seat and squeezed his eyes shut. Bunny's brilliant blue gaze burned into his brain. Try as he might, Nate couldn't deny his body's reaction to Bunny. Bert had noticed. And Aunt Martha had noticed. Nate had spotted the concern right through her phony blue contact lenses.

He wasn't a fool. He knew Martha's attempt to set up Bunny with Jeremy was a means to an end. Well, she didn't have to worry. Nate was a man of his word, and he'd given his word to Melanie Brittingham.

Melanie. He let out a frustrated breath. Their relationship was anything but steamy and passionate, but he'd never hurt her.

He patted his sizzling forehead and focused on slowing his pulse.

Bunny Love.

He supposed letting his mind wander to the what-ifs was harmless. After all, Bunny might be able to unblock his chakras, but his was a life filled with expectations, and McNultys delivered on their expectations.

Whether they were happy doing so, or not.

Chapter 9

Bunny stared at the art deco style of the Loews Hotel lobby, having just finished a walk-through with the hotel conference coordinator. So this was how the other half lived.

Rich, male laughter tickled her ear. She turned in time to see Armand Miller usher a slim, well-dressed woman into a waiting cab.

He straightened, a bright smile spreading wide across his face as he spotted her. He stepped briskly back into the lobby. "Beatrice. Have you just finished an appointment?"

She nodded.

"Marvelous." He took her hand, tucking it into the crook of his arm. "I could kill for a bit of espresso. How about you?"

She was completely out of her league. Her years of working from home hadn't done a thing to hone her social skills. But something nagged at her about Armand. He was too . . . polished. *Really*. What person was this smooth? He probably practiced his moves in a mirror, but then, they *were* spectacular moves.

"That sounds lovely," she managed to answer.

"Splendid."

They settled at a window table in the hotel bar. Bunny shoved down her feelings of inadequacy, focusing instead on exuding an air of sophistication. Armand's smile never ceased—a true study in practiced perfection.

The waitress slipped their espresso cups onto the table. Armand swirled the black liquid in his tiny cup and crooked a brow.

"Perhaps you'd honor me by accompanying me to dinner sometime?"

All thoughts switched from the man's arrogance to the topic at hand. Why would a man like Armand invite her to dinner?

"Me?" Her voice squeaked and she cringed.

Armand leaned across the table, gazing deeply into her eyes. She fought to keep herself from drowning in the depths of his bottomless stare.

And then reality struck. Her current employer and the source of the paychecks necessary to secure financing on her condo loathed Armand Miller. She believed *despised* was the actual word Nathan had used.

"Aren't you and Mr. McNulty rivals? I'd hate to do anything to jeopardize my job, as much as I'd love to have dinner."

"Oh, Beatrice." Armand clucked his tongue. "It's refreshing to find someone so loyal to her employer, but you needn't worry. Nathan McNulty and I have a healthy spirit of competition that goes back to our high school days. I hardly think what you do on your personal time is any business of his. Do you?"

"You're right." And he was right. It was an excellent point. "I'm sure Mr. McNulty would understand."

"Well, there's truly no reason to tell him." Armand drank down his espresso and reclined against his stool back. "Tell me, he doesn't require you to call him Mr. McNulty, does he?" His voice was light and teasing.

Bunny shook her head.

Armand slowly tipped his perfect male head to one side. Bunny's gaze followed the movement of the rugged chin, the sharp angles of his cheeks, the full lower lip, the . . .

"Well that's good. I'd always imagined his employees had to salute good old Nate when they passed him in the hall."

Bunny laughed politely, but guilt nagged at her belly. Nate was a good man—albeit a bit stifled. "No, sir," she answered softly. "No saluting."

Armand leaned forward, pulling Bunny's fingers to his mouth. He pressed his lips to the top of her hand. "Beatrice. You are the most delightful creature I've met in a long time. But, please, I can think of far more endearing terms for you to call me than sir."

A hot blush fired in Bunny's cheeks. She glanced at the table to hide her embarrassment. It wasn't every day a man of Armand Miller's caliber kissed her hand. Well, okay. It was never. He was no match for Nate Mc-Nulty, but darned if he wouldn't do in a pinch. And Nate was spoken for. Right?

"Promise me you'll call me Armand." He gave her hand a squeeze. "At least until we get to know each other better. Then you can call me whatever you want."

The waitress brought their bill. Armand tossed a platinum credit card onto the small leather folder, scrutinizing Bunny. She did her best not to wiggle beneath his piercing gaze.

"Perhaps you're free for dinner this evening?"

Nate's warm, brown eyes flashed through Bunny's mind and she hesitated. *Why?* The man was as good as engaged. More importantly, he'd never give Bunny a second thought.

"I have information that will help you with The Worthington Cup. Would you like that?"

"Very much so." Bunny smiled. Dinner with a handsome man *and* job advice? "Sounds perfect."

Armand signed his credit card slip then sat back, his

lips twisting into a crooked, sexy smile. "You and I, Miss Beatrice Love, have a date."

Nate glared at the bottom of his coffee mug. This afternoon's pot hadn't provided the pick-me-up he craved. He ran a hand over his exhausted face, but straightened when a knock sounded at his office door. "Come in."

Jeremy's blond head appeared in the opening. His layered cut would look unkempt on most men, but on Jeremy it was the perfect statement of his casually elegant style.

"You're becoming a regular here," Nate said suspiciously. "To what do I owe this unexpected surprise?"

"I didn't come to see you." Jeremy jerked his thumb toward the row of cubicles. "Bunny in?"

Anxiety flickered in Nate's gut. "Why?"

Jeremy's deep blue eyes narrowed to slits. "Since when do you feel justified in questioning my actions?"

"Since your 'actions' involve my event coordinator— who happens to be working on a very tight deadline."

Jeremy crossed the office and sank into one of the rich leather chairs opposite Nate's desk. He raked a hand through his blond mane, each piece slipping effortlessly back into place. Jealousy flicked to life in Nate's belly at the sight of the familiar move. It was insane to be jealous over hair, but he was.

"Aunt Martha thought I should stop by."

Warning bells chimed in Nate's brain.

"She thought I should ask Bunny to the Autumn Harvest dinner dance." He leaned forward eagerly. "Hell, I'd love to get to know her better, so, I figured, why not?"

Nate reflected on his earlier conversation with Bunny and the ache that had flashed through her eyes when she thought he didn't want her at the dance.

"Why not?" Nate shrugged, his voice tight, but steady.

Jeremy rocked back against the chair. "Did you see the way she filled out that dress this morning?"

Nate sucked in a deep breath and counted to ten. "Melanie and I will be there. We'll get a table together."

Jeremy unfurled himself from the chair in one smooth, sleek motion. "Great." He beamed. "Tell Bunny I stopped by. I'll give her a call later."

Nate trained his focus on a financial report. "Will do."

"Hey, Nate?"

He looked up to meet his brother's bright gaze. "Death by ruffles." He winked. "Heck of a way for a man to go."

Nate watched his brother close the door, then flipped open the report. He did his best to focus on the columns of numbers, but try as he might, he couldn't shake the image of Bunny's hand beneath his—or the way she filled out her ruffles.

Later that afternoon, Nate stood just outside Bunny's cubicle and watched her work. Her head tipped down toward the notepad she scribbled on. He admired the soft curve of her neck, chastising himself for the desire simmering in his gut.

He tapped on the edge of the cubicle door. "How did the walk-through go?"

She spun to face him and his heart caught in his throat. Her eyes were brilliant. Soft wisps of reddish-brown hair feathered her cheeks, flushed with color.

"It went well, I think. They're ready for the dogs. Lots of cleaners, plastic runners. You name it." A grin spread across her face and soft smile lines crinkled the corners of her eyes. His stomach tightened. "I took the checklist you gave me and didn't forget a thing."

"Perfect." He sank into the extra chair in her office, dragging a hand through his hair. "This is extremely important to the firm. You know that, correct?"

She tipped her head to one side, her expression growing intent. "I understood the first several times you told me."

"Right." He glanced briefly at his shoes then met her stare. "My brother stopped by to see you while you were out."

Her gaze widened, and Nate's heart caught. Damn it. He shouldn't care that she brightened at the news.

"Really?"

He nodded. "Seems Aunt Martha's already spoken to him about this weekend." Nate stood, moving toward the cubicle's door. "He'll call you later." He tapped on the metal edge of the partition. "Listen. Kitty wants an update on our plans. I thought we'd head out to her estate in the morning. I can pick you up at your apartment."

"Sure." Surprise washed across Bunny's pert features. "I can meet you here if it's easier."

Nate shook his head. "I'll pick you up. Make sure you leave me the address before you head home."

"Will do."

He hesitated as she turned back to her desk. "The slippers are fine as long as you confine them to your work space."

She turned to face him, her upturned eyes huge saucers of blue beneath her long lashes. Fresh fire colored her cheeks. "Thank you."

"Anything else I should know about? Other surprises?"

A sheepish grin spread across her face. "A boxful actually."

Nate winced. "Why doesn't that surprise me?"

"They're all wonderful tools for freeing creative energy." She straightened defensively.

"I'm sure." He leaned against the wall. "Just make sure they stay within these four walls."

"These four gray walls," Bunny teased.

"These four pewter walls."

She smiled, sending warmth straight to his center. "I'll see you in the morning. Nine o'clock."

"Just wait until you see my apartment," she quipped. "Its energy will knock your socks off."

Her vivid blue gaze met his and his stomach gave another twist. A *serious* twist. That couldn't be good.

A sudden vision of Bunny in lounging pajamas and bunny slippers flashed into his mind. She'd be curled up on a lovingly beat-up sofa and he'd be feeding her grapes, or sipping on wine, or nibbling on her ear lobe. *Good grief.* What on earth was wrong with him?

"How about you, Nate?"

"What about me?" he sputtered.

"Don't you want a bit of life in your office?" Her features brightened, as if issuing a dare.

"I have pictures." His voice tightened, and he mentally berated himself. What did it matter what this woman thought?

"Yes. Each frame exactly two inches from the next." She shook her head, clucking her tongue. "Blocked chakras."

"Order." Nate cleared his throat then stepped into the hall. He needed a tumbler of scotch or a splash of cold water on his face. One of the two. *Or both.*

Nibbling on her ear lobe. Absurd. As if she'd ever let him. *Or would she?*

He shook the vision out of his brain. *Control, McNulty. It's all about control.*

Bunny knocked on the open door to Nate's office. His chair sat empty and he was nowhere in sight. Just as well. She quickly crossed the room to his desk, positioning the slip of paper with her apartment address and number in the middle of his blotter. His *empty* blotter.

She reached into her briefcase, lovingly stroking the

three Chinese coins she'd bound together by a red thread. Energy. Luck. Prosperity.

She shot a quick glance toward the hall, then opened the top desk drawer and pulled the coins from her bag. Working quickly, she tucked them into the far back corner and slid the drawer shut. With any luck, the coins would create positive chi.

She pondered the stark, gray space, glancing from one wall to the next. Lord knew the office needed an energy shift. It was no wonder the guy was stifled. She turned to scrutinize the symmetrical grouping of frames.

This time she recognized the faces. Nate. Jeremy. Melanie. Martha. The only smile was on a very small photo of a young Nate. What looked to be a motorcycle helmet sat tucked into the crook of his arm. *Nate on a motorcycle?* Bunny stifled a snort. That would be the day.

An unfamiliar man had his arm draped around Nate's shoulders, the resemblance between the two uncanny. Nate's father. Bunny's heart twisted.

She let out a deep breath and briefly considered another attempt at rearrangement, then shook her head. One thing at a time. Otherwise poor Nate wouldn't know what had hit him.

Nate gazed out his office window onto the street below, watching Bunny's slight figure bob in and out of the horde of pedestrians as she headed home for the evening.

Bert had mentioned her date with Miller. First Jeremy. Now Armand. Seemed Miss Love's ruffles had turned more than one male head since her arrival on the event planning scene.

Armand Miller. Nate had grown accustomed to Aunt Martha falling for the snake's phony persona, but Bunny?

His eyelid twitched and he flattened his palm against

the window, his gaze darting from one street corner to the other before he realized she'd slipped out of sight.

Bunny Love and her naive beliefs were like nothing and no one he'd ever known, and that scared him. He had no control over his body's reactions or his emotions when she was near. That terrified him.

He sank into his leather chair and pulled open a drawer, reaching for his calculator. His fingers brushed against something foreign, something cold. He pulled out the strange object, turning it over in his hand.

Three coins sat tied together by a red thread.

"What the—"

Bunny. Bunny and her feng shui.

Nate bounced the coins in his palm for several long seconds. *Cosmic life force.* She had a cosmic life force, all right, but it would never help him save McNulty Events. And right now, that was all he had time to deal with.

He refused to let his aunt throw away everything his father and uncle had worked to build. He'd keep the company in the family if it was the last thing he did.

Nate slid his leather-wrapped trash can from beneath the desk and let the coins slip between his fingers. They landed with a clank at the bottom of the can. He didn't need Bunny Love or her New Age mentality. He needed control. Nothing more, nothing less. After all, it hadn't failed him yet.

Martha McNulty sat in the lounge of the Union League, watching Armand Miller greet the other patrons as he prowled into the plush space. She took a sip of her cocktail, waiting for his gaze to find her across the crowded room. Their eyes locked and the practiced smile spread across his flawless face.

"Martha, darling. You look ravishing as always." Armand brushed his lips against the back of Martha's offered hand.

"Armand, as delightful as I find your usual adulation, let's cut to the chase. Shall we?"

She gestured to a chair, laughing internally at the startled expression in Armand's typically cool eyes.

He sank into the chair, crossing his legs elegantly. "At your service."

"Did you do as I suggested?" Her pulse quickened.

Armand nodded. "I was at the Loews when you called. I managed to bump into Miss Love in the lobby."

"And?" Irritation flickered through her. Armand of all people should know she had no patience for slow storytelling.

He leaned forward. "And she and I will be dining together this evening."

A slow smile spread across Martha's face. *Perfect.* If Armand could pull this off, she'd hand him McNulty Events on a silver platter, regardless of her promise to Nate. Guilt teased at her but she shook it off. Her actions were for Nate's own good. For his future. She lowered her voice. "You understand my request?"

His dark eyes narrowed, slight crow's feet appearing at their edges. "I'm not sure why you want this event to fail. You're talking sabotage, correct?"

Martha flinched. "Such an ugly word, Armand. I'm not seeking a catastrophic event. I'm looking for something that will cast doubt on Miss Love's abilities without discrediting Nathan." After all, her ultimate goal was to assure his security, not ruin him professionally.

"I was told you'd promised him the firm." One roguish eyebrow lifted.

"If he pulled off a successful Worthington Cup." Martha met Armand's curious stare full on. "He hasn't done that yet, has he?"

Armand rocked back in his seat. "Understood."

Martha's pulse kicked to an even faster clip. She was risking her reputation by trusting this man, yet she felt it the surest way to achieve her goal.

If she could ensure Nate's marriage to Melanie and sell the firm, her nephew would accept the position with Brittingham Insurance. He'd no longer have the stress of running his own firm. He'd be married to a solid woman of upstanding character. His position in society would be safe. *Secure.*

"Martha." Armand spread his arms and chuckled. "You look so serious. When have I ever let you down?"

He never had. She could only hope there wouldn't be a first time. "The firm is yours if you do this for me."

Armand's smile faded, his gaze intent, focused like a hawk calculating the distance to his prey. "Consider it done."

Chapter 10

Bunny pushed open the door to her apartment, all thoughts of her impending date scattering from her mind as she set sight on the mess inside. An empty Starbucks cup and assorted candy wrappers lay strewn across the coffee table, which, to Bunny's horror, sat at a terrible angle, blocking the energy flow for the entire apartment.

She scanned the rest of the room. Nothing was where it had been when she'd left that morning. "Alexandra?" Her voice sounded strained, tense. No wonder. The chi screamed stifled. Hell. The chi screamed Alexandra.

"Yes, dear." Her mother zipped past, picking up her clutter and depositing it in the kitchen trash. She zoomed back past, headed toward the bedrooms.

Bunny took a step backward, contemplating leaving altogether. The woman moved quicker than the Energizer Bunny on a sugar buzz. "Has Daddy called?" Maybe he could calm her mother down, if he'd only get up here and face the situation.

"No, dear." Alexandra reappeared in the living room, her overnight bag in hand.

"You're leaving?" Anxiety fluttered through Bunny. She might be driving her slowly insane, but as long as Alexandra stayed under the same roof, Bunny knew she was all right.

"Overnight greeting card seminar." Her mother's face glowed with excitement.

"With your teacher?" Bunny asked suspiciously.

"He says I'm a natural." Alexandra straightened.

"I'll bet he does," Bunny muttered.

"Speak up, dear. It's uncouth to mumble."

Bunny rolled her eyes. It was also uncouth to trash your daughter's carefully decorated apartment. Her mother probably thought feng shui was a small island in the Pacific.

"Why is it you left Daddy because of tidy canned goods, yet you insist on reorganizing my entire life?" Bunny asked.

"That's different, dear. You could use some order in your life."

Control was what she wanted to say. She couldn't fool Bunny. She'd lived this battle her entire childhood.

"I met an old friend of yours today." Bunny threw out the information, deciding a change of subject was in order. "Martha McNulty. I don't know her maiden name."

"Martha." Alexandra made a dramatic show of rubbing her chin. Bunny decided she might just be taking the tortured artist thing a bit too far. Suddenly, she jabbed a finger in Bunny's direction. "Talented artist. Pen and ink, correct?"

"Martha McNulty?" Bunny choked back a snort. "Doubtful."

Her mother nodded as she breezed toward the front door. "I'm sure I'm right. I should call her about the new card line. She'd be perfect." She yanked open the front door, pausing to give Bunny one last look. "I'll see you tomorrow, darling."

"Be careful, Mom. I don't know about this teacher of yours—"

Her mother waved her free hand toward the living room wall. "We need to talk about your color scheme.

I'm thinking eggshell. These jumbled shades can't be good for your eyes."

Bunny bristled. Now the woman had gone too far. "Did you ever stop to think I have things just how I want them?"

Alexandra paused, her expression horrified. "Oh, dear. This space is too colorful. Everything clashes."

Bunny glanced at the carefully chosen bright, warm colors, savoring the eclectic, yet vibrant, energy they created.

"What you need"—Alexandra gestured toward the kitchen—"is some eggshell."

Bunny shuddered. *Eggshell?* "I don't think so."

"Neutral is in, darling. You'll see."

She was gone before Bunny could rouse herself from her stunned silence. *Jumbled shades, my behind.*

She raced for the phone, frantically punching in her parents' number in Florida. Enough was enough.

"Daddy," she spat out when the machine picked up. "If you love me at all, you'll get on the next plane up here and save me from this sugar-munching, caffeine-guzzling menace." She glared at the horrible flow between the sofa and stuffed chair, clutching the phone tight to her mouth. "Or else the next verse she writes may be her last."

Bert stood at the curb. The evening was quickly growing dark and the air had the bite of a cold winter to come. He hoisted his hand in the air, signaling to an approaching cab. The yellow car whizzed past, its backseat already occupied.

"Damn." Tired and cold, he only wanted his warm apartment and a long, hot shower.

"Psst." A woman's voice sounded.

Bert pivoted but saw no one save the statue outside the building's revolving door. He turned back to face the street, completing another futile attempt to wave down a cab.

Soft feminine laughter rang out behind him, but the sidewalk remained empty, except for the statue. He must be losing it.

"Psst."

Bert spun again, glaring at the statue. Statue? There had never *been* a statue there before, and this particular specimen was quite lovely.

A familiar niggling tickled his brain and he took a step closer. Pale green, the statue stood like an ethereal vision—hands clasped, long hair upswept into a graceful style.

A cool breeze rippled down the street. Bert turned up the collar of his jacket just as the air caught the statue's dress. The soft material fluttered.

Wait a minute. Statues didn't flutter. Did they? He stepped closer and peered into the statue's eyes.

She winked.

"What the—" Bert stumbled backward.

The statue shook with laughter and dropped her arms to her waist. She bent to peer into an upturned cup at her feet. "How am I doing?"

"Matilda?" Bert's heart rapped against his ribcage. "Is that you?"

"Took you long enough." She hoisted up her skirt to step down from her platform. She plucked the cup from the sidewalk, rattling the contents as she peered inside. "Not bad."

"I think you gave me a heart attack."

Her grin was devilish and alluring. "We need to talk."

"About what?"

She frowned. "You're playing havoc with Bunny's energy."

His pulse quickened. "Me, personally?"

She jerked her thumb toward the building. "This job. Come on. I'll buy you a drink and we'll chat."

Bert hesitated for a moment then smiled. She was a vision in pale green. "You're on, Matilda."

She tucked her cup full of money into the folds of her dress, held out her arm and nodded. "Let's go, Parks. And call me Tilly."

Bunny wondered if her face looked as pinched as it felt. Armand Miller had positioned himself in such a manner as to watch his reflection in the restaurant's mirrored wall. Bunny rolled her eyes. There was no reason not to. After all, her dining companion certainly wasn't looking at her.

She twisted in her seat and frowned into the mirror. Armand's gaze slithered from his own perfectly reflected features to hers. His eyes widened with the realization that he'd been caught admiring himself.

"Thought I might have had a spot of food on my mouth." He made a show of dabbing at his upper lip.

Right, Bunny thought. As if anything could grab hold. His lips hadn't stopped moving long enough for a crumb to stick. Apparently, as enamored as the man was with his reflection, he was even more infatuated by the sound of his own voice.

Bunny had tuned out long ago. Somewhere between the entree and the Death By Chocolate dessert she'd ordered to put herself out of her misery, she'd stopped listening. And to think, she'd thought Armand harbored romantic feelings for her. "Ha," she sputtered out loud. The only eyes he'd been gazing into tonight had been his own.

Armand's brows puckered. "Yes," he said. "That's right. How did you know? That's exactly what I said."

Bunny shook her head and refocused on her tea. Lord help her, she'd never be swayed by a face as pretty as Armand Miller's again. She'd prefer another lecture from Nate to this torture. And it *was* torture. Armand had promised tips on The Worthington Cup and instead the night had been a nonstop litany of his Philadelphia social status.

"Now you really ought to pay attention to this, Beatrice."

Bunny downed the last of her herbal tea, hoping if she finished quickly, they'd be able to end the evening. She rolled her eyes impatiently.

"Something in your eye, gorgeous?"

Yes. Your ego, she thought. "It's gone. Thank you."

"I was explaining about the leads, Beatrice."

"The leads?" She narrowed her eyes. "Leads for what?"

"For the dogs. Kitty specifically wanted them to match the theme of the show." Armand sat back, cutting his eyes quickly to the mirror then focusing them on Bunny. "She loves the color purple, and I've found a source for purple leads." He leaned forward and held a finger to his perfectly pursed lips. "Kitty will think you're a genius." He slid a business card across the table. "Tell them you need the *special* leashes."

Okay, so perhaps the night wasn't a total loss.

"How about an after-dinner liqueur?" He did a quick scan of the room. "I thought I saw the Monroes, didn't you? I hear they're looking for someone to handle this year's tournament."

That got Bunny's attention. Thurston Monroe? Here?

"I have an early meeting tomorrow." She reached for her clutch purse. "If you want to stay and mingle, that's fine. I'm quite tired actually." She stood and pushed her chair beneath the table. "I've had a lovely time."

"Armand," a high-pitched woman's voice cooed. "Lovely to see you."

Miller stood, smoothing a hand quickly over his glossed hair as he stepped around the table. "Lovey. It's been too long."

Oh my God. First she had to spend the evening with

the most self-centered man in all of Philadelphia and now she was stranded on Gilligan's Island.

"Beatrice."

She winced. Thurston's deep voice sent the small hairs on the back of her neck popping to attention. Bunny plastered on her warmest smile and turned to greet them.

"Bunny." Lovey Monroe's bright smile lit her face. "I hear your mother's launching a new line of greeting cards."

Bunny squinted, the only expression she could muster to avoid rolling her eyes.

"And you're working at Martha McNulty's firm," Lovey continued. "Glad to hear you gave up the drawing." She wiggled her fingers. "Or whatever it was."

"Drawing?" Armand cocked a questioning brow.

"Graphic design," Bunny chirped. "I handled graphic design for several of my clients."

"Clients?" Lovey's voice rose two octaves. "Thurston told me you were bro—"

"Look." Bunny pointed to the hostess who gestured impatiently at the Monroes. "I think your table's ready."

Thurston and Lovey made a beeline for their seating. Bunny took her time before she turned to face Armand.

"Bro—?" he questioned.

"Brilliant." Bunny gave a quick shrug. "Thurston's forever saying how brilliant I am." She cast a wary glance at the silver-haired grouch's head then smiled. "He's a big fan."

Bunny crossed her fingers behind her back. If Armand ever asked Thurston to corroborate the story, her total lack of experience would be exposed. Even worse, the Monroes knew Martha McNulty. Cold chills danced down Bunny's spine.

If Martha learned Bunny's event planning experience was a lie, she'd be out of a job before the ink dried on her mortgage application.

She stole one last look at the Monroes as they settled at their table. She could only hope they had no occasion to run into Martha until The Worthington Cup was over and her mortgage was a done deal.

Nate rapped on the door and waited for Melanie to answer. Her garden's late season roses filled the evening air with a sweet, warm scent. He glanced at his watch. Nine thirty. She must be home.

He rapped the knocker again and heard her voice call out from inside. "Who is it?"

"It's Nate." His voice boomed in the quiet of the upper-class neighborhood.

The door creaked open and Melanie ushered him inside. She was covered head to toe in a pale velour robe. Its zipper looked ready to choke her, she'd pulled it so high. Bright blue shimmering heels sheathed her feet. Even more odd was the cold cream slathered all over her face.

"Bad time?"

She shook her head. "Just taking off my makeup."

Nate nodded to her feet. "And those?"

Melanie glanced downward and gasped. "Forgot those. I need to return them," she stammered. "They're all wrong."

Nate narrowed his eyes, suspicion growing inside him. "I didn't interrupt anything, did I?"

She rapidly shook her head. "Come on in. I'll wash my face and be right back. What can I get you?"

"How about some scotch?"

"Coming right up."

Nate settled in Melanie's warm, white living room. He sat, leaning his head back against her leather recliner and closing his eyes. What in the hell was Melanie doing wearing such outrageous high heels?

She looked like a stripper, quite frankly. Well, except for the head-to-toe robe.

Guilt gnawed at his belly when he realized he hadn't even kissed her. To be honest, the thought hadn't crossed his mind. Nothing had crossed his mind tonight other than the image of Bunny out on a date with Armand Miller.

If the bastard touched her, he'd . . . he'd . . .What? Nate had no right to do anything. He shoved a hand through his hair. Hell. He didn't even have the right to care.

He glanced toward the hall. The sound of running water filled the house. Right now his fiancée-to-be was washing cold cream off her face, dressed only in a robe. He should sneak up behind her, caress his hands over her naked flesh, and make love to her. He dropped his face to his palms and moaned. Melanie had never inspired those urges in him. Not once.

Bunny's smile flashed through his mind. His eye twitched. Damn it. Did the mop-headed woman have any idea what havoc she'd wreaked on his libido? He should be putting the moves on Melanie, but here he sat thinking how bright and alive Bunny's eyes were. He wondered what they'd look like after making love. Would she trace one finger down his cheek, along his jaw, down his neck to his bare stomach and . . .

"Nate? Are you listening to me at all?"

He jerked to attention, hoping his arousal was well hidden beneath his trousers. "Sorry. What?"

"I said I don't have any scotch. What else can I get you?"

He scrutinized Melanie's face for several long seconds. Her pale skin had been scrubbed clean of all traces of cold cream—smooth and beautiful. He should be proud she'd have him for a husband.

"Nate?" Concern wrinkled her forehead. "What's wrong?"

"Do you love me?" he blurted out. He'd intended to broach the subject more delicately. So much for good intentions.

Her pale eyes grew huge and she took a step backward. "What kind of question is that?"

He stood, meeting her shocked expression head-on. "It's a fair question."

Melanie clutched the neck of her robe tightly at her throat and turned away. "I'm not comfortable talking about these things."

"Why?" Nate closed the distance between them and touched her elbow, coaxing her gently toward him.

She searched his face. "I don't know," she whispered. Tears glistened in her eyes. "Don't you want to marry me?"

His heart lurched. *Did* he want to marry Melanie? He didn't know. All he knew was that he'd been expected to marry her for so long he'd never questioned their future together. Now he found himself longing for something more. And he wasn't quite sure what that something was.

"Don't you, Nate?" she repeated. A tear slipped over her lower lid and trailed down her cheek.

He brushed the moisture from her cheek then leaned to kiss her nose. He straightened, looking intently into her sad face. No fireworks. No stomach tightening. No earth tremors.

"I'm sorry." He shook his head. "I had a bad day and I shouldn't have stopped by unannounced."

She hugged herself. "It's okay. You just frightened me."

"I didn't mean to." He brushed his thumb across her cheek, giving her a reassuring smile as he stepped onto the front step. "We'll have a great time at the dinner dance this weekend."

She nodded, closing the door behind him.

Nate followed the brick walkway to the drive, breathing deeply of the night air. The moon winked out from behind a cloud and he wondered what Bunny was doing right now. He wondered if Miller had touched her or kissed her.

He leaned against the car and blew out a long sigh. Glancing back toward Melanie's front door, he chastised himself. He had promised himself to Melanie, and he wasn't going to let her down.

A soft breeze brushed his face—sweet, subtle. Like the soft, vanilla scent of Bunny Love.

Bert stepped off the elevator into the lobby of Tilly's apartment building just as Bunny rushed in from outside. Her pinched features warmed the instant she recognized him.

"What are you doing here?" Her tone was light with surprise, and Bert wondered again just what scared Nate about falling for this woman. There was the issue of Melanie. But everyone knew that relationship had been forced on them both.

"Just seeing Tilly home." He fought to keep his features expressionless.

A bright smile spread across her face. "Really?"

Bert nodded. "We ran into each other on the street. She wanted to read my aura again."

Bunny's smile morphed into uninhibited laughter. She pointed to his neck. "Looks like she left a little of her aura on your collar."

He twisted, trying in vain to see what she was talking about. Bunny stepped close, giving his shoulder a quick pat.

"That makeup she wears for her street performances is murder. She got some on my sofa one time and I had to redo my entire color scheme." She winked.

Bert decided the only way to avoid this conversation was to change it. "How was the date with Miller?"

Her bright features fell slack. "Ugh. I'd rather talk about your aura."

He shook his head. "No plans for a repeat?" He hoped the question wasn't as obvious as it felt. If she fell for Miller, the plan Tilly and he had hatched wouldn't stand a chance.

Bunny wrinkled her nose as if the suggestion horrified her. "One word: No."

Relief washed through him. "That bad?"

"Worse." She squinted. "I've never met someone so self-absorbed."

Bert chuckled, unable to hold back his pleasure. "Truer words were never spoken. Can you imagine working for the guy?"

Bunny rolled her eyes. "Trust me. I'll do whatever it takes to make sure Martha doesn't sell to him. Or anybody," she added. "I know how important this is to Nate."

Soft color flushed her cheeks and Bert warmed optimistically. Maybe he and Tilly wouldn't have as much work to do as they thought.

"You didn't happen to hear any loud noises coming from my apartment, did you?"

Bunny's words jolted him from his thoughts, and he narrowed his eyes. "Is that a frequent problem?"

"My mother showed up unexpectedly. Bit of a distraction."

Tilly's pixie face flashed through his mind. Distraction seemed to be the flavor of the week. He shook his head. "None that I heard." He stepped toward the door. "Better get going. Boss is a stickler for punctuality."

"Good night, Bert." Bunny pressed the elevator button. "I'll see you after our meeting with Kitty."

Bert stepped out onto the sidewalk, hoisting his arm to hail a cab.

Step one. Force proximity for Bunny and Nate.

Planning The Worthington Cup ensured that much.

Their out-of-the-office meeting tomorrow was an excellent first step.

He chuckled as he pulled open the taxi door. Nate McNulty might think he had things completely under control, but Bert suspected he was in for a rude cosmic awakening.

Chapter 11

The next morning, Nate stood at the door to Bunny's apartment and knocked. He willed his body to have nothing more than a professional reaction to her smile.

She snapped open the door with a grin. The sight of her rumpled hair sent warmth seeping through him. He had thought twinkling eyes cliché until he met Bunny. Hers sparkled.

"Morning," she chirped. "I'm almost ready, come on in."

Nate's gaze raked down her body. Skintight leggings hugged the curves of her calves and a short robe wrapped her upper body. Sky blue polish winked from her toenails.

"You aren't . . . dressed." Nate's voice thickened and his pulse picked up a notch.

"I know." Bunny gestured to a large, overstuffed tapestry chair. "I lost track of time during my morning meditation." She winked. "Which is the whole point actually."

Nate sank into the chair, wondering if the creation actually possessed a seat. The soft fabric enveloped him, forcing his knees dangerously close to his chin. The mixed scent of spices and vanilla toyed with his nose.

Bunny tugged her robe close around her throat. "Can I get you something?"

"I don't suppose you'd have a cup of coffee?"

Her nose wrinkled as if he'd said something grue-some. She propped one fist on her hip. "How about some echinacea tea?" Her gaze scanned him head to toe. His body tingled under the heat of her turquoise eyes. "You look a bit stressed."

"No, thank you."

She tipped her head, arching one brow. "You don't know what you're missing."

Yes, I do, he thought, letting his mind imagine exactly what feminine features Bunny's robe hid. He tamped down the desire to loosen his collar. "Is it warm in here?"

Bunny gave a knowing nod. "Your suit's stifling you."

He narrowed his eyes. "This suit is professional, which is more than I can say for that getup."

The terry cloth robe hugged her hips as she sashayed away. "Don't worry. I'll look professional." She slipped through an orange doorway, calling out over her shoul-der, "But first, I'm making you some tea."

"I don't need tea," he hollered. "And we need to get going."

"We're early. There's plenty of time."

"Early is good," Nate said, trying to pry himself from the chair. "It's also professional."

"No." Bunny peeked out from the kitchen, a devilish gleam in her eye. "It's annoying."

Heat flared in Nate's cheeks. He unfurled his body from the seat, catapulting himself across the small room. He landed face-to-face with a grouping of photos atop a small mantel. A variety of stained glass and cloisonné frames haphazardly cluttered the limited space.

Nate shook his head. He straightened each one, ar-ranging them symmetrically, evenly spacing one from the next.

"Here you go." Bunny's voice sounded brightly from behind him. "This will help your immune system."

Nate spun around, his gaze following the line of the robe's collar to where Bunny's creamy neck lay exposed. He took the offered cup, forcing his eyes to meet hers. Her focus, however, had shifted to the mantel behind him.

She blinked. "Someone's been rearranging my photos." It took mere seconds for her to return the frames to total disarray. "Much better."

She smiled and pointed to the man-eating tapestry chair. "Sit. Wait." She rolled her eyes. "And for gosh sakes, don't touch anything else. There's so much positive energy in this space you're bound to explode."

"I can handle positive energy," Nate protested.

Bunny let out a rather unladylike snort. "Yeah, right." She headed down the hall, her laughter building as she increased the distance between them. "That's a good one."

Bunny snickered as she slipped into the emerald green suit. It was rather fun to have Nate on her turf. Just think of the chakras she could unblock if he'd give her a chance. The tea alone should get his juices flowing.

Thank goodness Alexandra was away at her seminar. She and Nate together would have been all Bunny needed. The two of them could start their own chapter of control freaks anonymous.

Bunny spun to admire her reflection in an antique mirror. The flared skirt skimmed the top of her knees, while the fitted jacket nipped in at her waist. The outfit perfectly combined her personality and the corporate look Nate preferred.

She gave her hair one last toss and pulled open the bedroom door. Nate sat in her favorite chair, knees to chin.

"Comfortable?"

He pulled himself from the depths of the seat. "Your chair is smothering my chakras." His gaze widened as he scrutinized her outfit. "Good color for you."

"Thanks." She reached for his mug. "Can I freshen your tea?"

He shot her a sheepish look. "I didn't drink it."

"I'll grab a to-go cup. A little herbal tea never hurt anyone."

"Just great," he mumbled.

"Pardon?"

"I said, we're late."

Bunny frowned and poured the tea into a stainless steel cup. The man was a mumbler, but the habit was rather endearing.

They rode in silence much of the way to Kitty Worthington's. As controlled as Nate was in the office, he was more so in the car. Bunny glanced at the speedometer. Fifty-five on the nose. Not a mile over or under the speed limit.

She chuckled softly.

"Does my speed meet with your approval?" Nate's tone teased.

His words sent white-hot electric scorching through Bunny's nerve endings. "I'm not surprised to see you sticking to the posted limit, but it wouldn't kill you to walk on the wild side. Go a mile or two over. I dare you."

He grinned, never taking his eyes from the road. "Well-measured control is a sign of fine breeding."

Bunny admired the clean-shaven line of his jaw. "You don't say."

"Speaking of fine breeding, how was your date with Miller?"

Bunny cut her eyes at him. "It wasn't a date, and it was horrid."

A smile played with the corner of his mouth. "What happened?"

"It's none of your business." Bunny glanced out the passenger window. "Let's just say Armand Miller is an egocentric, self-centered, self-adoring jerk."

Rich, male laughter filled the car. "That good?"

"Hmph." Bunny crossed her arms over her chest, then turned back toward Nate. "He did give me a tip for The Worthington Cup, though."

"I'm listening."

"He's got a source for purple dog leashes." She watched as Nate's brow furrowed. "What's the matter?"

"Nothing." He spoke slowly. "He told Kitty purple was gauche. That's why she dumped him as her planner."

Bunny shrugged. "Maybe he hopes to redeem himself."

"Not his style."

Nate took the next expressway exit, slowing carefully at the yield sign. Large, Tudor-style houses appeared between expansive stretches of stone walls. "Welcome to the Main Line."

Bunny let out a long, low whistle.

Nate flicked on the turn indicator, slowing the car into a gated drive. "Here we are. Annoying poodle central." He shot her a quick wink.

Bunny's stomach caught and tightened. She hadn't been prepared for the comment or the wink. Who would have thought Nate capable? See that? A few minutes inside her apartment, and his energy had become freer already.

Nate turned off the ignition and climbed out.

"You forgot your tea," Bunny nagged, rushing to grab the cup and exit the car.

One dark brow arched with amusement. "You really want me to drink this stuff."

"Yes." Bunny nodded emphatically. She tapped the steel cup with a fingernail. "This is seriously good for you. Your chakras won't know what hit them."

"Fine," he grumbled. He yanked the cup from her grip, draining the contents in several large gulps. He handed the cup back to Bunny and rubbed his stomach. "I feel like a changed man. Let's go. Your tea's awful, by the way."

* * *

Nate admired Bunny's vitality and the grace with which she fielded each of Kitty's questions. She was a natural—born to make others feel comfortable with what was going on.

He also couldn't help but appreciate the way her suit hugged her feminine curves. As she moved, the soft fabric moved with her, accentuating her delicate build and offsetting her fair coloring. The green was the perfect complement to the red tones of her hair. His cheeks warmed. He wasn't a man to notice such things, but he noticed them in Bunny Love.

She'd moved on to an explanation of the slogan and Web site plans for The Worthington Cup. Kitty clapped her hands together and nodded her head vigorously. Excellent. There was nothing better than a happy client—especially one with as many society ties as Kitty. It must have been a lucky stroke of fate that brought Bunny into his office on Monday. Was it really just a few days ago? He felt as though he'd known her far longer.

Nate tugged at the throat of his shirt. Warm. The air was unbearably close in the room. His throat felt as though it had sprouted cactus needles. He coughed, or rather tried to cough.

He glared at Chablis and Chardonnay. *Little menaces.* As if reading his thoughts the smaller of the two approached his leg, snuffling his cuff. With his luck, he had a hairball stuck in his throat. Nate opened his mouth to shoo the dog away, but succeeded only in choking.

"Nathan, darling. Are you quite all right?" Kitty's voice was tight with concern. "You look rather flushed."

"Fine," he bit out. "Just a bit warm."

Bunny took one look at Nate and gasped. His face glowed like a ripe tomato.

"Have you consumed anything out of the ordinary this morning?" Kitty asked. "You look as though you're having a reaction."

The tea. Bunny's heart fell to her toes at the precise moment Nate's nervous eyes met hers.

"You don't think?" He winced.

Bunny swallowed and gave a quick shrug of her shoulders. "Do you have allergies?" she asked tentatively.

"Certain flowers." He shook his head. "Certainly not to tea."

Dread pooled in Bunny's stomach. Echinacea came from sunflowers. She stood and stepped closer to Nate. "I think we should get you some water." She fought the panic that clutched her throat. "Kitty? Water, please."

The poodles had each seized the opportunity to frantically snarl and tug at the cuffs of poor Nate's trousers.

Bunny leaned close, staring into his eyes. "How about sunflowers? Allergic to them?"

His brown eyes grew steely. "Why?" he snarled.

"That's what the tea's made from," she muttered. "Think that's a problem?"

"I can't swallow." Annoyance dripped from his words. "Think *that's* a problem?"

She tugged on his arm. "We should probably go."

"Where?"

"To the nearest hospital."

Kitty returned with the water, but stopped dead in the doorway. Her eyes narrowed to tiny slits, apparently mesmerized by the changing state of Nate's complexion.

Bunny snatched the water from her hand and foisted it on Nate. "Drink this. Now."

"Can't swallow," he croaked. "Burning up."

Without thinking Bunny tossed the water in Nate's face. His already glassy eyes popped wide then squinted in disbelief.

"Sorry," Bunny stammered. "Nerves."

Water dripped from his nose and chin, saturating his

suit jacket and tie. Bunny winced. Not her best move. Oh well, no use dwelling over spilled water.

She grabbed his arm, spinning him toward Kitty. "Where's the nearest emergency room?"

"Lankenau."

Bunny gripped Nate's elbow, pulling him toward the door. "Let's go."

"The meeting," he croaked.

"It can wait." She dragged him out onto the front step. "I've poisoned you or something. We need to get to the emergency room."

His stunned brown eyes were the size of saucers. "Poisoned?" he whispered.

Bunny thrust her open palm in his face. "Keys."

"Do you drive stick?" He cast a nervous glance toward his BMW.

"I do now."

Nate gripped the door handle and braced himself against the dash. Heaven help him, his life was in the hands of the Tasmanian devil. The car screamed in protest as Bunny downshifted into a turn. The fact his vision had blurred into a narrow field of focus was probably for the best.

Over the course of four days, Bunny's creative life force had spun his orderly existence out of control. She'd reduced him to a mumbling, twitching—and now swollen—shell of the polished executive he'd been just last week. She and her damned turquoise eyes.

"Right here." He could barely manage the husky rasp. A blue hospital sign flashed past and he uttered a silent prayer of thanks. They were close. If he had any luck left at all, he'd survive the herbal tea poisoning long enough to recover whatever shred of dignity he had left. If this was what unblocked chakras felt like, he preferred his good and stifled.

The gears shrieked as the car jerked violently to one side. Bunny gripped his knee and squeezed. Her touch was like an electric prod sending a jolt straight to his groin—swollen nerve endings be damned.

"Sorry. I had no idea you'd be allergic."

Nate stole a glance at her cheek, blanched of all color. He must be in pretty bad shape to elicit such a frightened expression from the normally fearless woman.

As pale as she appeared, and as exciting as he found the feel of her hand on his leg, nothing could contain the frustration and anger rolling in his gut. He had let his guard down for a brief moment in time and where had it gotten him? Poisoned and at the mercy of the queen of chaos.

Wasn't this exactly what Aunt Martha had worked to pound into his skull for as long as he could remember? Control was safe. Chaos was anything but.

Bunny downshifted, whirling the car around a corner. "Hang on." She slammed the car to a stop next to the emergency room entrance.

The next few minutes were a blur of activity. Bunny confiscated his wallet and insurance information, while a nurse ushered him into a treatment room. Within moments, he sat on the edge of the examination table, staring down at the tiled floor.

A pair of powder blue clogs entered his line of vision as a male voice clucked his tongue. Nate looked up into the grinning face of the youngest doctor he'd ever seen.

"Well, well. Looks like you went a few rounds—and lost."

Nate glared at the doctor, but kept his thoughts to himself. It wasn't fair to direct his anger at this stranger. No. His anger should be directed, quite simply, at Bunny Love.

The source of all his woes.

* * *

Exhaustion seeped through Bunny as she crossed the apartment lobby and stepped into the elevator. The rest of her day had been uneventful back at the office. Once Bert had called to say Nate would recover, she'd headed for home.

Nate hadn't wanted her at the hospital. Could she blame him? She'd poisoned him. Thankfully, one shot of epinephrine had been all Nate had needed. Cripes. She scrubbed a hand over her weary face as the elevator doors closed.

She couldn't have just given him the damn coffee. No, she had to pour herbal tea down his throat. Maybe she was no better than her mother, forcing her ways on everyone around her. For some crazy reason, the thought calmed her. Blaming the entire fiasco on her mother held great appeal, actually. Wasn't that the excuse most serial killers used?

Strains of Nat King Cole wafted down the narrow hall as the elevator doors slid open. Bunny's breath caught. *Daddy.* She dashed for her apartment, bursting through the front door. She spotted her father in the kitchen and reached for the volume on the stereo. The pantry door stood open wide. The only visible portion of the man who'd raised her was his backside, moving to the rhythm of the music.

"Daddy?"

He stilled, straightening to peer around the door. "Hey, cupcake. Got your message."

"Weren't you going to come after her?" Bunny crossed to where he waited, planting a warm kiss on his clean-shaven cheek.

Even though John Love had recently turned fifty-six, he didn't look a day over forty. His sandy blond hair camouflaged the slight touches of gray flirting at his temples, and his turquoise eyes sparkled with vitality.

"She wanted to find herself." He shrugged. "I didn't

think she'd try to find herself in your apartment. Sorry."

"It's okay." Bunny leaned around the pantry door to see what he'd been doing. "I'm glad you're—"

Holy cow. Every item in the pantry had been organized by color and size. Either her life was flashing before her eyes, or she was suffering from some serious déjà vu.

"Like it?" He beamed. "You can't go wrong when you follow the color wheel."

"Mm." Bunny nodded, biting back the urge to run screaming.

Her father pointed toward the front door. "You know you really need to get those locks—"

"I know," Bunny interrupted.

As if on cue, the front door eased open. Alexandra entered, looking bedraggled and upset. Tears glistened in her normally perky eyes. Bunny rushed to take her mother's bag, lowering it to the floor and wrapping an arm around the crying woman. "What happened?"

Alexandra focused on John. "What's he doing here? It's supposed to be just us girls." She sniffed.

"He missed you. He flew all the way up from Florida to be with you." Bunny glared at her father, nonverbally coaxing him to jump in anytime.

"House was empty without you," he offered.

Alexandra sniffed again and Bunny's heart ached. "What happened?"

"That horrid man was no more a greeting card instructor than you are. He was after a little hanky-panky, nothing more."

Bunny wasn't sure, but she could have sworn she heard her father's blood pressure explode. "He what?"

Alexandra shook her head. "Nothing happened. I'm no floozy."

"Maybe it's for the best." Bunny struggled to find

soothing words. "You did rush into the greeting card thing."

Her father cleared his throat, capturing Alexandra's attention. "I've done some thinking about the idea."

Alexandra dabbed at her moist eyes, gazing hopefully at her husband.

"You knew about this?" Bunny asked.

He nodded. "Spoke to a former associate of mine. He runs a printing business outside the city."

Alexandra stepped closer, her excitement palpable. Bunny fervently hoped the next words out of her father's mouth would be positive, or the woman would probably go into a cleaning frenzy the likes of which Philadelphia had never seen.

"I made an appointment for tomorrow. Let's get this show on the road."

Bunny's heart swelled. The man might be obtuse at times, but with a little prodding, he was a regular Romeo.

"Really?" Her mother now stood just inches from her father. "You like the idea?"

John leaned forward and kissed Alexandra on the nose. "I love the idea," he said softly. "Sorry I wasn't more encouraging when you first brought it up."

Bunny's vision blurred, relief washing through her. "So you two will be heading back to Naples."

"Oh, no." Alexandra shook her head. "We've got business plans to develop. Artists to line up." She tapped a finger to her chin. "Distribution. Sales."

John nodded. "Help me finish the pantry, sweetheart. A little organization will get the planning juices flowing."

Alexandra gave her husband a hug, and Bunny pulled open the front door, headed for Tilly's apartment. Between the latest development in the evolution of her parents' marriage and Nate's trip to the ER, she was ready for a batch of Tilly's Celestial Margueritas. And how.

* * *

An hour later, Bunny snuggled deeper into Tilly's battered sofa, trying not to imagine the havoc her parents were wreaking on her apartment. She hugged a pillow to her chest, eyeing her friend through tear-filled eyes.

"I blew it," she sniffed. "I'll get fired and lose my apartment."

"He won't fire you." Tilly scowled. "What grounds does he have?"

Bunny rolled her eyes in disbelief. "Hello. I tried to destress him and sent him to the ER instead. My positive chi's morphed into bumbling failure since I met him."

Tilly winked. "You two were destined for each other."

Bunny lowered her face to the pillow. "Yeah, like the *Titanic*. Only I'm the iceberg."

"It's not that bad," Tilly urged. "At least you didn't kill him."

Bunny blinked. A lone tear slid down her cheek. "Whoever heard of someone being allergic to echinacea tea?"

A knock sounded at the door. Bunny shot Tilly a confused look. "Expecting someone?"

"Bert."

"My Bert?"

"No." Tilly grinned. "*My* Bert."

Tilly pulled the door open. Bert planted a kiss on Tilly's cheek, then glanced at Bunny, a devilish glint twinkling in his pale blue eyes. "Miss Love."

He stepped to where she sat and patted her shoulder. "At least we can't say things at McNulty Events have been boring since you arrived on the scene."

"How is he?" Bunny asked, almost afraid to hear the answer.

"Glowing, but no worse for the wear."

"Am I fired?"

"Just in the doghouse." He winked. "Pun intended."

"Bert and I have a plan," Tilly said.

Bunny lowered the pillow. Bert's and Tilly's faces wore equally bright, mischievous expressions. Her stomach rolled.

"I'm afraid to ask."

Tilly clapped her hands, then dropped to her knees in front of Bunny. She planted her palms on either side of Bunny's face, her eyes growing wide. "We're going to do a creative energy intervention."

"A creative energy what?"

"Intervention," Bert answered. "And I can't think of anyone more deserving than Nate McNulty."

Chapter 12

Nate sat in the Warwick Hotel ballroom watching Philadelphia's finest gather for the Autumn Dinner Dance. Aunt Martha busied herself doing the same. An awkward silence had fallen across the table, and Nate sipped his scotch as Melanie vapidly drank her wine.

He sighed inwardly, wondering when Bunny would arrive. He hadn't seen her since she'd deposited him at the emergency room two days earlier. Try as he might, he couldn't tamp down his lingering anger. Obviously, the entire incident had been an innocent mistake, but the woman was a walking menace.

He jerked his focus to an approaching couple. Jealousy tangled with the anger in his gut at the sight of Bunny's arm tucked against his older brother's elbow. *Jealousy.* As if that wasn't the last emotion he needed. Bunny's gaze flickered to his as Jeremy held her chair. Soft pink blossomed in her cheeks.

"You look lovely, dear." Aunt Martha nodded approvingly.

And she did. The color of a warm summer sky, her dress hugged her curves, making Nate long to touch what lay beneath. Her bare shoulders glowed under dimmed ballroom chandeliers. Nate fought the protective urge to ask if she was too cool.

He snuck a peek at her feet, wondering if her toenails

were still painted the same sky blue. Closed-toe pumps obscured his view. *Damn.*

"How are you feeling?" Bunny's tone was cautious and light.

"Full recovery."

Her expression shifted from timidity to hopefulness. "I've taken steps to make it up to you."

Dread pooled in Nate's stomach. "I need you to focus on order and control, not feng shui."

Melanie mumbled something incoherent and took a long swallow of wine.

"Did you say something?" Aunt Martha questioned.

The pale blonde shook her head, her blue eyes huge. Nate squinted at her, and she quickly turned away. He redirected his attention to Bunny, whose cheeks had flushed to a distractingly attractive shade of deep pink. Her full lips pressed into a defensive line. "I'm asking you to toe the line from now on."

She met his glare unflinchingly.

"There will be no more tea, or chipmunks or positive chi. Understood?"

Bunny made no move to agree. Not even a nod.

"If I want coffee, I'll drink coffee. If I want gray carpet, I'll have gray carpet. If I want a boring life, I'll—"

Bunny interrupted. "I never called your life bor—"

"It is boring."

Melanie's words stunned Nate, silencing his rant. He turned a disbelieving stare toward his fiancée-to-be. She returned a watery smile. "Aren't you tired of gray, Nathan?"

She lowered her head to the table. Nate held his breath. Perhaps she'd pass out, sparing them her uncharacteristic outburst. No such luck.

She straightened as if steadying herself for battle. "Your trip to the ER was the most exciting thing that's happened to you in what? Forever?"

Nate opened his mouth to respond, but Martha beat him to it.

"You, my dear, are drunk. Your behavior is inappropriate."

Melanie scraped back her chair and stood. "I'm not drunk." She leaned toward Nate and whispered, "I'm bored."

Nate flinched. A tear slid over Melanie's lower lid, and she turned, making a beeline for the ladies' room.

What had gotten into her? If he didn't know better, he'd swear Melanie harbored the same doubts about their impending engagement as he did.

Nate, Martha and Jeremy sat in stunned silence. Bunny squirmed uncomfortably. At least Melanie's little outburst had deflected the attention from her. She looked around the table expecting someone—anyone—to go after her. When she couldn't take the silence a moment longer, she glared at Nate. "We should do something."

"She's drunk," Martha hissed.

Bunny rose from her seat, not willing to let Melanie cry alone in the ladies' room. She navigated the dance floor and slipped into the restroom, hesitating in the ornate dressing area just inside the outer door. Visible through the archway, Melanie stood at the bank of sinks, dabbing her cheeks with a tissue. Bunny's heart twisted.

She reopened the outer door, letting it close with a thump. She cleared her throat, crossing to where Melanie stood. "Are you okay?"

Melanie's eyes shone bright with tears, and a phony smile lit her features. Even distraught, the woman was gorgeous. The jacket of her pink evening suit lay draped across a bench. Melanie hugged herself as if she'd been caught half-dressed.

The halter-style bodice accentuated her shapely upper arms and shoulders, sending a ripple of envy through Bunny. The woman was a vision.

"I'm sorry."

Bunny dabbed at her lipstick, watching her reflection in the mirror. "Do you want to talk about it?"

The pale eyes grew wider, softer. "Just a bad night, that's all." She reached for her suit jacket.

"You should leave that off." Bunny swallowed. She didn't know the proper restroom etiquette for commenting on another woman's outfit, but she'd never been one to keep quiet.

Melanie spun to face Bunny. "Leave off the jacket?" She emphasized the last word as if the idea were unthinkable.

"It's not as if I'm telling you to go out there naked."

Melanie blinked.

"Your gown is gorgeous." Bunny pointed to the fine beadwork. "You should show it off."

"I couldn't do that." Melanie plucked the jacket from the bench, slipping it over her bare arms. "A lady wouldn't do that." She glanced at Bunny, standing bare-armed in her sheath. "I mean . . . I didn't mean to hurt your feelings."

"You didn't," Bunny lied, sadness uncoiling in her chest.

"Your dress is lovely." Melanie's lips curved into a gentle smile. "It matches your eyes."

Bunny thought of the woman modeling the cobalt blue cocktail dress at Daffy's—the woman who had looked so much like Melanie, but with a look of happy abandon on her face.

"I can picture you in cobalt blue. Something vibrant against your pale coloring. A sequined sheath perhaps." Bunny grinned. "That would be a sight to see."

Melanie's pale brows arched and a soft flush spread up her cheeks. "Cobalt blue?"

Bunny nodded. "Don't get me wrong. Pink is fine, but it's got so much yin." She pressed her lips together, carefully choosing her words. "It can be a problem."

"Yin?" Melanie's eyes grew huge, her gaze flickering from Bunny to the front of her dress, frantically searching the delicate material. "Where? I don't see it."

A soft laugh slipped from Bunny's lips. "It's not on you. It has to do with energy." She took a step closer. "You can change your energy fields through your choice of color."

Melanie's gaze narrowed incredulously. "Energy fields?"

"Mmm hmm." Bunny patted Melanie's arm. "Try cobalt blue. It'll liven up your aura."

"I'll remember that." Melanie blinked again, then stole one more glance at her reflection. "Cobalt blue?"

"Definitely."

The women locked eyes for a brief moment. Bunny relished the happier expression on Melanie's face.

"I'd better get back before Nate thinks I've passed out." She gave Bunny a genuine smile. "Thank you for checking on me."

The bathroom door whooshed shut, and Bunny stared into the full-length mirror, scrutinizing her reflection. Her auburn hair fell carelessly into the choppy bob, so different from Melanie's smooth, pale strands.

She reached to tame the unruly waves, tucking first one side, then the other, behind her ears. No earrings hung from her lobes, never had. A simple pearl necklace adorned her throat, a treasured sweet sixteen gift from her grandmother.

Bunny stared at her narrow face and frowned. Bending at the waist, she shook her hair free. She stood upright and smiled at the exaggerated tangle surrounding her cheeks.

Maybe she didn't belong with the country club set. And maybe she didn't know well enough to cover her bare shoulders. But she was being true to herself. And that was one thing she'd never sell out on.

Nate watched the soft drape of Bunny's dress as she headed off after Melanie. As for himself, he was too shocked by Melanie's words to give thought to much else. Talk about a total loss of control. He'd never dreamt Melanie had it in her to speak her mind.

"Anything you need to tell me?" Ice tinged Martha's words. The palpable heat of her glare seared into the back of Nate's head. For a fleeting moment he considered pretending she hadn't spoken.

Nate cringed. Melanie had the right idea. Getting too drunk to remember the evening had definite merits.

"I'm speaking to you, Nathan."

He turned to face her. "Sadly, I'm well aware of that."

Surprise registered on her face. Nate took some small measure of pride in being the cause. Jeremy stood, excusing himself. *Coward.*

Martha stood, pushing back out of her chair. "Don't make a mess of this."

Guilt rippled through him as she walked away. Maybe he'd been wrong to speak to her so harshly. Someone slapped his shoulder. He turned to meet Jeremy's questioning gaze.

"Okay?"

Nate nodded. Jeremy handed him a fresh drink.

"Rough crowd." Jeremy waggled his brows. "And you wonder why I got the hell out when I could."

"Why did you?"

Jeremy sank into a chair, meeting Nate's gaze head-on. "If I'd followed her rules, I'd be the one whose most exciting experience in years had been an allergic reaction."

A few moments later, Melanie returned. In true Mc-Nulty fashion, neither brother asked about her outburst. It was the family way. Emotions were for denial, not acknowledgment.

Nate took a sip of his scotch, watching gratefully as Melanie and Jeremy headed for the dance floor. She'd been right, of course. His life *was* boring. He'd played by the rules his aunt had spelled out for so long, he wasn't sure he knew how to do anything else.

"Everything okay?" Bunny's voice whispered close and soft.

Or at least, his life *had* been boring. He glanced up at her concerned smile. The corners of her eyes crinkled and his breath caught in his throat.

"Everything's fine." He glanced guiltily to where Jeremy spun Melanie around the dance floor, their bodies disappearing momentarily among the throng of partygoers.

Bunny slipped into the seat next to him, her warm, vanilla scent washing over him.

"I apologize for my lecture." He smiled at her surprised expression. "I was out of line."

A soft pink blossomed in her cheeks. "I had it coming."

He narrowed his eyes. "I didn't mean what I said in the cab the other day—about Aunt Martha asking you here out of pity." He spun his glass from one hand to the other.

A soft laugh slipped from Bunny's ruby red lips. "But you were right. I *am* out of my league."

His pulse quickened. "I never said that."

"You didn't have to." Her features softened, saddened. "It's true. I don't even have a proper jacket for my dress."

Nate's gaze slid over her figure, from one enticingly bare shoulder to the other. Desire fired low and heavy. He swallowed. "It would be a crime to cover up that dress." He took a quick sip of scotch, watching the shock register on Bunny's features. He stared at his empty glass, wondering if it had been the liquor or his libido talking. Either way, the observation was true.

From her mop-topped hair to the way the soft filmy material of the dress's hem shimmered against her ankles, she was a vision. A sudden wave of need surged through him. "You look like a young Audrey Hepburn tonight. Except for the hair." He stood, extending a hand. "Dance with me?"

Bunny slipped her slight hand into his, sending countless sparks of awareness radiating from her touch. She beamed, launching Nate's heart into a rapid rhythm.

Damn Aunt Martha *and* her McNulty rules. For once in his life, he'd do what he wanted—and he wanted to dance with Bunny. The orchestra slid into a slow number, and he curled an arm around Bunny's waist, inhaling deeply when her hair brushed his chin. His pulse roared in his ears.

He wished he weren't a McNulty, Bunny wasn't an employee, and they weren't standing in the middle of the Warwick ballroom. He longed to sweep her into his arms, take her mouth with his, slip the straps of her filmy dress from her shoulders and cover the valley between her breasts with slow, sensual kisses.

If only.

Bunny didn't think her knees capable of supporting her. They'd turned to rubber the moment Nate had compared her to Audrey Hepburn. Her muscle tone had gone downhill from there.

He tightened his grip on her waist, and her breath caught. Desire coiled in her belly. She fought the urge to tuck her head into the hollow where his shoulder met his neck.

He smiled down at her, his dark eyes soft and smoky. Bunny knew she must look like a schoolgirl, but for the moment, didn't care. Her only thoughts centered on the warm spot where Nate's palm pressed into the small of her back, and on the heat burning where his hand held hers, tension simmering between them.

For all his talk of control and decorum, Nate Mc-Nulty oozed raw, masculine heat. Bunny intended to drink in every drop offered. She swallowed hard, thinking of the changes she, Bert and Tilly had made to the conference room and Nate's office. A wide grin spread across her lips. He'd be so pleased when he experienced the improved energy flow.

"What's that look for?"

Bunny met his questioning gaze with a shrug. "You'll see."

The music stopped. For several long seconds they stood staring at one another—the silence anything but awkward. In fact, it was the most comfortable moment Bunny could remember.

"Statements like that make me nervous," Nate teased.

"Trust me."

"The last time I trusted you I ended up in an epinephrine-induced stupor."

Bunny winced. "I didn't know—"

"There's a lot you don't know about me." His rich brown eyes darkened, his gaze softening.

The orchestra began a new number, but Nate and Bunny remained still, staring intently into each other's eyes. He gave her hand a squeeze and Bunny's stomach tightened. He leaned close, his lips parting ever so slightly.

Bunny's heart beat a rapid staccato against her ribs, and she fervently wished he'd brush his lips against hers. She longed to know how his kiss would feel. How he would taste.

"What's the matter?" Jeremy's voice whispered roughly. "You two so caught up in conversation you forgot to dance?"

Nate blinked and straightened, releasing Bunny's

hand. "Actually, Bunny and I were discussing The Worthington Cup." He gave her a long, wistful look.

Jeremy took Bunny's arm, spinning her away from Nate. "Melanie's looking a bit green around the gills."

The breath rushed from Bunny's lungs and she silently berated herself. An unmistakable thread of attraction pulled her and Nate closer and closer together, but they'd never share more than words. Nate cast one last look in her direction before he disappeared into the crowd of people near the tables.

Just like that, the thread snapped, and a chill replaced the contented glow that had momentarily infused Bunny's veins.

Martha watched from a far corner of the banquet room as Jeremy whisked Bunny away from Nate. Thank goodness one nephew showed some common sense. She bristled at the longing look Nate cast toward Bunny as they parted. Shades of his father. Bad news all the way around.

She'd loved Nate's father—and his mother. But the two had created an explosive combination. Their love had been legendary, but they'd gotten careless. Tears stung her eyes at the memory of the boys' faces. Orphaned. Alone. Young.

She'd dropped her dreams and career aspirations to give them what they'd never had. Security. Safety. But now she was tired of being the glue that held the family together.

Once she sold the firm and Nate married Melanie, she'd be free to walk away. Nate would settle into a safe life with his bride and a secure job with his new father-in-law. He'd never want for anything.

She glared at Bunny, waltzing slowly in Jeremy's arms. She was the factor that had to be controlled. Martha stiffened with grim determination. When Armand delivered on his promise to discredit Miss Love, Nate would do the right thing. He'd drop his immature infatuation faster than the little troublemaker could say positive chi.

Guilt flickered through her, but she slapped it away. Her plans would ensure Nate's long-term happiness. And safety. His heart would heal. Eventually.

Chapter 13

Nate dropped the morning paper onto Miss Peabody's desk. "Is Kitty Worthington here yet?"

"She's waiting for you in the conference room, sir. Bunny and Bert are in with her."

"Very well." He glanced at his watch. Five minutes late. How had *that* happened? He hadn't deviated from his morning routine, had he? There had been no distractions. Oh, who was he kidding? He'd been distracted ever since he held Bunny in his arms Saturday night.

For the briefest moment he remembered the feel of her delicate curves beneath his fingers. And her scent—soft vanilla—sweet, warm, alluring.

He cleared his throat and straightened his tie. There was no time for fond memories. As much as he'd wanted to taste her ruby red lips on Saturday night, he had to snap out of it. He needed to focus on work, the Cup and regaining control.

He couldn't afford distracting thoughts of Bunny Love. A chuckle slipped from his lips. No, sir. He'd learned that lesson the hard way when he'd sampled her herbal tea. Just think what might happen if he tasted anything more.

"Feeling all right?" Concern tinged his secretary's voice.

He nodded, heading for the conference room as laughter sounded from inside. Excellent. Nothing bet-

ter than a happy client. Perhaps Bunny had left her
mumbo jumbo at home. Clients expected decorum,
plain and simple. He put on a wide smile and pulled
open the door. "Good mor—"

What in the hell had happened?

Soft chimes sounded in the background. Water trickled down the face of a stone sculpture, and a shocking
shade of maroon covered the far conference room wall.

His eye twitched. *Damn it.* He pressed his finger to
his lid and leveled a glare at Bunny. Her hopeful smile
faded, anxiety flashing across her features. He had no
doubt who was behind this atrocity, he could only wonder *why*.

"Still feeling the effect of the tea, Nathan?" Kitty sat
at the head of the table, today's safari suit some shade
of brown. "Something wrong with your eye?"

He refocused on Bunny's nervous face. "It's not the
tea."

Bert cleared his throat and pulled out a chair—
directly in front of a grouping of plants. *Plants.* "Have
a seat, Nate. We were just going over the final plans
with Kitty. Bunny's done a superb job of pulling this
together on such short notice. I left an agenda on
your desk. Did you get it?"

"No, I haven't been to my office yet this morning."

Nate sank into the chair, never taking his eyes from
Bunny's pale gaze. "I wish to speak with you when
we're through." Soft curves, or no soft curves, she'd
gone too far.

She nodded, a nervous swallow working her throat.
Nate felt some small satisfaction in watching her
squirm. He'd tolerated enough of her whimsical influ-
ence on the firm and its employees. He glared at Bert,
who barely concealed his smug amusement. It was time
for decorum to return to McNulty Events.

"Now then." Nate dug deep to muster his most charming tone. "Let's review plans for the Cup. Shall we?"

* * *

Bunny wished the gray carpet would swallow her whole. She never dreamed Nate would be upset with the changes. Surprised? Yes. But angry? No. How could he not sense the improved energy in the room? The changes were genius. Sheer genius.

Color flushed his cheeks and that darn eyelid of his danced a jig. What was it that helped with spasms? She had just read an article in her herbalist guidebook. *No.* She caught herself. The poor guy had forgiven her on Saturday. She should have been happy with that. Of course, the conference room had already been changed by then. Damage done.

She stole a brief glance at the revamped space. It was lovely, actually. If Nate couldn't appreciate the improved flow of chi, he was worse off than she thought.

"Bunny." His voice had grown strained. "We're waiting."

She gave him a weak smile before she began. His glare only intensified. Anxiety simmered in the pit of her stomach. If he was upset with her now, just wait until he saw his office.

She ticked off the list of preparations underway for the Cup, meeting Nate's gaze each time Kitty voiced her pleasure. His glare never softened. Not once. Not even for a moment.

Bunny shot a wary look at Bert whose only reply was a shrug. Great. So much for backup. The whole feng shui intervention had been his idea—he and Tilly. There was a match made in Heaven. Talk about yin and yang.

"Bunny?" Nate's growl startled her attention back to the meeting. "Taking a creative pause?"

One of his dark brown brows arched so high it kissed his rumpled hairline. Warmth mingled with the butterflies in her stomach, and she opened her mouth to speak. Daggers shot from Nate's gaze. She snapped her mouth shut.

"Can we turn off this blasted music?" Nate stood and began pacing the small space.

"I find it soothing." Kitty leaned forward, releasing Chardonnay and Chablis from her lap.

Bunny shot Nate her best *so there* sneer just as the teacup poodles lunged for the potted plants. A small ficus tree hit the gray carpet, sending up a cloud of loose dirt and gravel.

Kitty clutched her chest. "We just came from the groomer."

Chablis dragged a peace lily under the table while Chardonnay disappeared into a large ceramic pot. A chime sounded loudly from the recorded music and both poodles burst into hysterical yapping.

"Heel!" Kitty yelled in a futile attempt to stop the poodles' rampage. "Heel!"

Bunny swallowed down the nausea clawing its way up her throat. Bert lowered his head in an attempt to either hide his laughter or imitate an ostrich. She wasn't sure which. One thing was crystal clear, however. Nate McNulty was about to blow a gasket.

He stood still as a statue, staring at the frenzied destruction taking place. The poodles had knocked over all but one potted plant, and countless dirty paw prints covered the once pristine gray carpet. He pressed a finger to his eyelid as his jaw muscles worked feverishly. A large, angry-looking vein pulsed in his forehead.

Deciding retreat was her safest option, Bunny slid her notes into her leather folder and silently pushed her chair back from the table. She had taken one step toward the door when Nate's voice stopped her dead in her tracks.

"Miss Love."

Drat. Seconds from a clean getaway. Cold chills raced down her spine and her knees went weak. She hadn't felt so scared since . . . well . . . since she'd poisoned him. She stood still, not daring to meet his gaze.

"You and I need to speak privately. Kitty, will you excuse us? And send me the groomer's bill for removing the potting soil. Bert, you'll see Kitty and the girls out."

Bunny gasped when his palm gripped her shoulder and squeezed. "My office," he snarled in her ear. "Now."

She stepped into the hall and watched, horrified, as he crooked his finger in her direction and stepped quickly away.

"Wait." She had to keep him from seeing the redecorated office. "We should talk here."

Nate stopped, pivoting sharply on one heel. White hot anger scorched from his mocha glare. And to think, it had been such a sensual gaze just Saturday night.

"This creative chaos has got to stop." He took a step toward her, shoving a hand through his hair and releasing a frustrated breath. "How long have you been here? A week?"

Bunny nodded, swallowing down what little saliva she had left.

"Well," Nate growled. "It seems like a lifetime, and feels like a lifetime sentence." He jabbed a finger in the air. "We're going to have a refresher on just who is, and isn't, in charge here at McNulty Events." He leaned close, lowering his voice. "Here's a clue. It isn't you. Let's go."

He turned and sped for his office. His hand hit the doorknob and he paused, nodding toward his secretary. "Hold my calls."

Miss Peabody lowered her gaze to her desktop, avoiding all eye contact with Nate or Bunny. "Yes, sir."

Nate turned to Bunny, keeping a firm grip on the doorknob behind him. "Move it, Love."

"No!" Bunny cried out. Dear God in Heaven. He was going to kill her if she didn't stop him from seeing his office before she could put things back as they'd been.

"No?" Incredulity flashed across his already strained features. "You're telling me no?"

Miss Peabody opened a desk drawer and bent below the top of her desk—completely out of sight. The woman wasn't stupid. She'd be out of the line of fire when objects started flying.

"Let me make something perfectly clear." Nate's voice had grown eerily calm. "If Kitty Worthington wasn't such a big fan of yours, you'd be fired. Right here. Right now." He opened his office door. Bunny's heart leaped to her throat.

"Nate. Stop."

"No." He shook his head. "I won't stop. I've tolerated all of the positive chi I'm going to tolerate." He took a step backward into his office.

Bunny shot a panicked look at the rearranged furniture, the plants, the paint. Her nerves threatened to choke her. "Nate. I'm begging you."

"No." Anger boomed in his voice. "Begging won't help. *I* am the boss, not you." He continued his backward progress, eyes fixed on Bunny, frustration etched across his features. "This has gone on long enough."

The coffee table she and Bert had added to his office sat mere inches behind his feet. One more step and he was toast. *She* was toast.

"And another thing," he barked out.

"Stop!"

Too late. His calf hit the edge of the coffee table and he tumbled backward, onto the gray carpet.

Now what? Could this day get any worse? Could this week get any worse? Nate stared up into Bunny's terrified turquoise gaze. Hell. Could his *life* get any worse?

"I tried to warn you." Her voice was little more than a whisper.

Nate glanced around his office. At least he *thought* it

was his office. Candles burned on the bookshelf. Some sort of tapestry hung on the far wall—the wall that had been blessedly gray and empty last he checked. And what the hell had he tripped over? He frowned at the alien coffee table.

"*What* did you do?" he snarled.

Bunny dropped to her knees, pressing a palm to his shoulder. His body defied his anger by shooting heat straight to his groin. Great. Why should his lower back be the only body part afflicted by throbbing pain?

"I only meant to help." She reached for his cheek. "I'm so sorry. I wanted to surprise you."

"It worked." He twisted his face away from her touch and winced as pain shot down his spine. "Son of a—"

"You're hurt." Her pale gaze widened and moisture glistened in her eyes.

"Your detective skills are to be commended," Nate quipped. "Your decorating skills are not."

"I only wanted to improve the energy flow."

Nate tried to pull himself to a sitting position, but pain racked the small of his back. "Remind me to put that on your tombstone after I kill you."

Bunny scrambled behind him, wrapping her arms around his waist, her body tight against his back. "I'll help you." Her soft, warm breasts pressed through his suit jacket.

He jerked away from her grasp. "Let go of me."

Miss Peabody appeared in the doorway, her eyes wide with what appeared to be a mix of shock and amusement. "Shall I call for assistance?"

"No," Nate ground out. "Just make sure Kitty Worthington and her poodles have left the building and find Bert. *Now.*"

Bunny's heart was doing its best to jackhammer out of her chest. At least she hadn't killed him. But it had been close. Again. She wrapped her arms around his waist and tried once more to help him to his feet.

"I told you not to touch me," he snapped.

He couldn't mean that, she rationalized. It was the shock talking. "Let me help you. You need me. You do."

Nate sank to the floor flat on his back. Even from that position, his fury was palpable.

She lowered herself on top of him, one arm on either side of his shoulders. A swallow worked in his throat.

"Please," she whispered. "Don't call Bert. I can get you up."

He blinked, his eyes appearing unfocused for the briefest moment. "Let's get something straight right now." His voice had grown thick and robotic. "I am not interested in *you* getting me *up*. I am only interested in you getting off of me and out of my sight, as quickly as possible."

"But I can help." She gripped his shoulders, and he tensed beneath her touch.

"No."

His dark gaze locked with hers, sending nervous heat skittering to her toes. "I'll massage your back."

"No." He scowled.

"I'll be gentle." She slid her touch from his shoulders to his chest.

"No." Nate's eye twitched and he winced.

"Please. I'm quite good with my hands." She worked her palms against the rough fabric of his jacket, hoping the motion would soothe the anger boiling in his glare.

"No!" The force of the word reverberated in Bunny's bones.

She flinched and scrambled backward, out of range should he decide to start kicking. Her throat tightened and tears welled in her eyes. "I only wanted to—"

Nate thrust up one palm. "Not . . . another . . . word."

He rolled onto one hip, leveling a glare that shook her to the core. "From this moment until The Worthington

Cup takes place, I do not want to sense your positive chi in this firm. Is that clear?"

"But I—"

"I do not want to see plants, or bunny slippers or candles. I do not want to hear chimes, or tiny waterfalls or hamsters. I do not want to hear your voice. I do not want to see your smile. I do not want to gaze into your eyes. Do you understand?"

Bunny nodded meekly. He couldn't mean it. She clasped a hand over her mouth to keep herself from throwing up. Vomit was just about the last thing this office's energy needed.

"If you need assistance from me, you'll speak to Miss Peabody. And if you pull off the Cup, perhaps—just perhaps—you'll keep your job."

Dread pooled in her stomach. *Her job.* She winced. Without her job, she'd lose her condo. Somewhere in her mission to free Nate's energy, she'd lost sight of the whole reason she was even at McNulty Events. "I only wanted to improve the flow of energy in your office."

Nate looked up disbelievingly from his prone position, his scowl mixed with pain. "Well, your plan worked beautifully."

She gulped down her distress just as a knock sounded at the door.

Bert cleared his throat. "Am I interrupting something?"

Bunny scrambled to her feet.

"Miss Love was just leaving," Nate snarled. "Please see her to her cubicle and chain her there if necessary. Pull my door closed behind you so that I may salvage my dignity."

Bunny shot Nate one last desperate glance as she headed for the door. His eyes were closed, his chin turned defiantly away from her.

Bert took her elbow and escorted her into the hall.

He pulled the office door shut and winked. "May I surmise the changes knocked him off his feet?"

Bunny turned to Miss Peabody's trash can and tossed that morning's herbal tea.

Chapter 14

Barry Manilow seeped into Bunny's brain as soon as her alarm clocked chimed. *Copacabana*. That couldn't be good.

She glanced at the clock. One hour before she had to meet Bert at Nate's apartment. Nate had finally agreed to see her, though only for an update on Cup planning.

She winced. A dislocated back. So much for the positive effects of feng shui. Thanks to her efforts, Nate would be laid up for days, maybe even weeks.

She headed straight for the bathroom, definitely needing a hot shower before facing whatever Alexandra had organized this time.

A few minutes later Bunny pinched her arm furiously, hoping the lack of color on her apartment walls was part of a really bad dream. "How long have you been at this?" She stared in shocked horror at the bland color. *Eggshell.*

"Isn't it glorious?" her mother beamed. "I started around three this morning. I was blocked, dear."

"Blocked?" Disbelief flickered through Bunny's belly. Life had been so simple before Alexandra had buzzed into town.

"Creatively." Her mother waved the paintbrush at the wall, sending a drop of acrylic to the floor.

Bunny bit back a whimper.

Alexandra narrowed her eyes. "This is a much better color scheme than what you had going, honey. All those colors were rather juvenile. Don't you want to be taken seriously?"

Not particularly. Bunny opened her mouth to argue, but realized sooner or later, her mother would go back to Florida. Then she could reclaim her space. Until then, if Alexandra needed to paint, she could paint. Why stifle a creative awakening? Even if it was eggshell.

She shrugged, pasting on a fake smile. "Get unblocked soon, okay? Every time you hit a wall, I'm losing valuable square footage."

Alexandra plucked a handful of jellybeans from a ceramic bowl typically used for fruit. "Funny, dear," she mumbled around the mouthful of sugar. "Very funny."

Bunny couldn't help but notice they were one family member short. "Where's Daddy?"

"At the Four Seasons. I kicked him out."

"You what?" Bunny squeaked.

"The printer was a setup. Your father thought he could overwhelm me by talking business plans. He thought I'd give up my dream and scamper back to Florida."

See? Bunny would be insane to fall for a control freak like Nate. Just look at her mother and father. Her mother was completely smothered even now. God, the woman thought eggshell was a hot decorating color.

Alexandra straightened, slapping a fresh coat of paint onto an innocent wall. "I told him he must have me confused with some other wife."

Bunny sputtered on her cup of tea. "You said that to *Daddy?*"

Her mother raised her brows. "And a whole lot more that you're too young to hear."

Bunny nodded, pride swelling in her chest. "Go, Alexandra." She set down her cup to flip through the pile of folders she'd left on the coffee table.

"Lose something, honey?"

Frustration rippled through Bunny's chest. *Yes.* But she wasn't about to admit that to the queen of control. "I just need some forms for my mortgage. They're due today and I wanted to drop them off on my way to my meeting." Suddenly, she spied the documents and breathed a sigh of relief. "Got them."

"You should keep a list," Alexandra's voice chirped.

"List?" Bunny's head pounded. She couldn't tell if the sensation stemmed from paint fumes or her mother's constant desire to organize her life. She headed for the front door, now with only twenty minutes to make it to Nate's.

"A *to-do* list." Alexandra enunciated the words carefully, as if Bunny might not be able to grasp the concept. "Keeping a list of things to do never hurt anyone."

"Tell that to the trees." Bunny pulled the front door closed behind her, eagerly gulping down the fresh hallway air on her way to the elevator.

Bunny watched Bert slip the key into the door of Nate's apartment. Sudden nerves threatened to strangle her. "We're just going to walk in?"

"He knows we're coming. Besides, he's supposed to stay off his feet."

"I thought he'd like the changes we made to his office," she said softly.

"He fell for them," Bert teased. "Quite literally."

"It was your idea."

Bert winked mischievously. "He doesn't know that."

"I could tell him." But she wouldn't. Not her style. Bert knew it and shot her a wide grin.

She followed him into the apartment, her gaze locking on a wall of windows overlooking Fairmount Park. Breathtaking. Orange and yellow leaves still clung to the trees, painting the view with an artist's brush.

"Nate, my boy," Bert called out. "The troops have arrived."

Bunny stood still, her feet riveted to the carpet. The gray carpet. Her heart fell. Even here, in his home, with the stunning beauty of nature providing a breathtaking backdrop, Nate clung to gray. What was he so afraid of? Life?

She scanned the living space for a sign of vitality. The only thing that caught her eye was the arrangement of photos above the fireplace. Symmetrical. Stiff. So much like the arrangement in his office that a shiver cascaded down her spine.

She sniffed the air, hoping for a fragrance—something masculine . . . musky . . . Nate. Nothing. Heck, he'd managed to sterilize the air along with the rest of his life.

She shuddered, tamping down her disappointment. After all, what had she expected? Splashes of color and wild artwork? Fragranced candles? Incense? This was Nate. A sad sigh slipped from her lips. She guessed she'd hoped he hid his vitality at home—or let it free here.

Bert eyed her suspiciously. "Problem?"

Bunny shook her head. "It's just so . . . ."

"Nate," he said softly. "Come on. Embrace the order."

She followed him down the hall toward Nate. *Embrace the order*? Never. She'd rather shrivel up and die than have her life force sucked as dry as Nate's.

Nate sat propped against a pile of pillows. He repositioned himself, grimacing as he straightened. Bunny's stomach tightened. What had she done?

"I'm so—"

Nate shook his head, interrupting her apology before she could begin. "Let's stick to business. What's done is done."

"I've got to go." Bert glanced at his watch. "Breakfast meeting."

"Go?" Bunny blurted, her already tense stomach twisting into a knot.

"Breakfast?" Nate frowned.

Bert was across the room and out the door. "You two have a good catch-up session."

"Traitor," Nate mumbled.

"What?"

"Nothing."

Impatience bubbled in Bunny's chest, overriding her nerves. "You're a mumbler."

"You're a bumbler." Nate's dark brows arched tauntingly.

Bunny felt the air rush from her lungs. So much for sticking to business. "I beg your pardon?"

"Let's review, shall we?" Warm color flushed his cheeks. "You poisoned me." He held up a finger. "You destroyed the so-called energy in the conference room." Another finger. "And you turned my office into an obstacle course." A third finger.

Heat flared in her face. "If I'm so incompetent, why don't you fire me?"

"I'm sure I would if I wasn't so heavily drugged."

She smiled then quickly straightened her features. "Do you think I'm incompetent?"

"No." He stared at her, his fiery gaze sending hot, electric pulses to her toes. "I don't think you're incompetent. Overly enthusiastic, perhaps. But not incompetent."

The words cheered her, bolstering her mood. "Thank you." She pulled several folders from her briefcase. "I brought the Cup files to update you on our progress."

"Let's get to it, shall we?" Nate pointed to a rocking chair. "Pull that over."

Bunny did as she was told, numb with the realization Nate was being gracious about his injury. Just how strong were his meds? And where could she get more to keep him this way?

As she positioned the rocker, her gaze fell onto an exquisite framed pen and ink. A family of four. *A definite sign of life.* Mother. Father. Two boys. Her heart swelled. Nate's family—she recognized the faces.

"My mother's," Nate volunteered, having obviously noticed her open-mouthed stare.

The piece of art apparently held a special place in Nate's heart. Bunny warmed. There was hope after all. "Did Martha do this?"

Nate frowned. "Why would you think that?"

Bunny met his confused look. "Alexandra mentioned your aunt was quite the artist."

Nate's rich, brown eyes widened. "I had no idea."

"Doesn't the rest of this bother you?" She gestured to the stark bedroom walls. "Don't you crave color?"

"What I crave is coffee, if you think you could manage a cup."

"I don't know how to make coffee," she admitted. "How about a nice cup of—"

His warning glare froze the word on her lips.

"Coffee," she stammered. "Coming right up."

"There's a jar of instant," Nate offered as she headed for the door. "You can boil water without any major catastrophes, can't you?"

"You're so set in your ways." Frustration bubbled in Bunny's chest. He could free his energy. He could *live.* "This whole place is rigid and stiff," she blurted out.

"Sometimes stiff is good." One dark brow arched.

Bunny swallowed, heat infusing her cheeks. "I'll get that coffee." She was out the door and into the hall in three strides.

Nate leaned back against the pillow, chuckling softly to himself. Where had that inappropriate comment come from? Must be the pain pills talking.

He scanned the room, his gaze following the clean

lines of the walls, the knickknack-free expanse of chest and bureau. Finally, he turned to stare at the pen and ink. He'd had it so long he never noticed it anymore, to tell the truth.

Nate plucked the frame from the nightstand and stared into the captured expressions of his family.

Bunny was right. His gut clenched. This was the only sign of life in his apartment, and two out of four pictured were dead. Regret welled in his chest as he remembered his argument with Aunt Martha's and Jeremy's words.

If I'd followed her rules, I'd be the one whose most exciting experience in years had been an allergic reaction.

Maybe Bunny Love had breezed into his life for a purpose. She'd shown him just how dead inside he'd become.

Bunny stepped back into the room, chattering something about how he could use curtains to warm the living room to complement the view of the park.

He studied her then, noticing how her own colors suited her perfectly—the reddish brown hair softly framing her pert features, the long lashes a dark contrast against her pale skin and her bottomless blue eyes. Bunny stood frozen, her gaze locked with his.

His stomach tightened and he remembered again how much he'd wanted to kiss her on Saturday night. How much he wanted to kiss her right now.

"Is something wrong?" She leaned forward, reaching toward the nightstand with the coffee mug, her voice nothing more than a whisper.

He never took his eyes from hers, nor she from his. Nate shook his head, extending a hand. "I'll take that. Thanks."

A swallow worked in Bunny's throat as she handed him the cup, brushing the ceramic against his fingers.

"What colors did you have in mind?" Nate asked.

Her eyes popped wide.

"For the curtains," he explained.

A slow grin curved up the corners of her mouth and she laughed, sloshing hot coffee onto the blanket covering Nate's lap. "Cripes."

Nate closed his eyes, the moment lost. Was it his imagination, or did chaos prevail each and every time he weakened in the woman's presence?

She thunked the cup onto the nightstand, pressing a napkin to Nate's lap.

"It's not that bad." Nate's voice tightened. "Honestly, let's just get to work."

Bunny pressed and patted, her cheeks flushing to a deep red. "I'm so sorry. You mentioned color and I got all . . ." She tipped up her chin, giving Nate a look that rocked him to the core. "Excited."

She isn't the only one. Nate winced with the realization that Bunny's inadvertent lap massage was having a similar effect. His eye twitched and he slapped his hand over hers. "You need to stop."

"What on earth is going on here?" Aunt Martha's voice boomed from the doorway.

Nate winced and all color drained from Bunny's face. Damn. Just what he didn't need—more ammunition for his aunt's ire. Bunny straightened, moving quickly away from the bed. "Coffee spill." She pointed her finger.

"I'm sure." Martha's tone could have frozen hell.

"Miss Love was updating me on the Cup." Nate's voice felt tight and he silently berated himself. Why did he let his aunt's approval matter so much?

Her expression softened for a moment and he realized she'd spotted the pen and ink. "I brought you some updated financials," she said flatly, forcing her gaze away from the drawing and onto Nate. "You'd be wiser to focus on numbers than on coffee, I'd say."

Nate watched her wordlessly. Had Bunny's mother

been right? Had Aunt Martha had a creative side once, penning the drawing his mother had so loved?

"I should get back to the office." Bunny nodded toward Nate as she gathered her folders. "I'll fax you an update."

"Very good." He did his best to keep the regret seeping through his body out of his voice. He'd been decidedly susceptible to Bunny's charms today. Must be the pain pills.

Martha watched the young woman scamper from Nate's bedroom, her nephew's dejected expression not going unnoticed. "I'll walk you out, Bunny."

She yanked the coffee-stained blanket from Nate's bed, tossing it into the hamper and pulling fresh linens from the closet. As she covered Nate's lap, she shot him a glare, hoping she left no room for misinterpretation. "Tread carefully."

He said nothing, returning her glare with the same intensity she'd given him.

Martha caught up to Bunny at the front door, following her into the hall. Bunny spun to face her. "My mother mentioned your talent for pen and inks."

The young woman's impossibly blue eyes sparkled, and Martha fought to keep her shock off her face. She'd expected her to apologize for her behavior, not question Martha's past.

She'd tried to avoid all thoughts of her long forgotten artwork, much as she ached for the creative outlet. Seeing the drawing in Nate's bedroom had been surprising enough. She'd have to cut off Miss Love's line of inquiry quickly.

"Your mother must be mistaken. She never was one to pay much attention."

Bunny blinked then nodded, as if accepting she'd be

getting no further information. "I thought perhaps you'd done the drawing on Nate's nightstand. It's exquisite."

For the briefest moment, Martha longed to hear more, but she straightened, brushing past Bunny to press the elevator button. "I'm sure the artist would be thrilled to hear you liked his or her work."

Bunny's warm vanilla scent tickled Martha's nose as she stepped near, her expression a toss between understanding and sympathy. "It would be a sin to waste a talent like that."

Martha focused on the illuminated numbers above the elevator doors, ignoring the regret whispering at the back of her brain. She knew all about wasting her talent, but then, what choice had life left her?

Chapter 15

Nate leaned against the back of his chair and glowered at the office wall. *Maroon.* The color gave the space a feel not completely horrible, he decided. Not that he'd admit that to Bunny. Hell. Not that he'd admit that to anyone.

He gingerly rubbed the tender area just between his spine and right hip. He'd been laid up on his back for three and a half weeks thanks to Bunny's campaign for improved energy. The injury had kept him on bed rest, safely distanced from the mop-topped menace—with the exception of their one rather interesting meeting. If Aunt Martha hadn't interrupted when she had, Nate might have done something he'd regret.

He'd safely overseen agency business via fax and laptop from that point forward, instructing Bert to keep him updated on all Cup preparations. A knock sounded at the door and he wrestled his thoughts to the present.

"Miss Love left these for you." Miss Peabody deposited a stack of folders on the corner of his bare desk. "She thought you'd like to see the media coverage the Cup's received."

"Mmm."

She frowned at his brilliant display of verbal skill then continued. "She also wanted to remind you that Jeremy will be here this morning for your final approval on the Web site. Call me if you need anything."

Nate slid the files to the center of his desk. The soft

aroma of vanilla wafted up from the papers sending warmth seeping through his chest. His eye twitched. *Damn.* That hadn't happened since he'd seen Bunny last. Not once.

He flipped through the rundown of media hits. This year's event had received more coverage than he could remember for the past five. A smug grin tugged at the corner of his mouth. This would show Armand Miller. What had Bunny called him? An egotistical, self-adoring jerk? Nate laughed. She might be a menace, but the woman was an expert judge of character.

A picture of her vibrant blue eyes flashed through his mind, and he groaned. He'd been able to tamp down most thoughts of Bunny until today. His eyelid twitched again. Damn the woman and her positive chi. Perhaps the Cup would be so successful another firm would hire her away. He could only hope. His stomach tightened in protest.

Bunny Love might have succeeded in sending his nerves and libido into turmoil, but she had not succeeded in corrupting the staff at McNulty Events. From what Bert had reported, she'd been subdued and low profile during his absence. Apparently, she'd finally accepted the rules of decorum.

Now all Nate needed to do was focus his thoughts on anything and everything but her.

Owen Carruthers, McNulty's chief financial officer, sank into the straight-backed chair next to Bunny's desk. "He's back." His worried brow wrinkled. "Have you seen him?"

Bunny shook her head. Nor did she want to. Well, she wanted to, but she was afraid to. Their last conversation had resulted in a lap full of coffee and an unfortunate groping incident. Okay, not *entirely* unfortunate. In the meantime, she'd done what she considered to be a fine job for The Worthington Cup, including evading Armand Miller and his endless event planning tips.

"Do you have my package?" Owen's expression grew anxious and Bunny realized Nate's return would require her to rethink the creative goody distribution. "Right here." She slipped a brown paper bag from beneath her desk and handed it over. "Keep them under wraps until you're in your office."

"Will do." The man pulled himself upright and stepped toward the door. He tucked the bag under his elbow and looked back at Bunny. "We appreciate you, even if he doesn't."

A twinge of sadness tightened Bunny's chest. Her unorthodox methods had garnered the approval of most everyone in the firm, but not the one opinion she coveted most. During Nate's absence, she'd supplied just about every McNulty employee with tools for improving energy and creativity—from Slinkies, to singing hamsters, to slippers. She turned back to her desk and picked up the phone.

Oh well. She refused to pine away over Nate McNulty. He certainly wasn't missing her. Whenever she'd suggested subsequent visits to his home, he'd refused. He'd made it clear he wanted nothing to do with her. Knowing Nate, he'd probably counted the days until the Cup was over so he could fire her creative rear end.

Bunny let out a frustrated breath, listening to the ringing at the other end of the line, doing her best to ignore the persistent ache in her heart.

"Saslow Sundries," a deep voice barked out.

"It's Bunny Love. You ready for me?" She listened intently for several moments, staring at her watch. "Sounds good. I'll be there in twenty."

She called down for a taxi, slipped off her bunny slippers and stepped into her black leather pumps. It was a good thing she had plenty of running around to do before the cocktail party tomorrow night. All the better to avoid Nate McNulty and his deep, dark, smoldering eyes.

Nate frowned at Jeremy's laptop perched in the middle of his desk. His brother clicked through the final Web site design. "You don't like it?"

"No." Nate shook his head. "I mean, yes. It's great." He met his brother's narrowed gaze. "You did a great job."

Jeremy laughed. "Now I know something's wrong. You haven't given me a compliment since my grand-slam homerun in seventh grade."

Nate scowled. "That can't be right."

Jeremy waggled his blond brows and nodded. "Want to tell me what's wrong?"

"Everything's fine."

Jeremy powered off the laptop and snapped it shut. "I know you better than that." He crossed his arms. "Fess up."

Nate drew in a deep breath. "I've had a lot of time to think." He reached to pluck the smallest photo from those behind his desk then handed it to Jeremy.

His brother's smile grew wide. "The day you got your dirt bike. Dad was so proud."

"They had their accident the next week." Just saying the words made Nate's stomach catch.

"And Aunt Martha sold our bikes before they were buried."

"She did the right thing." Nate nodded.

"No"—Jeremy shook his head—"she didn't."

"They died because they were on a motorcycle." Nate stood and slowly paced the office, remembering his aunt's many lectures on control and safety. "They were careless."

"But they were happy." Jeremy leaned back in his

seat. "It was their time. Call it fate, call it whatever you want." He shrugged. "It is what it is."

"You've been spending too much time with Bunny."

"Sounds like you could stand to spend a little more."

Nate's pulse quickened. "As if I could survive it."

Several long beats of silence fell between them. Nate walked to the window and scrutinized the street below. "What if this is as good as it gets?"

"Wow," Jeremy teased. "Deep thoughts by Nate McNulty."

Nate spun to face his brother. "I'm serious."

Jeremy stood and closed the gap between them. "It's about time."

Nate blinked.

"You've been a robot for a long time. It's nice to see you coming back to life." He rapped Nate's chest with his finger. "Looks like someone's flipped your switch back to on."

"Bunny?" Denial shimmied through Nate. Jeremy wasn't saying anything he hadn't said to himself, but the idea was nuts. He and Bunny couldn't be more opposite.

Jeremy smiled and nodded.

"What about Melanie?"

Jeremy moved back to the desk and picked up the laptop. "Couldn't help but notice she's not exactly Mary Poppins herself these days."

"What about Aunt Martha and her grand plan?" Nate turned back to the window, as if somewhere out there everything would make sense. "What about her?"

"Live your life, not the one she's planned for you." Jeremy turned to leave. "See you tomorrow night. Call me if you need anything."

He was halfway into the hall when Nate called out, "Hey, Jer?"

His brother stopped and looked back, a surprised grin etched across his face. "You haven't called me that in years."

"Thanks."

* * *

Bunny made it to the revolving exit doors just as Kitty Worthington stepped out of a long, black sedan.

"Bunny, darling." She waved her hand. "You're just in time to take the girls."

"Take the—" Bunny flinched as Chablis and Chardonnay emerged from the backseat, sporting matching purple collars and leashes. Rhinestones covered their tiny canine accessories and purple bows adorned each of their powder puff ears.

Kitty tucked the leash grips into Bunny's hands.

"What's going on?"

"You're watching the girls." Kitty frowned. "It's standard Cup procedure. Surely you knew that."

Bunny squinted at the gaudy leashes she held. "Why?"

"I'm off to the salon. With the cocktail party tomorrow night, I've got to look my best."

Bunny paused then forced a weak smile. "What about Chablis and Chardonnay? Don't they have to get ready, too?"

Kitty clucked her tongue. "No, no, no. The girls don't show. They're not a recognized AKC breed. Plus, they've just come from the groomer. Surely you can tell." She eyed Bunny expectantly.

"Surely," Bunny murmured. "You do realize I've got a lot of running around to do."

"Oh, they love errands. Absolutely adore them."

"But, Kitty, you can't expect me to watch them with all I've got going on."

Kitty's expression grew serious and intense. "Armand always watched the girls for me while I went to the salon."

Armand. Bunny should have known. For all the worthless details he'd provided, he'd left this one out. The rat.

Bunny sucked in a deep breath. "How are they in cabs?"

Kitty's eyes popped wide. "My girls can't ride in a taxicab. You'll have to make other arrangements." She glanced back to the curb. "My driver's waiting. I'll see you later."

"But—"

"I'll call you."

Bunny stood in silence as Kitty's car eased away from the curb. The only thing that broke her frustrated stare was the sensation of gnawing at her heel. She looked down to find Chablis fang-deep in patent leather.

"No," Bunny shrieked, doing her best to shake loose the tiny pedigree's teeth.

"Problem, Miss Love?" The doorman glared nervously at the two small fur balls, no doubt more concerned about the marble foyer than Bunny's shoes.

"Any idea where I can borrow a car for the afternoon?"

His bushy eyebrows drew together. "Most everyone here takes the train or walks." His expression brightened. "The big boss drove in today. You could ask him."

Bunny's heart fell. "Anyone else?" There was no way she'd ask Nate for his car. No way at all. "Anyone at all?"

He shook his head. "Shall I cancel your cab?"

Bunny nodded, dragging the girls toward the bank of elevators. The tiny poodles danced around her feet, succeeding in winding their leashes into a snarled, rhinestone mess. The middle set of doors slid open and the three shuffled on.

Bunny pressed the button to return upstairs, anxiety sitting like a knot in her chest. Nate had made no secret of the fact he did *not* want to see her. She pondered the two poodles at her feet, now sitting politely, pink tongues wagging. He wouldn't be thrilled to see these two, either.

Oh well, if nothing else, perhaps he'd lend Bunny his BMW just to keep the three of them out of his sight.

* * *

Nate straightened, glaring at Bunny and the furry monsters draped around her ankles. He couldn't believe his ears. "Absolutely not. Have you learned nothing from your past escapades?"

"It's for the Cup."

"No." Disbelief welled in his gut. "Not even for the Cup."

Bunny planted one fist on her hip and tipped her head. "I'm perfectly capable of driving your car. I've done it before."

"And it still sticks in third. You destroyed the transmission. All of you—out of my office. You're bad luck."

Her brilliant eyes grew huge. "I've brought nothing but good luck to you. You're just too stubborn to admit it."

"What?" This time she'd gone too far. He stood and leaned on the desktop.

"Good luck? You sent me to the ER, sprained my back, spilled hot coffee down my crotch, and I can't sit for more than five minutes without a cushion under my ass." He raked a hand through his hair. "Is that a fair summary?"

Bunny stood quietly for several seconds, her gaze narrowing on his. "Is your eye twitching again? You really should try meditation."

"Did you hear me?" he bellowed. "You're bad luck."

She took a step closer. Nate instinctively backed up, bumping the credenza and sending his family photos tumbling from their easels.

"It's not uncommon for a series of mishaps to occur when someone's energy is shifting. Perhaps the worst is over and you're on your way to becoming a new you." A bright grin spread across her luminous face.

Nate's traitorous stomach twisted and caught. Damn

her and his body's reaction to her insanity. "The old me is just fine."

Bunny made a tsking noise with her tongue, then gave several quick nods of her head. "You're loosening up."

Nate pressed a finger to his quaking lid. "I am not. I'm just as uptight as I ever was."

Bunny lowered her gaze to hide her laugh.

"You know what I mean." The woman was exasperating, and he had a sudden urge to pull her into his arms and kiss her senseless. "Here." He grabbed his car keys from his top drawer and tossed them across the blotter. "Take the damn car and go—you and those little long-haired rats."

"Thanks." Bunny plucked the keys from the desktop and turned for the door, Chablis and Chardonnay in tow. "Here's another tip for you." She stopped long enough to shoot an alluring wink over her shoulder. "It's two days before the big show. I'd suggest you stop calling the clients 'rats.'"

She and the fur balls were out the door before he could respond with anything more than a grunt. He sank into his chair, swearing softly as pain knifed into his back.

Meditation. As if that would cure what ailed him.

Oh, what the hell. He lowered his face to his palms and closed his eyes, but no matter how hard he tried, the only mantra he could muster consisted of two words. Bunny Love.

The resulting chant was anything but soothing.

Martha disconnected the phone, returning her attention to her sketching. She'd stopped at a Center City art supply store on a whim and now traced the point of a fine nib along a crisp sheet of paper. A heady rush filled her at the sight of the line, entirely at the control of her own hand. She'd forgotten how complete the act of drawing made her feel.

She trained her thoughts back to the phone call from Armand. His plans were going well, he'd assured her, though he'd offered no details, saying it was best she didn't know specifics. She made a face at the paper before her. The man had obviously been watching too many spy movies. All she'd requested had been a bit of mayhem at a dog show. How difficult to arrange could that be?

Before long, Miss Love would be a distant memory for Nate and for McNulty Events. It was unavoidable, even if the girl's words had spurred Martha to rediscover her beloved pen and ink.

While Melanie's behavior might have been atrocious at the dinner dance, she was the wisest choice for Nate. Safe and secure. Martha had always secretly envied the passion Nate's parents had shared, but look where that frivolity had gotten them. She shook her head, setting her chin determinedly. She would not weaken now.

The plans in motion would secure Nate's future. She had only to make sure nothing—and no one— got in the way.

Chapter 16

Bunny loaded the poodles into the BMW's back-seat, contemplating her argument with Nate as she slammed the door. She leaned against the silver sedan and frowned. Their reunion hadn't been exactly warm, but there had been several redeeming moments. Okay, not several, but a few. Well, maybe one. And that had been her epiphany.

Nate's energy was changing, whether he realized it or not. Heck, *she* hadn't realized it until she'd seen him today. His whole demeanor screamed *alive*. Bunny's frown twisted into a grin. *Alive.* She had known he had it in him.

She leaned forward and laughed, softly at first, then deep and loud from her belly. Holy cow. Nate McNulty had displayed emotion. *Serious* emotion.

He'd screamed at her, openly dragged his hand through his hair, slammed his palm against the desk-top, and hollered—good and strong—with *passion*. That hadn't been the pain pills talking. No, sir. Nate had come to life with a bang, and her positive chi had been part of the transformation.

The crucial step would be to help him channel his energy. He'd been completely bottled up at first, but now energy seeped through his voice, his hands, his eyes. Ooh, those eyes.

A shiver shimmied down Bunny's spine. Nate's rich,

brown gaze was the most incredible she'd ever seen, and each time she saw him, his heat grew more intense. More *alive*.

A yap sounded from inside the car. Bunny jumped. Sheesh. The dogs. The leashes. She snapped herself from her thoughts, pulling open the driver's door. Her heart pitched. Chablis lay sprawled across the passenger side, gnawing on the leather trim.

Yowza. Bunny winced. She had a sneaking suspicion she hadn't begun to see Nate's full emotional range.

Nate applied pressure to his twitching eyelid. The encounter with Bunny had not gone well. Definitely not his finest display of control. Damn the woman. Damn her bright eyes, her lunatic rationale and the ratty poodles she'd shuffled in with.

He squeezed his eyes shut. Perhaps if he concentrated hard enough, the previous month would be nothing more than a bad dream. The flaw in that reasoning was that there had been several intriguing episodes during the past month—all of them centered on the life force known as Bunny Love. Her chaos-loving grin played across his mind and his heart twisted.

Nate opened his eyes, turning to look at his fallen photos. He let out a frustrated sigh. *Chaos*. That's what Bunny had brought. All his life he'd strived for control, yet now he found himself in the midst of pure chaos.

He picked up the framed photo of Melanie, scrutinizing her controlled pose. Hell, everything about her screamed *control*. Controlled hair. Controlled pink suit. *Controlled*. Like their relationship and their passion—or lack thereof.

What was it Jeremy had said about their parents? They may have been careless, but they had been happy. He was right. Their relationship had been anything but

controlled. What it had been was full of love, and life.
Even Nate had been old enough to understand that.

His father had been born into a family of Philadelphia bankers. He and Uncle Arthur had been raised to
become society leaders, but then his father had met his
mother. Their explosive chemistry had been legendary.
She'd been as free-spirited as his father had been controlled. Where she challenged rules, Nate's father had
worked to keep life orderly.

Nate shoved a hand through his hair. *My God.* He was
his father and Bunny was his mother. No wonder he
couldn't keep his mind off of the woman.

The thought of Bunny's brilliant, blue eyes sent heat
zinging from his chest to his groin. Damn. Was he willing to risk all he'd worked for? For Bunny? For smiling
turquoise eyes? For chaos?

His stomach tightened. He couldn't. He *wouldn't.*
The most important thing in his life was saving his father's firm. To do that, he had to control Bunny's
chaos. He had to maintain a sense of order. Nate
slapped away the vision of Bunny and the raw need
surging through his body.

A knock sounded, and Owen Carruthers stood in
the doorway, holding a ream of paper in the crook
of his arm. "Brought you the revised budget figures
you asked for."

Nate patted the top of his desk, welcoming the in-
terruption. "Bring 'em on, Owen."

The man dropped the printouts in the center of the
desk, pausing for a beat. "How's the back?"

Nate straightened. "Coming along. Thanks. And
thanks for these."

Owen nodded, heading for the door.

"Owen?"

The burly man stopped, twisting to meet Nate's gaze.
"How were things while I was out?" Nate narrowed

his eyes, curiosity simmering in his belly. "How about the new hire? Miss Love? She fitting in well?"

Owen visibly swallowed, almost appearing nervous. "Why?"

Nate shook his head, wondering. "No reason." He had surprised the man with the question. That was evident. Owen would have had no reason to encounter Bunny, but Nate's intuition had snapped to attention.

Intuition. Hell. Four weeks ago the word hadn't been part of his vocabulary. Now Bunny had him thinking about intuition. *His* intuition. "Thanks again," he called out as Owen stepped into the outer office.

That's when his eye caught the flash of pink. The flash of pink furry ears. *Fuzzy bunny slippers.* On his chief financial officer's feet.

"Whoa!" Nate bolted around his desk and out of his office.

Carruthers looked like Thumper in a hunter's scope, his brown eyes huge in his pale face.

Nate pointed to the man's feet. "What . . . in the hell . . . are those?"

"Slippers."

"No shit." Nate's blood boiled. "*She* did this, didn't she?"

Carruthers shook his head, clasping his hands together. "It's not her fault. She asked me to be discreet and, well, the things are so comfortable, I forgot I had them on."

Nate spun to Miss Peabody. "Ring my car. Get Miss Love on the phone."

"Yes, sir." The woman's features tightened. She discreetly slid a ceramic dish of greenery behind her computer monitor.

"What is *that?*" The words hissed from Nate's lips.

"Lucky bamboo, sir." Unlike Carruthers, Miss Peabody straightened, holding her chin high. "And I like it."

"Well, *I* don't." He rapped his fist on her desk. "Miss Love. Now." He turned back, fully intending to rip the rodent slippers from Carruthers' feet, but the coward had vanished.

"She's not answering, sir."

"Well, keep trying. I'll be in Bert's office."

Would this darn phone never stop ringing? Bunny swerved as Chablis attacked the handset for the second time. "It's a phone, you furry idiot."

Bunny scowled at the ancient contraption mounted between the seats. Couldn't the man carry a cell phone like a normal person? She refused to answer his personal line. *No way.* With her luck it would be Melanie. Bunny had no intention of adding to that woman's identity crisis.

Over the past few weeks, Melanie had paid more visits to Bunny's cubicle to garner information on color therapy and feng shui than employees had ordered bunny slippers. The poor woman desperately searched for her life's direction. Bunny only hoped she'd find it before she and Nate made the mistake of marrying each other. Their energy fields were completely wrong for each other.

Guilt flickered through her. Who was she kidding? Her thoughts were probably motivated solely by her attraction for Nate. She clucked her tongue. Shame on herself.

The phone began a third round of ringing. Chablis catapulted herself from the backseat to the front, frantically biting and snapping at the handset. Bunny groaned. "For gosh sakes, don't leave teeth marks."

Chardonnay took up a rousing chorus of yapping from the well behind Bunny's seat. Bunny gritted her teeth. She pressed down on the gas pedal, focusing on reaching the warehouse quickly. The gears protested noisily, the car bucking, jerking her neck.

You know, for an uptight guy, Nate really should take better care of his car—especially if he was going to let other people drive it.

Nate burst into Bert's office without knocking. His vice president scrambled to right himself from a lounging position, sending a stack of folders sliding onto the carpet.

"To what do I owe this pleasure?" Bert quipped.

Exasperated, Nate raked a hand through his hair. "She's a menace."

Bert waggled a finger in Nate's direction. "Did your hair explode?"

Nate paced the office, pivoting sharply, hands on hips. He stopped, leveling a glare at Bert. "Do you know why I look like this?"

Bert put a hand over his mouth, shaking his head.

Nate stomped toward the desk and leaned, hands pressed flat against the gleaming gray resin surface. "She's making me crazy."

Laugh lines crinkled around Bert's eyes as he rocked back in his chair. His easy laughter usually cheered Nate, but right now the sound only added to his frustration. "She's a complete and total menace."

"She's a breath of fresh air," Bert said softly. "And you know it."

"No, she's not." Nate's voice had thickened. "She's infuriating, that's what she is." He resumed his pacing. "She has no sense of decorum. I mean, my God, what was she, raised in a barn? A workplace is for work—not for lucky bamboo and bunny slippers."

Nate closed his eyes, trying to calm his soaring blood pressure. "The woman is a blue-eyed, mop-topped leader of the pack, and I will *not* let her creative chaos take over this firm. We've succeeded through control, and we will continue to do so."

Bert's lips twitched into a mischievous grin. He

slowly repositioned himself in his chair. Leaning back, he put one foot, then the other, on top of the desk. Pink, fuzzy, bunny slippers covered both.

Nate felt the color drain from his face. He pointed a shaking finger, but found himself speechless.

"You know," Bert said slowly, "you shouldn't knock it until you try it." He crossed his legs at the ankle and laced his fingers behind his head. "They're just the thing for letting your toes wiggle."

Nate did his best to focus on Bert, not on the pounding headache pulsing over the center of his eyes. "McNulty Events does not condone wiggling. Of any type."

Bert swung his feet to the floor and walked to where Nate stood. "Life's short, Nate. Try to enjoy some of it."

Nate glared down at the offensive pink foot coverings. "How can you stand there in *those* and criticize me?" He raised his gaze to Bert's. His friend's features softened, but his posture did not.

"Don't make her color inside your box. She's the best thing that's ever happened around here."

Nate turned, walking quickly toward the door. "Don't quote pop psychology to me, and get those things"—he jabbed his finger in the direction of Bert's feet—"out of this office."

Seconds later he towered over Miss Peabody's desk. "Did you track down Bunny?"

"No." His secretary flinched, as if bracing herself for another outburst. "But the manager at the Loews just called. Seems to be some sort of altercation among the guests."

"The menace has my car," Nate snarled. "I'll take a cab." He turned toward the elevator, but yelled over his shoulder, "I don't care what you have to do. Find her and tell her to meet me at that hotel."

* * *

Bunny pulled Nate's BMW onto the pothole-riddled parking lot of Saslow Sundries. Armand had better be right about this. Seemed a bit ridiculous to supply the handlers with leads, but she supposed the purple theme was worth the expense. "Move it, ladies," she called out to Chablis and Chardonnay, now asleep, exhausted from pillaging the interior of Nate's car.

The trio trotted across the lot, Bunny's heel catching twice in the rough surface of the drive. Once behind the heavy metal entrance door, Bunny blinked, trying to adjust to the dingy interior.

A balding Soprano wannabe sauntered out of a tiny office. A stogy stuck out one side of his mouth. He tugged down the hem of his blue and white warm-up jacket, stretched to its limits across his paunch. "Can I help youse?"

Anxiety coiled inside her. This particular moment was not one for her event planner's scrapbook. "I came about the leashes," she said tentatively.

Chablis and Chardonnay jerked Bunny's arm, obviously intrigued by the possibilities of the dark warehouse aisles. "Miss Love. From McNulty."

The man nodded. "Yeah." He plucked the stogy out of his mouth then scratched his belly. "Gave them to your assistant about five minutes ago."

Bunny squinted, trying to make sense of his words. "I don't have an assistant."

"Nice-looking guy." The man straightened. "Buff, know what I mean? Little taller than me."

Wild thoughts raced through Bunny's mind. Who on earth would have picked up the leads? Hell, the only person who knew about this dive was Armand.

"Said he wanted to surprise you. Save you some work."

"Brown hair?"

The man nodded.

"Very polished?"

Another nod.

Her anxiety had morphed to full-blown urge-to-kill. "Did he say his name was Armand?"

"Dat's it." He waved the stoey in her direction.

Bunny pulled Chardonnay and Chablis close to her side, out of the arc of falling ash. "But I told you I was on my way."

"Didn't tell me, lady." He shrugged.

"I told someone."

"All I know is he was here to pick up favors for some other gig and asked if the leashes were in. The rest is history."

"Great," Bunny grumbled.

She thanked the man and hustled the dogs back into the car. She plucked Armand's card from her purse, alternating stares between the number and Nate's phone. Finally she pulled the phone from its base and punched in the digits. Armand answered on the third ring.

"Speak to me."

Bunny rolled her eyes. Could the man be any more in love with himself? "Why did you pick up my leads?"

"Bunny, gorgeous. How are you?"

"The leads, Armand."

"I just left you a message. Thought I'd do you a favor."

"It's my account, Armand, not yours."

His rich laughter filtered through the phone, sending a shudder up her spine.

"Chill, babe. I'm on my way to drop them off at the Convention Center. Just wanted to be sure they were the correct ones."

She squinted. "A leash is a leash, right?"

"Not for the Cup, babe." He paused for a beat. "These are special, just for you."

His words set off alarm bells in her head. Call-waiting beeped. Drat. Now she'd *have* to answer the phone. "All right. I'm on my way. Just leave them with the show manager and I'll take it from there."

"Will do. Ciao."

Bunny clicked the disconnect button. She cleared her throat to answer the second call. "Nate McNulty's car."

Miss Peabody spoke softly and quickly. "You'd better get to the Loews and fast."

"What happened?"

"Some kind of commotion. Nate's on his way."

Bunny winced.

"And, Bunny?"

"Yes?"

"He's a little hot under the collar."

Hot under the collar. Awareness rippled straight to Bunny's core, but dread quickly replaced the warmth with a chill. "Is he angry with me?"

"*And* your positive chi."

Bunny tamped down her growing anxiety. "What did he find?"

"Owen's slippers, Bert's slippers, my bamboo."

"Oh." It could have been worse. Far worse. But knowing Nate, that had been bad enough. "I'm on my way."

She disconnected then cranked the ignition.

If she could beat Nate to the hotel and put out whatever fire simmered there, perhaps he'd forgive her creative meddling back at the office.

At least long enough to close on her mortgage.

Chapter 17

By the time Bunny screeched Nate's car to a halt in front of the Loews valet stand, Chablis had dismantled two Beatles CDs and started on her third. Chardonnay apparently preferred Elvis Costello. Bunny shrugged. Who didn't?

She and the fur balls jumped from the car, hurrying through the front doors of the grand hotel. They came to a dead stop when they spotted the mayhem inside. A thirty-something couple engaged in a heated argument while their long-nosed dog stood sheepishly to one side.

On the far side of the lobby, what appeared to be a motorcycle gang congregated—laughing, loud and raucous. Anxiety clawed its way from Bunny's stomach to her chest. Uh-oh. What were a bunch of bikers doing in the same hotel as her breeders and owners?

She hurried to the desk, dragging Chablis and Chardonnay behind. The tiny terrors growled and snarled, as if sensing trouble in the air. "Miss Love." Eugene Quigley, silver-haired hotel manager extraordinaire, peered down his nose.

Bunny tipped her head toward the leather-clad bikers. "What are they doing here?"

"They are showing their champion German Shepherd." Quigley thinned his lips, tipping his chin toward the arguing couple. "*They* are the problem."

Bunny turned to size up the well-dressed pair. Their

voices had risen a few notches, their postures had become more agitated. She sucked in a breath. "Not happy with their room?"

"No," Quigley snapped. "Apparently not happy with each other. They reserved separate rooms."

Bunny handed the manager the poodles' leashes. "Hold these for a minute." She headed toward where the couple stood arguing.

As she neared, the dog clambered to his feet, stretching to his full elegant length, his enormous, narrow snout snuffling the air. "Why the long face?" Bunny murmured. The sad-eyed dog scrutinized her, his brown gaze swimming with moisture.

"He's a Borzoi," the woman replied, a chilly clip to her tone. Anger had twisted her features until she resembled a bad caricature on the Atlantic City boardwalk.

"Pardon?" Bunny squinted, trying not to laugh.

"Borzoi." The elegant man offered Bunny his hand. "I'm Timothy Goodloe. His elegant head is the sign of fine breeding. We call him Goodloe's Gentleman Poindexter."

Bunny shook the man's hand then shared a sympathetic stare with the dog. "I feel your pain, buddy."

"Did you say something?" Impeccably dressed from his tweed jacket to his tasseled loafers, the man screamed *old money*.

Bunny flashed her brightest smile. "I said my name's Bunny. Bunny Love. Coordinator for The Worthington Cup. I understand you two are having some sort of disagreement." She looked from the woman to Mr. Goodloe, arching a brow.

The woman let out a huff of breath. "I don't see that this is any of your business." Her raven bob swung about her chin, red splotches blooming in her flawless cheeks.

"My wife." Goodloe jerked a thumb toward the woman who now held her arms tightly crossed over her chest. "Mitsi Goodloe."

"Ex-wife," Mitsi hissed.

Bunny nodded. She was beginning to get the picture.

"And Poindexter?" Cripes, Bunny could barely say the word without laughing. Poor dog. "Poindexter is your dog?"

"Yes." Goodloe and Mitsi barked the word simultaneously.

"It's my weekend," Mitsi snarled. "*Mine.* The terms of our agreement are very clear."

"But, Mitsi, darling—"

"Don't ever"—the suede-clad woman jabbed a finger in the direction of her ex-husband's face—"call me darling. Not after what you did."

Bunny puffed out her cheeks. This wasn't going well. She cast a hopeful glance at the manager, hoping for backup. He gave her nothing more than an impatient arm gesture. She seriously doubted he'd learned the move at hotel manager school.

"The custody settlement clearly states I get Poindexter on show weekends," Goodloe explained. "It's rather common sense, Mitsi. I am his handler."

The woman snorted. "And whose fault is that? If you hadn't slept with the last three, we might have a real handler."

And so the plot thickened. Bunny held her hands in a time-out signal. "Let's take a moment."

The Goodloes shot matching angry glares. Brrrr. Did they keep the thermostat low in this place, or what?

"May I suggest some deep breathing?" Bunny pressed her palms together, nodding toward the couple. "Close your mouths and take a deep breath through your noses. From the belly."

Mitsi's eyes narrowed to golden, spark-shooting slits. Timothy's sapphire orbs widened, the color draining from his cheeks. Poor Poindexter dropped to the floor, tucking his head beneath an end table and draping one paw protectively over his snout. *Major issues,* Bunny thought. *Major* issues.

"Come on," she urged. "Breathe in. One. Two. Three. Four." She smiled enthusiastically. "It'll change your energy, give it a try."

The couple exchanged a glance. Bunny could have sworn she saw a smile flicker across Timothy's lips. Progress. If nothing else, she'd give them something to laugh at together.

The Goodloes breathed in as told. Perfect.

"And out. Slowly through your noses. One. Two. Three. Four."

She led them through several successive cleansing breaths, watching as the tension eased in their shoulders and the lines on their faces lessened. When their eyes reopened, their energy was far more positive than it had been. Even Poindexter pulled himself to a sitting position.

"Now then," Bunny said. "Let's reach a compromise so you both can enjoy the weekend."

"Well I—" Mitsi's voice was still too tight-sounding for Bunny's taste.

She held up a hand. "You both want to be here with Poindexter, correct?"

The Goodloes nodded.

"And how about you?" Bunny bent down to Poindexter's level, holding out her hand. "You want your humans here?"

Poindexter placed one gentlemanly paw on Bunny's palm. She gave it a shake then patted his furry head.

"Do you both have reservations?" She scrutinized the couple's faces.

Both nodded.

"I'll be right back." Bunny pivoted on one heel, crossing quickly to the registration counter. The manager waited eagerly, arms crossed, foot tapping. "It's simple." She flattened her palms on the counter. "Adjoining rooms. Custody battle solved."

The manager's carefully trimmed eyebrows snapped together. "We are sold out for the show, Miss Love. Do you think I can simply snap my fingers and find two available adjoining rooms?"

"No." Bunny jerked a thumb over her shoulder. "But, unless you want to watch the battle of the tweeds all weekend, I suggest you make this work."

The man glared at the Goodloes, scrutinizing their adversarial stance. "Will they survive adjoining rooms?"

Bunny peered at the couple, now standing with their backs to each other. Poindexter sat between the two, looking from one backside to the other.

"There's a lot of love left in their energy," Bunny explained. "This could be good for them."

A few moments later, she handed the Goodloes their card keys. "You'll have a door between your rooms," she explained. "Poindexter will be able to come and go as he pleases. Joint custody for the weekend. Fair enough?"

"Thank you." Mitsi extended her hand. She allowed herself a tight smile.

"Anytime." Bunny patted Poindexter's head. "Good luck this weekend, buddy." She glanced back at the dog's owners. "Remember, a little decorum never hurt anyone."

She shuddered as she turned back toward the registration counter. *Decorum?* When had that word slipped into her vocabulary?

The spot where the manager had stood holding Chablis and Chardonnay was empty. He was nowhere in sight. *They* were nowhere in sight. Bunny's heart fell to her toes. They might be two little pains in the derriere, but she hadn't set out to lose them—at least not intentionally.

Sharp yapping sounded from the opposite side of the lobby. The two had cornered a motorcycle. The

gang must have wheeled in a bike, and the duo of ter-
ror had chosen the pristine machine as their next
target. Just beyond them, a large German Shepherd sat
still as a statue, watching the poodles charge and
bounce off the motorcycle's tires.

Bunny cleared her throat. The poodles paused for a
beat. Chablis turned to ponder Bunny over her tiny
furry shoulder. Bunny crooked a finger then cleared
her throat again. "Now!" she ground out through
clenched teeth.

The poodles came scurrying. Bunny gathered their
leashes in her hand, glancing quickly to where they had
been, hoping no damage had been done to the motorcycle. A small, yellow puddle sat just next to the
bike's rear tire. Cripes.

She leaned over the counter, frantically looking for
help. "I need a little cleanup." She glanced to where
the leather-clad bikers gathered mere feet from the
poodles' indiscretion, then back to the counter. "Mr.
Quigley? Anyone?"

"Hell!" a very loud, very mad, male voice bellowed.
"Someone's dog took a piss on my Indian."

Bunny flinched. "Anyone?" Swallowing down her
fear, she turned slowly, only to find herself nose to snap
with a massive leather-covered chest.

Nate blew out a frustrated breath, wondering if the
cabbie could drive any slower. "Buddy, I'm in a rush
here."

The driver shot a threatening look in the rearview
mirror.

"Listen, bud." The cabbie's voice was clipped and
angry. "You'll get there when you get there. What do
you want me to do, sprout wings and fly?" He gestured
out the window. A sea of red brake lights clogged the
Parkway.

"How long until we get to the Loews?"

"Five minutes. Twenty minutes. An hour. Who knows?"

"Thanks for nothing," Nate muttered.

"What's that?"

"I said, I'm smothering. Mind if I roll down a window?"

"Suit yourself, mack."

Nate cranked a window open, glaring at the non-ending mass of autos. He should have hopped on the subway. Hell, he should have walked. A horn blared in the distance. Loud swearing followed. "How many blocks from here to the Loews?"

"No idea."

"You're a real wealth of information." Nate pulled his wallet from his pocket. He couldn't sit still a moment longer. "How much do I owe you?"

"Seven fifty."

"For sitting in one spot for fifteen minutes?"

The driver threw an arm up in the air. "Hey, buddy, you don't like it, you should get out of the city."

"Thanks." Nate tossed the guy a ten. "Keep the change."

"Gee, I'll try not to spend it all in one place."

Nate shook his head, climbing out into the stalled traffic. He beelined toward the sidewalk, setting off in a quick clip toward the Loews.

His first day back to work was going beautifully. Bunny Love and two poodles had hijacked his car. His staff had launched a mutinous bunny slipper revolt. And now, he had to mediate an altercation among dog people. He groaned. Amazingly enough, all of his troubles shared a common thread.

Bunny Love.

He snarled and picked up his pace. A little feng shui may never have hurt anyone, but one thing was certain. When Nate got his hands on the woman, he'd strangle her with her own positive chi.

* * *

"Did your dog piss on my bike?"

Bunny tipped up her chin to meet the man's angry gaze. His dark gray eyes glittered from beneath two furry brows. She grimaced. He rubbed his full, gray beard and groaned. "Lady, I asked if your dog pissed on my bike."

"Well . . ." Bunny stalled for time, hoping the desk clerk would magically appear with a roll of paper towels. "She didn't actually piss on your bike. She pissed next to your bike. And to be honest, I believe her disrespect may have been directed toward your dog."

A low laugh rumbled its way from the man's stomach to his massive shoulders. His features broke into a wide grin. He slapped Bunny's shoulder, sending her flying into the counter. Leaning back toward his group, he shouted, "Bertha, grab the doggie wipes, would ya?"

Bunny blinked. A petite leather-clad woman nodded, pulling a package of wipes from her leather fanny pack.

"Sorry," Bunny whispered. "I feel just terrible."

"Hey"—the burly man shrugged—"piss happens." He waggled his brow. He looked down at Chablis and Chardonnay who stood analyzing his leather boots, probably wondering if their fangs were big enough to take on the monstrosities. "Are these Teacups? Beautiful." He squatted down and the girls froze midsniff. "Hey, little ladies." He adopted the tone of voice most people reserved for infants and toddlers. "How are you?"

To Bunny's dismay, Chablis launched into a beard-licking frenzy. Chardonnay shimmied into a butt-wiggle dance. The man looked up at Bunny, who stood stunned by the surreal scene. "Don't tell me," he said. "You're the event planner."

Surprise flittered through her. "How did you know that?"

He turned his attention back to the poodles. "I can see it in your aura."

Bunny gasped. "You read auras?"

"Actually, I saw your picture in the paper."

Bunny's mouth gaped open. The man howled with rich laughter. "Jimmy Monroe." He thrust out a hand.

"Bunny Love." The force of his shake bounced her feet off the floor. "You're not related to the—"

"Jimmy!"

Bunny flinched. She'd know Lovey Monroe's high-pitched squeal anywhere. Jimmy rose to his feet and lumbered away. Chablis and Chardonnay scrambled to follow their new best friend, succeeding only in wrapping their leashes tighter around Bunny's ankles.

She watched in open-mouthed amazement as Jimmy swept Lovey Monroe off her feet. Thurston patted the man's broad shoulder, his smile genuine and wide. Bunny shuffled toward the three. *This*, she was not going to miss. "Thurston and Lovey," she called out.

Thurston's features fell slack. "Bunny," he snarled.

"I see you've met our Jimmy." Lovey now stood firmly on the marble floor. "The apple of my eye."

Giant of her eye was more like it. There was no way this huge, bearded, bike-loving man had come out of tiny, blue-blood Lovey Monroe's womb. And Jimmy was far too kind to share *any* blood with Thurston.

"This is my son, Jimmy," Lovey cooed. "From my first marriage."

Thurston mumbled something incoherent then smiled. Bunny began to wonder if poor enunciation was the country club method for venting frustration. Her eyes had glazed over five minutes later, partway into Lovey's dissertation on Jimmy's German Shepherd breeding.

She couldn't help but notice Thurston had taken on a dazed appearance of his own. He caught her scrutinizing his features and frowned. Bunny straightened.

She'd show him. Come Monday she'd own her apartment. Then he'd be stuck with her. Permanently. She chuckled to herself.

"Well, it's not funny, dear," Lovey admonished. "It's quite serious work."

Bunny winced. "Pardon me. I was thinking of something else." She smiled. "A million things to do before tomorrow night."

"How about a cup of chamomile tea for everyone?" Jimmy asked. He waved to Bertha, who approached the small group, doggie wipes at the ready.

Bunny squinted at Jimmy's bushy beard, leather cap, and studded leather vest. Chamomile tea? Was this guy for real? "I'd love to," she said, slowly stepping away from the odd grouping. "But I need to get back to work."

"Here, dear." Bertha handed Bunny the container of wipes. "In case you need them again."

Chablis and Chardonnay strained at their collars, locked in a stare down with a newly arrived Rottweiler. The massive dog snorted, then turned away. The poodles snarled and snapped.

"What is it with you two?" Bunny quipped. "You've got a Napoleon complex or something?" She yanked at their leads as she waved good-bye to the Monroes, Jimmy and Bertha.

She had just started the ignition when she realized she didn't have her purse. She lowered the windows for air and climbed out. "Be right back, girls. Try not to eat anything."

She dashed into the lobby, found her purse sitting on the registration counter and sprinted back to Nate's car. Chablis had managed to climb into the driver's seat and stood with her front paws on the steering wheel. Bunny pulled on the handle, but the doors were locked. Little furry menaces.

She squeezed her arm through the narrow opening, doing her best to shoo the fur ball into the backseat as she struggled to reach the lock. "Off. Get in the back. Now. Heel."

The poodle launched herself in a snarling fit directed at Bunny's arm.

"It's me, you idiot. The one who's tolerated your attitude all day. Be nice to me."

With that, Chablis jumped back onto the center console. Searing pain shot through Bunny's arm as the window slid closed, wedging her arm between the glass and the door frame.

She let loose a shriek that sent Chablis diving into the passenger seat. She yelled for help, doing her best to breathe through the pain. Could this day possibly get any worse?

"What in the hell have you done?"

Ice-cold fear seeped through Bunny's bones.

Nate sounded intent on murder.

Chapter 18

Bunny stood trapped, one arm wedged in the window. "Not . . . my . . . fault." She squeezed the words through gritted teeth. "Her . . . fault." She glared at one fuzzy ball of fluff, sitting on the passenger seat.

"Hang on." Nate dashed to the passenger side, reaching in to unlock the door. One sharp glare sent Chablis hurtling into the backseat, where Chardonnay cowered next to a small puddle. Nate grimaced. His *car*. "I suppose you're going to tell me that's positive energy?"

Bunny shook her head. "Sorry."

Nate reached across the seat to press the down button, releasing Bunny's arm. He scrambled to where she stood, rubbing the inside of her upper arm. "Let me see." Genuine concern had tempered his anger.

Bright pink fired in Bunny's cheeks. "Things are under control here." Her voice dropped. "Honest." She rotated her arm to expose the inside. A sharp line of purple marred the delicate skin.

Nate reflexively reached to touch the bruising. Awareness rippled through him as he met Bunny's vivid gaze.

She nonchalantly shrugged, although the color in her cheeks grew deeper. "I'm okay."

"Shouldn't have given you the damn car."

Her pert features twisted into a frown. "I drove your car just fine."

Nate peered into the driver's side. Several CDs lay strewn across the floor, half-chewed. The corner of the passenger seat appeared ripped, and there was the puddle. "I can see that."

"I'll pay for everything." Bunny's voice had grown timid, a definite change for her. "And I'll clean that up." She pulled a small container from the floor well and opened the rear door. The poodle demons maintained their cowardly positions. One dared a peek at Nate. He snarled and the fur ball ducked her head. "They don't mean to be destructive," Bunny said defensively.

"Yes they do." Nate nodded. "It's what they live for."

She wiped the backseat, the motion sending her body into a wiggle and Nate's thoughts back to the first time Bunny's path had crossed his own. Her interview. Heat raced through him, much as it had then. All thoughts of damaged leather, ruined CDs and stripped gears flew out of his brain with one simple, alluring wiggle.

"You sure you're all right?" He mentally berated himself at the sound of his thick voice.

Bunny straightened, grinning. "All in a day's work." Her smile vanished as quickly as it had appeared. "We . . . ah . . . I need to get to the Convention Center."

Dread tickled Nate's gut. "Why?"

She pasted on a phony smile. "No reason. I wanted to check on the setup." She shrugged unconvincingly.

Nate narrowed his eyes, his newly found intuition screaming. "I'm not buying it."

Bunny sighed visibly then planted one fist on her hip. "There may be a small issue with Armand."

"Issue?"

"When I went to pick up the leads for the show, the warehouse manager told me Armand had already picked them up."

Nate did nothing more than raise a brow.

"Exactly," Bunny said. "That can't be good."

"I'll drive." He jerked a thumb toward the hotel entrance. "What about the problem here?"

She smiled. "All taken care of. I know what I'm doing."

He scowled, and Bunny scampered around to the passenger side. She slammed her door, glancing at Nate, who'd dropped into the driver's seat and stared at the handset of his phone.

"Are those tooth marks?"

"Dinosaur."

He peered at her suspiciously. "The tooth marks?"

"No." She rolled her eyes. "The phone."

"I *like* the dinosaur."

She shook her head, fastening her seat belt. "No kidding."

Bunny watched Nate's profile as he drove. She massaged the underneath of her arm, longing to let out a yelp. It hurt like heck. Maybe Nate would rub it again. She looked at the window, waggling her eyebrows. His touch had felt . . . *hot.*

"Bunny?"

She turned to face him, shrinking under his intense glare. Suddenly, she remembered Miss Peabody's warning. She and her creative goodies had been found out.

"Would you like to explain why bunny slippers have multiplied and taken up residence among my senior staff?"

Bunny swallowed, dread puddling in her stomach. She was so close to pulling off the Cup and her mortgage. Surely Nate would forgive a little well-intentioned creativity. She opened her mouth to explain, but snapped it shut as he continued.

"I'll save your breath." His sensuous gaze narrowed. "I'm sure you believe you were helping improve energy, or whatever claptrap you call it. I, however, prefer to run a dignified firm. I'm not sure why you're incapable of grasping that simple concept, but you need to try harder." His voice tightened, as if he were battling to keep his anger under control.

"You're angry."

His eyes popped wide, heat scorching from their depths. A thrill of victory whipped through Bunny as she scrutinized the rugged lines of his face. His life force had been enticing before, but now he smoldered.

"Good display of emotion, Nate."

His mouth gaped open, obviously stunned by her bold assessment.

"See?" she teased. "Change is good."

Nate pressed his lips together then trained his focus on the road. "This conversation is not finished."

Bunny stifled a sigh. He and Melanie were so wrong for each other—like topping vanilla ice cream with more vanilla ice cream. Everyone knew you needed a little hot caramel to make the ice cream sing. Heat flushed her cheeks. What she wouldn't give to be Nate's hot caramel. Yum.

She peeked at the speedometer. Whoa. Thirty miles per hour on a city street. Nate McNulty speeding? There was hope after all.

"Am I going too fast for you?"

His sudden question made her jump. A sudden shiver traced its way across her shoulders. "Never."

Nate glanced at her. For a moment their eyes locked, the shared heat unmistakable. He looked away as he pulled the car into the Convention Center loading zone. Bunny turned, looking out the window to hide her reaction. She'd been wrong. The man's life force didn't just smolder, it *smoked*.

A few moments later, they stepped into the main Convention Center arena. Armand stood in the distance, herringbone jacket draped over his shoulder, barking out orders to the work crew. Bunny frowned. The man could be a walking billboard for narcissists anonymous.

Chablis and Chardonnay broke into shrill yaps. Miller turned, eyes wide, polished smile perfect. "Bunny." He opened his arms as if welcoming her home from an extended trip. When he spotted Nate, his grin morphed into a sneer. "McNulty."

"Miller." Palpable disdain tinged the word.

Two large boxes sat next to where Armand stood. Bunny pointed, tipping her head. "Are these our leashes?"

He flashed an overly dramatic wink. "You can thank me later for delivering them."

"Oh brother," Nate mumbled.

Bunny tamped down a grin. "I appreciate the gesture, but it's not your account. You had no right to—"

Nate interrupted. "What's done is done. Armand, thanks for dropping them off. I'm sure you have to be somewhere."

Armand frowned as he slipped on his sport jacket. "If you can't appreciate my generosity, that's on you." He nodded toward the show manager. "You owe that gentleman twenty dollars for unloading my car." He tossed a perfect smile over his shoulder as he left the arena. "Ciao."

Bunny squinted. "Do you ever wonder if he practices—"

"In the mirror?" Nate finished her thought.

Their eyes met and held. Synchronicity. The connection was more serious than Bunny had thought.

"I'll put these in the staging area." Nate hoisted one large box from the floor.

"I'll help." Bunny moved to grab the second box, but Nate vigorously shook his head.

"No, you take it easy with that arm. I'll do this."

She warmed at his protective tone. "Okay." She

tipped her head. "I want to check out the backstage area. The girls and I will be over there."

Chardonnay and Chablis raced ahead, pulling their leashes taut as Bunny watched Nate carry the first box away. What would it be like to wake up next to him tomorrow? Or next year? Or in fifty years? She shook off the idea. What was she? Nuts? Just look at her parents, for crying out loud.

"Hey wait a sec," Bunny called out to the tiny fur balls. "Let's try out the new leads." She reeled them backward until she could reach the second box. She stretched to pop the seam, then slipped two leads from the hundreds inside.

Bunny fastened one metal clasp onto Chardonnay's collar and the other onto Chablis', removing their rhinestone leads as she did so. "Let's feng shui some furniture, shall we?"

The dogs jumped in the air, wiggling and dancing. They headed across the floor, under the large purple draping hung ceiling to floor at the edge of the show arena.

"Watch it there," a male voice bellowed. "Tie-down's not finished. Stay away from those knots."

Bunny glanced at the large ropes dangling from the curtain, tied haphazardly along the wall. She waved back to the concerned worker. "No problem. We won't cause any trouble."

Looping the handles of the two leashes over her wrist, she crossed her arms, scrutinizing the layout of the backstage furniture. Not good. The energy was completely wrong. She worked quickly to group the seating area into a pleasing arrangement, then shimmied the table onto an angle.

"Yo!" the same male voice called out. "Lady! Your dogs!"

Cold fear washed through Bunny's veins. Nothing tugged at her arm. She glanced down at the empty leashes. The poodles had somehow pulled free from the metal closures.

Chablis and Chardonnay had engaged in a frenzied tug-of-war with one large loose knot. As Bunny watched, the curtain sagged ominously. "Stop!" She raced toward the pair as the curtain sank farther and farther from the ceiling. Too late.

The massive satin draping cascaded down on top of her, enveloping both her and the dogs in a pool of purple satin.

Nate saw the curtain sag just as he stepped back into the main arena.

"Stop!" Bunny's voice rang out.

The huge purple drape fell toward the floor. He broke into a run, but the curtain buried Bunny and the poodles in less than a second.

The two hairballs wiggled for survival, burrowing their way out of the fabric like two moles beneath soft earth. Bunny, on the other hand, resembled a large purple blob, thrashing wildly. Nate stepped across the satin and wrapped his arms around her. She shrieked.

"It's me." Her body stilled beneath his touch, the heavy fabric sliding between his fingers.

"This isn't good for my aura," she mumbled from beneath the material.

He grinned. "Or your chakras."

"Them either."

Nate held tight while the stage manager and crew rolled the material toward Bunny. One kind soul corralled the poodles, holding them by their tiny, troublemaking necks. Static from their ordeal had made them resemble tiny exploding sheep.

Nate did his best to stifle a laugh.

"What's funny?" Bunny's muffled voice squeaked.

"What's not?"

The show manager worked the folds of material close to Bunny. "She's gotta crawl out."

"You've got to—"

"I heard him. Which way?"

Nate released his grip, watching as she lowered herself to all fours. "Toward your left hand."

She obediently turned, scrambling for the opening. He rubbed his chin, admiring her shapely rear end wiggling beneath the satin. Damn, but the woman had curves.

Bunny emerged from the trap of purple fabric, her blue eyes huge. She smiled when she spotted Nate, her reaction sending electricity tingling through his nerve endings.

He pulled her into his arms, stroking her hair. "You okay?"

Bunny nodded, relaxing into his embrace. He savored the feel of her body pressed against his own, inhaling deeply. Vanilla. He smiled. Oh, how he'd grown to love the scent.

Bunny closed her eyes, praying the moment would never end. She took a deep breath and sighed— wrapped in Nate's warm, strong embrace. His musky scent enveloped her and she snuggled closer. "Where are the fur balls?" she whispered into his broad chest.

"Who cares?"

His body shook with laughter, the rich, deep rumble music to Bunny's ears. After all of the chaos she'd put him through, he laughed. She'd never heard a sound more sweet. She pulled back, lifting her chin to meet Nate's gaze. Raw heat oozed from his dark eyes. "And you call yourself a positive chi expert."

Their stares locked, and Bunny thought of the moment they'd shared at the dinner dance. The memory couldn't hold a candle to how much she wanted to kiss him now.

He lowered his mouth to hers, and she was instantly lost in the sensation of his lips caressing hers. His fingers tensed into her back with light pressure, the heat of his body pressed flat against her own. His tongue and lips teased and tasted.

Heat pooled between Bunny's legs. With any luck at all, Nate would ravage her right here on top of the damn curtain. A girl could dream. The stage manager cleared his throat. Nate broke the kiss. Bunny staggered from the loss of contact.

"Everyone all right here?" the man asked.

"Yes."

Was it Bunny's imagination or had Nate's voice grown deeper than usual? She stared at her toes, wondering how on earth she should react to what had just happened.

The work crew scattered. Nate touched her chin with his finger, raising her gaze to meet his. "I shouldn't have done that." His brown eyes sparked with life, sending a thrill rippling up her spine. "Caught up in the moment, I guess."

"That makes two of us." Bunny touched her fingertips to her lips. *Zing*.

Nate nodded to where a lone worker stood holding Chablis and Chardonnay. "We'd better get them back to Kitty." His handsome features broke into a wide grin. "They may need a touch-up at the salon." Laughter tinged his voice.

He wrapped an arm around her waist. Bunny happily tucked her body tight to his side, planning to milk this moment for all it was worth.

Nate silently reprimanded himself. Talk about a total loss of control. What had he been thinking? Hell. He hadn't been thinking—he'd been feeling. And what a feeling it had been. The small sample only made him crave more.

He wrapped his arm around Bunny's waist, pulling her close. He was only being cautious. After all, the woman had been trapped in a car window and engulfed in a tidal wave of purple satin within the course of an hour.

Yeah, right. Who was he kidding? The signals his libido was sending to his brain were anything but gentlemanly. He tightened his grip on Bunny, intending to savor the feel of her body pressed to his as long as he could.

Chapter 19

Nate sat in his car, staring at Melanie's house. He knew what he had to do. He'd known from the moment his lips had touched Bunny's. Hell. He'd known longer than he cared to admit, but holding Bunny had made the decision an urgent one.

He wanted to taste more than her lips. He wanted to feel more than the curve of her waist beneath his fingertips. Nate wanted to touch and taste every inch she had to offer. He inhaled deeply, trying to calm the pounding of his heart.

Had this been how his father had felt whenever his mother was near? Had he been unable to imagine a life without her?

If anyone had told him a month ago he'd fall for a mop-topped, feng-shui-practicing live wire, he'd have told them to have their head examined. But now? Now all he thought about was the creative lunatic and the way her smile lit up a room.

Nate pushed open the driver's door and stepped into the cool October night, steeling himself as he glanced at Melanie's house. She deserved someone who loved her with all of his heart, and he wasn't that someone. He'd never been more sure of anything.

Loud rock music blared from inside the stately brick home as he stood on the front step and knocked. Nate frowned. He peered through the side window, but could see no movement. What in the hell was going on?

Several minutes later, he gave up, choosing to return to the car. Maybe Melanie had gone out and left the radio on to deter burglars. Who knew? He only knew he couldn't deny his own needs any longer. He needed Bunny, and he needed her now.

Bunny swallowed the chocolate syrup and dragged a hand across her mouth. Her brain hurt. Her heart hurt. Only days away from closing on her apartment and pulling off The Worthington Cup, her verse-spouting mother had pillaged her apartment, her parents had decided to *date* after thirty years of marriage, and she'd kissed Nate.

"I think you're overreacting." Tilly glared at her from the overstuffed chair. "Kissing Nate was a good thing."

Bunny tipped the syrup bottle over her open mouth and squeezed, savoring the sweet comfort before she swallowed. "His energy is changing so fast. He's acting . . . he's acting . . ."

"Human."

"Scary." Bunny shook her head. She upended the bottle for another mouthful. Lord, she was turning into her mother—seeking solace in a vat of sugar.

Tilly crossed the room and plucked the syrup from her grasp. She plunked the bottle on the counter, then turned to shake Bunny's shoulders. "Get a grip."

Bunny's stomach caught and twisted. Her heart tattooed against her ribs. She pushed Tilly out of the way, reaching for the chocolate. "Look at my parents. They've been married for thirty years and suddenly my mother decides she's had her creativity sucked dry." She searched her friend's face. "I don't want to end up like that."

"You won't." Tilly hopped onto the counter, her

short pixie legs swinging like a child's. "Your energy will adjust."

"What?" Bunny talked around a mouthful of syrup. "Why should my energy adjust? My energy's just fine."

Tilly shook her head. "Your energy was fine for you, but now that Nate's in the picture, you need to shift."

Bunny narrowed her gaze. "Shift?"

"To the dark side." Tilly threw back her head and laughed.

"Very funny." Bunny set the syrup on the counter. She crossed her arms over her chest, frowning. "You think I'll be stifled?" Her voice tightened.

Tilly let loose with a belly laugh. "Honey, there isn't a man alive capable of stifling you."

Bunny breathed a half-hearted sigh of relief, hoping her friend was right. Tilly padded to the door and pulled it open. Bunny's breath caught in her throat.

Nate stood in the doorway, his fist poised to knock.

"You must be Nate," Tilly said.

He nodded without looking at her, his gaze locked on Bunny.

Tilly tossed Bunny an exaggerated eyebrow wiggle, then pulled the door closed behind her as she left.

Nate stepped inside. The door clicked shut, but Bunny said nothing, her turquoise eyes the size of saucers. Had he been wrong to show up at her door unannounced? He'd feel less guilty if he'd been able to talk to Melanie, but there was no denying what he wanted—and that was Bunny.

An older, shorter version of Bunny bustled out of the bathroom, dressed in a figure-hugging red dress and clutching a coffee mug. "I'm off to get lucky with your father." Her words bubbled out as she came down the hall, eyes focused on her feet.

Bunny rolled her eyes. "Alexandra, this is my boss, Nate McNulty. My mother, Alexandra Love."

The older woman stopped in her tracks, her gaze zeroing in on Nate. A slow grin tugged at the corners of her mouth.

"Sorry, I should have called," Nate mumbled.

Bunny shook her head.

Alexandra waggled a finger in his direction. "*McNulty.* I should have made the connection. You look just like your father." She took a few steps closer, a shadow crossing her face. "So tragic. Martha raised you, didn't she?"

Nate nodded, fighting down the lump growing in his throat.

"I asked Bunny if she was still drawing."

"Drawing?" Nate frowned. "Aunt Martha?"

Alexandra drained the contents of her cup then patted Nate's arm. "She's quite talented, your aunt. You should ask her about it sometime."

She stood then, staring at him as if she hoped to memorize his every feature. She suddenly turned to Bunny, placing her palm on her daughter's cheek. "No wonder you've been so bright lately." Bunny's pale eyes grew even wider.

Alexandra breezed into the kitchen, thunked her mug onto the counter and crossed to the door. She plucked an overnight bag from the floor and stepped into the hall. "I'm sure you two have lots to talk about." She grinned. "Don't wait up."

The door clicked shut, and she was gone. Nate stared at the empty space for a beat, wondering if he'd imagined the whole episode. He slowly turned toward Bunny.

She wrapped her arms around her waist, scrutinizing his presence. "And you think I'm a menace?"

He laughed, stepping closer. "What happened to your walls? Weren't they all different colors before?"

Bunny flinched. "She painted them."

Nate grinned, amusement seeping through him. "Imagine."

She eyed him expectantly, his comment obviously lost on her. "To what do I owe this visit?"

"I needed to see you."

He took a step closer. Bunny held her ground. A faded denim shirt hung large and loose on her slight frame. Black leggings hid her legs, and pink fuzzy bunny slippers covered her feet. He smiled. "So you keep a pair at home and at work." He moved closer still.

Bunny glanced at her feet then back at Nate. A deep, rose-colored blush blossomed on her cheeks. "Yes." She stepped toward him, erasing the space between them, her eyes locked on his. "I highly recommend it."

Nate focused on her mouth—her sweet, soft lips. He'd thought of nothing else since this afternoon. "Maybe I should try a pair."

Bunny stood so close heat radiated between their bodies. Several long, silent seconds passed. "About today—"

He interrupted. "I'm going to kiss you again."

Bunny's eyes widened. A slow smile curled the corners of her mouth as she wrapped her arms around his neck. Nate closed his mouth over hers as he pulled her into his arms, pressing her to him, aware of the fact he'd gone instantly hard.

Something deep inside him snapped. Every inch of his body hummed, as if he'd waited his whole life for this stolen kiss with Bunny.

Her fingers twisted into his hair, sending electric heat roaring to his groin. He slid his palms from her waist over her curves, cupping her bottom, pulling her close. She willingly arched into him. Bunny's mouth never left his, her lips and tongue working fervently, igniting previously unknown sensations within him.

Nate traced his lips along Bunny's cheek, feathering kisses down her soft skin to the line of her jaw. She tipped back her head, allowing full access to the creamy flesh of her neck. He slid his hands beneath her shirt, caressing her satiny smooth skin. He palmed one full breast, stroking his thumb across her taut nipple.

She gripped his shoulders, arching backward. He moved his hand just long enough to undo her shirt buttons. The denim fell open, and Nate gazed with open admiration on the beauty of her naked body. Bunny's brilliant eyes, hooded beneath long lashes, met his. Fire raced through him, his urgent need like nothing he had ever experienced. He cradled her breasts in his palms, closing his lips over one eager nipple. Caressing. Tasting.

He drank of her creamy flesh, working his tongue to tease, taste and savor. He'd imagined this moment, but not once had his thoughts come close to the sweet reality of Bunny's naked beauty.

Nate trailed kisses down the valley between her breasts to the flat plane of her stomach. She sucked in a sharp breath as he smiled against her skin, cupping his palms on her buttocks, pressing his mouth against the apex between her thighs. Heat filled his mouth—the heat of Bunny's desire for him.

He stood, sweeping her into his arms. Bunny pressed her lips to his neck as she fumbled with the buttons on his shirt. Her gentle touch slipped beneath the cotton and caressed. Nate's erection grew painful and he bit down on his lip as he carried her toward the bedroom.

Bunny wanted to scream. Any moment now she'd spontaneously combust. It had been a long, long time since she'd been with a man, but Nate McNulty had her feeling sensations she'd never felt. The man had some serious energy—all channeled in her direction.

The soft quilt of her bed pressed into her back as

Nate gently lowered himself on top of her. Hard, heavy and all male—at that moment he was hers. At long last.

Nate tugged at the waistband of her leggings. "These have to go."

Bunny eased the elastic with one hand, wiggling the soft material down over her hips.

Nate sat to one side, delicately pulling the material to her ankles. She kicked off one slipper, then the other. Nate pulled her legs free, and her shirt fell open. The combination of cool air and Nate's gaze sent shivers of desire racing across her naked flesh.

"Beautiful," Nate whispered.

Bunny swallowed down any earlier trepidation. He was the yin to her yang. Heat seared between her legs. She had never wanted any man as she wanted Nate—needed Nate.

He unbuttoned his shirt, leaning forward as he did so to press a soft kiss on the skin just above her belly button. Her body responded instantly. She arched into his lips, straining for his touch. He obliged by moving his mouth in a slow caress up the length of her belly to the rise of her breasts. His lips and tongue lavished the valley between them, then suckled one mound into the heat of his mouth.

A groan escaped from somewhere deep within her. "You're killing me," she whispered.

Nate straightened, arching one brow. "Can't have that."

The husky richness of his voice sent raw, carnal awareness rushing through Bunny's body. He stood, shrugging out of his shirt. In one deft move, he unzipped his trousers and stepped free of the clothing. For a brief moment, he stood naked before her. The rich chestnut strands she loved so much stood rumpled above his gorgeous mahogany eyes. His mouth twisted into a grin and Bunny's heart was his. Completely his. She drank in the sight of him, naked, vulnerable. So far removed from the man who had interviewed her just weeks ago in his gray office.

Nate gently lowered himself on top of her, his lips finding hers, drinking deeply. She held her breath, savoring the exquisite feel of his naked flesh pressed to hers.

He broke the kiss, lifting his face ever so slightly. "A practical question."

"Top nightstand drawer," she whispered. "I used to be a Girl Scout. Always prepared."

"That's my girl."

His girl. Her stomach tightened, thrilling to the sound of the words on Nate's lips. Her body cooled as he moved to the side of the bed to sheath himself.

As he lowered himself on top of her, he paused. "I wanted to do this in a more controlled manner." He grinned. "But that never seems to work when you're near." His lopsided smile grew wide. Carefree.

Bunny's heart raced, beating so loudly she was sure he must hear it. Excitement wound through her, coiling tighter and tighter, anticipating the feel of him inside her.

Nate lowered himself between her legs, hands planted on either side of her shoulders. Bunny wrapped her legs around his waist, opening to him body and soul. Her breath caught as he slipped inside, filling her. She took his face between her palms, pulling his mouth to hers. His hands moved beneath her, cradling her buttocks. He quickened his thrusts then slowed. Quickened. Slowed.

Nate stroked and caressed, building Bunny's desire to a frenzy. He held still for a moment and she realized he fought to control his release. He tightened his grip suddenly, rocking her hard against him. She gasped at the force of her orgasm, release splintering through her like a wave of Novocaine, numbing her every sensation but the pleasure of becoming one with Nate.

Their movements slowed and Nate slipped his fingers into the hot, tight space between their bodies. He stroked gently, lovingly, sending additional waves of pleasure rippling outward from his touch. She melted against the quilt, dazed by the power he wielded over her body's reactions.

Suddenly, Nate's touch was gone. Bunny opened her eyes, gasping at the intense need gleaming in his mocha gaze. His eyes locked onto hers as he drove deeper, harder inside her. He groaned, a shudder ripping through him. His eyes fluttered closed as their joined bodies pulsed to the rhythm of his release.

How had she ever thought this sizzling man stifled? She tried to move beneath him, but couldn't, her muscles overwhelmed by the power of their lovemaking. Nate pulled her tightly into his arms, cradling her spent body. Bunny closed her eyes, savoring the feel of his hot, damp skin pressed to hers.

"Next time," Nate growled, "we leave the slippers on."

Chapter 20

Nate rubbed the sleep from his eyes, watching Bunny move comfortably around her small kitchen. Shapely legs peeked from the hem of her bright yellow robe. She hummed as she worked, sexy little feet tucked into her bunny slippers. He chuckled.

Bunny caught him watching. A smile spread wide and bright across her face. "Morning."

He planted a kiss on the soft curve of her neck, then gave her waist a squeeze. "Same to you."

The teakettle whistled. Bunny turned off the burner and reached for two mugs.

"None for me." Nate waved a hand dismissively. "I learned my lesson."

Bunny pulled a jar of instant coffee from a second cabinet and winked. "So did I. I'm a quick study."

"So I've heard," he teased. He pointed to a coffee-pot, sporting several stalks of what he now recognized as lucky bamboo. "What happened there?"

Bunny grimaced. "I think we'd call that a little creative payback." She gave a quick shrug. "Not one of my finer moments."

Nate shook his head, deciding to let the subject drop. Bunny handed him a steaming mug, and he happily sipped the strong brew. Lord knew he hadn't gotten much sleep last night, and today promised to be long and tiring.

"Can I get you breakfast?"

He shook his head. "I'll grab something at home. I've got to get into the office." He waggled his brows. "So do you."

"I know." Bunny vigorously dunked a tea bag in her mug. "I'll be at the Convention Center most of the day, but I'll stop by the office first."

Nate blew out a long, slow breath.

"Say it." Bunny eyed him. "You want last night to stay between us. Remember decorum. Beware the McNulty image. Blah, blah, blah."

A twinge of guilt tickled Nate's gut. He hated to admit she was right, but she was. "You understand, don't you?"

"Not really." She shook her mop-topped head as she sipped her tea.

Bunny's honesty cut him like a knife.

"Look. I know this weekend is important to you. It's important to me." Her features softened, her eyes turning sad. "We'll pretend this never happened."

"Uh-uh." Nate set his coffee on the counter and tucked a hand beneath her chin. He tipped her face to meet his gaze. "This most definitely happened."

Lowering his mouth to hers, Nate covered her soft lips with his own. He deepened the kiss, smiling when Bunny's mug thunked onto the counter and she wound her fingers into his hair.

Nate slipped his arms around her waist, sliding his palms along her curves to the soft swells of her breasts. He rubbed his thumbs over the fabric of her robe, stroking her nipples into firm peaks. A soft moan slipped from her throat.

"Thought you had to get to work," Bunny murmured.

"Change of plans." He stepped back, drinking in her sparkling turquoise gaze. He slowly unwound the tie of her robe, letting the garment fall open. She wore nothing beneath.

Her eyes closed, long lashes splayed against her cheekbones. He hooked his thumbs under the robe's collar, easing it to the crook of her elbows. He pressed a kiss onto the creamy flesh of Bunny's bare shoulders. First one, then the other. She lowered her arms to her sides, allowing the robe to fall into a yellow puddle on the tile floor. She stood naked, more beautiful than anything he'd ever seen.

Correction. Naked except for her bunny slippers. Her sexy-as-sin bunny slippers. Nate grinned. As if reading his thoughts, Bunny moved to kick off the fuzzy foot coverings. "Leave them." Nate's voice grew thick with need.

He gently lifted her onto the counter, and she trembled as he set her on the cold, smooth surface. She leaned back, bracing herself against the cabinets. Nate palmed her ample breasts, suckling one and then the other until Bunny writhed. He lifted his gaze to hers. Bunny's vivid eyes blazed with desire, her skin flushed to a warm pink.

He pulled her to the counter edge, taking one firm nipple into his mouth, teasing the tip of her tender flesh between his teeth. She arched toward him, pressing her body to his lips. She wrapped her legs around him, feeding his arousal with white-hot excitement. Nate willed his body to wait, intending to pleasure Bunny as she'd pleasured him last night—fully, with nothing held back.

He trailed kisses down the smooth plane of her belly to the moist heat waiting between her thighs. He slipped one finger inside as he tasted, her body's slick response ratcheting up his desire. His heart jackhammered against his ribs.

A guttural moan slipped from her lips, kicking his pulse to a frenzy. "Nate. Please."

He slipped a second finger inside, slowly teasing, stroking, loving her. She white-knuckled the counter, her hips moving in a rhythmic dance to the beat of his touch. Bunny's need and desire pushed Nate to the edge of his control, his erection pulsing painfully against the constriction of his trousers. He moved his free hand to her taut nipple, caressing the creamy flesh, toying his thumb across the swollen peak.

Bunny's restraint broke, her body shuddering with orgasm. He stroked until her movements slowed, then trailed gentle kisses slowly up to the soft hollow at the base of her throat.

"Wow." Her words spilled like thick molasses. "I'll have to make you instant coffee more often."

Nate laughed, sweeping her into his arms and giving silent thanks for the day Bunny's chaotic presence had breezed into his life.

Two hours later, Bunny listened to the front door click shut. She lay tangled in the sheets, limp and spent. She hadn't felt this much sexual pleasure in . . . well . . . forever. *Such sweet pleasure.* She let out a satiated sigh.

If she'd known making love to Nate would feel this great, she'd have jumped him during her interview—not that she hadn't thought about it. She pulled her quilt to her chin, snuggling into the pillow. Somehow, she was fairly certain the waiting had made their lovemaking that much more . . . incredible.

A flicker of doubt traced its way through her. As incredible as he made her feel, Nate's control tendencies ranked right up there with those of her parents. Goodness knew they'd be dancing a jig to know he'd captured her heart, but was Bunny a fool to fall for him?

She glanced at her bedside clock. Nine fifteen. Holy cow. How had that happened? She had one thousand dogs to wine and dine—or rather *whine* and dine. She laughed at her own joke as she dragged her body out of bed, heading for the shower. It was time to put thoughts of Nate's naked body out of her mind. She had to focus on The Worthington Cup.

Boy. Talk about your day going to the dogs.

The elevator doors slid open. Nate stepped into the lobby of Bunny's building and glanced at his watch. Nine fifteen. Damn. He'd planned to be out of here earlier than this. He chuckled. His tardiness had been for a very good cause, however.

"Nathan McNulty, isn't it? Martha's nephew?"

Nate flinched, the deep male voice jarring him into focus. He smoothed a hand over his hair, wondering if he looked as though he'd just rolled out of bed. He turned toward the voice. Damn it all to hell. Thurston Monroe.

"Thurston." Nate extended a hand. "Good to see you."

The man raised a bushy white brow. "Early morning visit?"

"Yes." Nate's mind raced in a million directions. "I was just leaving. I stopped by. For a moment. To drop something off. To Miss Love."

A slow grin spread across Thurston's face. "I get the picture."

"I'm sure you do," Nate mumbled. Where was Bunny when he needed her? The woman could talk her way out of anything.

Thurston gave Nate a pat on the shoulder. "Good to run into you. We'll see you tonight at The Worthington Cup party, I presume." He shot Nate a condescending smile.

Nate nodded. "Looking forward to it." He hurried into the cool October morning. Running into Monroe had been bad luck. *Very* bad luck. Lord knew, the second Thurston repeated the conversation to Lovey Monroe, the society gossip lines would ring into action.

Great. Nate mentally berated himself. His carefully controlled persona had just gone straight to hell. Even worse, he needed to track down Melanie fast. He didn't want her to hear this from anyone but him.

Two hours later, Nate stepped off the office elevator, doing his best to ignore his anxiety. He'd repeatedly failed to reach Melanie. *Damn it.*

The door to the conference room sat ajar. Bert had the plans for tonight's cocktail party spread wide across the table. He looked up as Nate entered, then propped his slipper-covered feet on one corner of the table.

Nate paused, narrowed his gaze, but chose to ignore Bert's footwear.

"Late night?" Bert raised a pale brow.

"Had some things to take care of this morning."

"Really." Bert grinned, leaning onto one elbow. "I have a friend in Bunny's building—on the same floor. I could have sworn I heard your voice in her apartment." He leveled a grin at Nate. "Walls are like tissue paper in that place."

Nate held his breath. Had they been heard? Had they been *loud*? Warmth fired in his midsection. Hell, yes, they'd been loud. "Must have been a television set." He shrugged nonchalantly.

"Amazing." Bert chuckled. "Some actor has your identical voice." He rubbed his chin. "You learn something new every day."

Nate nodded to Bert's feet. "Thought I told you to get rid of those things."

"I chose not to listen." Bert straightened.

Nate scrutinized the slippers, imagining Bunny's fuzzy-footed legs locked around his hips during their lovemaking. He swallowed, tugging at his shirt collar. "Hot in here?"

"Not in the least." Bert grinned, gesturing at Nate's face. "Been drinking tea?"

Nate scowled. "Everything set for tonight?"

Bert tapped the layout for the cocktail party. "Perfect. Bunny's on her way over there now."

"Excellent." Nate headed back toward the door, but stopped short. "The slippers can stay." Heat flushed through his face, much to his chagrin.

"Thought you might change your mind." Bert smirked, returning his focus to the table. "See you later on."

Miss Peabody stopped Nate as he reached his office door. "Miss Brittingham's been trying to reach you all morning."

Damn. "Would you ring her for me?"

"Too late. She's got hair and nail appointments. Said she'd catch up to you at the cocktail party."

"Fair enough."

"She did say it was urgent that she speak to you."

Dread and guilt battled in Nate's stomach. His behavior during the past twenty-four hours had been totally out of character. Totally out of control. "What time did she call?"

"First thing."

Nate nodded.

"Then again at eight-thirty, nine, and nine-thirty." His secretary shot a disapproving glance over the top of her glasses. "I told her you must have been unexpectedly detained."

"Great," Nate mumbled as he pushed open his office door. "Just great."

Chapter 21

Cocktail party guests had begun to arrive in earnest. Bunny slapped away the nagging voice at the back of her brain that told her the evening would be a flop. All evidence suggested otherwise.

The work of the decorator she'd hired had been genius. Waist-high tables sat scattered in small groupings throughout the large space, each adorned with dog-bone-shaped arrangements of white tea roses. Strategically placed candelabra diffused warm light and the sweet aroma of freesia.

Bunny had done her best to encourage positive chi. A large grouping of plants sat tastefully arranged in the southeast corner. Ivory tulle draped the support pillars to counteract any negative energy caused by their sharp edges.

Her favorite decoration had nothing to do with feng shui and everything to do with fun. She pressed her fingers to her lips, attempting to hold back laughter. Pooch-high water stations, shaped like oversized martini glasses, offered a springwater pit stop for the discriminating—and parched—canine.

Kitty Worthington mingled with guests, Chablis and Chardonnay in tow. Bunny couldn't decide which was more ridiculous, the dogs' rhinestone-studded purple vests or Kitty's black, safari-style pantsuit complete with wide-brimmed hat.

Bunny had to hand it to her. What the woman lacked in fashion sense, she made up in energy. From the day Bunny signed on with McNulty Events, Kitty had called daily for updates, doing everything possible to ensure a successful Worthington Cup.

As for Bunny, the balls of her feet screamed in the high-heeled sandals she'd worn to complement her new cocktail dress. She groaned. What she wouldn't give to slide into her slippers right about now.

In a far corner, a polished couple and their Wheaten Terrier visited with Jeremy. At Bunny's request, he'd set up an interactive demo of the voting they'd planned for the final show day. *The People's Choice for Excellence.* Jeremy met her glance, tossing her a dramatic wink. She grinned. Maybe event planning wasn't so terrible after all.

A laugh slipped from her lips. Who was she kidding? She'd sleep for a week after this was over. If she survived. She was amazed she'd pulled it off. Okay, so she'd sent her boss to the hospital—twice—and been trapped beneath a giant curtain. It could have been worse.

"Bunny?" Melanie's soft voice captured Bunny's attention. Instant apprehension surged through her veins. Maybe the worst was yet to come.

She turned, then her jaw fell open.

"What do you think?" Melanie's pale blue gaze appeared cautious but hopeful.

"Wowza." Bunny could barely believe her eyes. Melanie's sequined cobalt sheath left little to the imagination. One thing was sure. Those pink Chanel suits hadn't done the woman justice.

"How's my energy?"

"Smoking." Bunny moved her head in a slow shake then let out a low whistle. "That's some transformation."

"I owe you." Melanie gripped Bunny's hands. "You gave me the courage to try this. You're a real friend."

Bunny swallowed. Her stomach fell to her toes. A

real friend. Right. A real friend who slept with your boyfriend. "Uh, Melanie?"

"Have you seen Nate?" Melanie surveyed the room, never letting go of Bunny's hands. "I've been trying to reach him all day. For some reason he wasn't at work this morning."

Because he was ravaging me on my kitchen counter. Bunny blinked. What had she been thinking? She'd slept with this woman's boyfriend. Chemistry or not, she'd messed up royally.

"I have to find him." Melanie tugged at the short hem of her dress. "You sure I look okay?"

"Yes." Bunny nodded reassuringly. "Can I talk to you for a second?"

Melanie flashed a wide smile, her confidence sparkling for a change. "After I find Nate, okay?" She sashayed away.

Bunny grimaced. How could she have slept with Nate? Okay. In all fairness, she had wanted to. *Really* wanted to. And the mind-numbing sex had made her forget Melanie existed.

Melanie and Nate.

Had he talked to Melanie? Broken things off? Did he plan to? Why hadn't she thought to ask?

Because you were otherwise preoccupied. Idiot.

Her heart lurched, dread puddling in her stomach. Surely Nate wouldn't go through with the engagement. *Right?* She longed to see his face to know she hadn't made a terrible mistake.

Martha McNulty entered, giving Bunny a polite wave from across the room. Thurston and Lovey Monroe followed close behind. Lovey tapped Martha on the shoulder and the two women exchanged air kisses. Next thing Bunny knew, the trio stood deep in conversation. *Great.* Just what she needed. Something *else* to worry about.

Thurston's mouth moved and Martha shot a glare in

Bunny's direction. Talk about negative energy. The gnawing pit in Bunny's stomach morphed into a black hole.

Suddenly, the perfect Whine and Dine didn't seem so perfect after all.

"Bunny." Tilly tapped her shoulder.

"You made it." Relief dripped from Bunny's words.

"You look like you could use a drink." Concern filled Tilly's eyes. "Everything okay?"

Bunny nodded. "Where's Bert?"

"Stuck at the office."

Bunny glanced again at Martha who now stared openly, a frown plastered across her flawless features.

"A drink sounds great." Bunny grabbed Tilly's elbow, pulling her toward the bar. Anything to move out of the line of fire.

"She's a charlatan," Thurston snarled.

"Well, yes, she does love her feng shui," Lovey chirped.

"No." Thurston paused for a beat. "She's a flake. A fruitcake. A fraud."

That got Martha's attention. "What do you mean she's a fraud?"

"She's no event planner." He shook his perfectly coiffed head. "I often wonder why you hired her. To the best of my knowledge, she's got zero experience."

"My nephew tells me she's well known. Had her own business."

"Designing logos for entrepreneurial wannabes. You call that event planning?"

Anger simmered in Martha's chest. Had Bunny Love deceived Nate? Or had Nate lied? "Perhaps you're mistaken, Thurston."

"No," Lovey chimed in. "I believe Thurston's correct.

The girl spent most of her days rearranging the lobby furniture."

Martha's impatience grew. She needed to extract herself from this conversation—and quickly.

"What was it she wanted, Thurston?" Lovey asked.

"Positive chi," Thurston snarled. He gave Martha a disgusted scowl. "Ruined my tennis game. That's the kind of nut job you've got running the show."

Martha pasted on a phony smile, frenzied thoughts whirling through her mind. "I'm sure you're mistaken." Was Bunny more than a personal distraction for Nate? Was she a professional one as well? "Excuse me." She stepped away before the Monroes had a chance to spot the angry flush spreading up her neck.

Martha scanned the room, taking in the ridiculous decorations and the huge martini glasses positioned for the dogs. Apparently she could have saved herself several conversations with Armand. It appeared Bunny had been quite capable of ruining the event with no additional outside help.

She searched the room one more time. Where in the hell was Nate?

Jimmy Monroe and Bertha stood at the bar, surrounded by a group of friends. Bunny kept a tight grip on Tilly's arm.

"I want you to meet someone. I think you'll like him."

"Bunny." A bright smile lit Jimmy's face as they neared.

A stunning German Shepherd sat by his side. The dog gave Bunny and Tilly a thoughtful gaze from beneath the bill of a leather cap. A red bandana knotted around the dog's throat accentuated his stunning tan and black markings.

"Who's this?" Bunny bent at the waist, offering the dog her hand. The canine sniffed then slapped a large paw into her palm.

"This is Harley." Jimmy's chest puffed out. "My pride and joy."

"He's a beauty." Tilly patted the dog's head.

"He's a bitch."

Tilly's face crinkled with delight. "Well, *she* has the aura of a winner."

"Gonna be a good show." Jimmy winked. "It's in her cards."

"You read?" Tilly's voice squeaked with excitement.

"Twenty years."

Tilly grabbed Jimmy's hand. "A kindred spirit."

Bunny gave herself a mental pat on the back. Something had told her these two would hit it off. She sized up the rest of Jimmy's gang. They ran the gamut from short and gray to tall, dark and handsome. "Friends of yours?"

Jimmy rubbed his chin. "Mainly family. Rode in to catch Harley's show." He patted the dog's head. "Always nice to have the support of loved ones."

Yes it was. Bunny scanned the crowd for any sign of Nate, wishing fervently he'd arrive before Thurston and Martha had too much time to talk.

"I'm a big believer in positive chi," Jimmy continued.

Bunny refocused on Jimmy, clasping a hand to her chest. "Me, too."

He winked. "Knew there was a reason I liked you, even if your dog took a piss on my bike."

"Near your bike," Bunny corrected. "And I am sorry. Not that excuses make piddle acceptable."

Jimmy's rich laugh filled the air. "Acceptable piddle. I'll have to remember that." He leaned against the bar. "I just ordered up a pot of chamomile. Why don't you ladies join us?"

"We'd love to," Tilly cooed.

"Well." Bunny turned, letting her gaze take in the roomful of dogs and people. "I'd better mingle. Don't want to get caught taking a tea break in the middle of my first event."

An ornery light flickered in Jimmy's eyes. He nodded toward one corner of the room. "Seems one of your guests is relieving himself in your plant corner."

Bunny's heart gave a jolt. She pivoted quickly, following the direction of Jimmy's nod.

"Well, at least it's a four-footed guest," Tilly snorted.

"Great," Bunny grumbled. "Maybe I should have given the watering stations a bit more thought."

The shrillest whistle she'd ever heard pierced the air. The dog stopped mid-spritz, scampering back toward his owner.

Jimmy's rich laugh sounded again, smoothing the rough edges of Bunny's nerves. "When in doubt, little lady, whistle."

Bunny shot him a narrowed look. "Whistle?"

He nodded. "Sure. These here are trained champs. They know a whistle when they hear it. The louder, the better. Stops 'em in their tracks every time."

"A whistle," she muttered to herself as she walked away. She'd have to remember that one. But first, she needed to find a mop, and, judging by the size of the offender, a big one.

Nate spotted Bunny the instant he entered the party. He smiled as she crossed the crowded space, gracefully winding her way through the room. Her requisite black cocktail dress hugged her figure, skimming her knees with a ruffled edge. His stomach tightened. There sure as hell was something enticing about the way the woman wore a set of ruffles.

Aunt Martha stepped into his path, eyes blazing.

"Aunt Marth—"

She jabbed a finger into his chest. "She has absolutely no credentials, does she?"

He stiffened. "Who?"

Her artificial blue gaze narrowed. "You know who."

"No." He gave her a nonchalant chuckle. "I don't."

"Miss Bunny Love." She planted her fists on her hips. "Or did you think I wouldn't find out she's not an event planner?"

"I hired Bunny because she was well qualified to learn." He swept his arm to one side. "Look at this party. Cocktails for dogs." He grinned. "Genius."

Martha pursed her lips. "A cocktail party for dogs is asinine. And McNulty Events is *my* business. Not yours."

"No." Nate blew out a breath. "McNulty Events was never your business. It was my Uncle Arthur's business and my father's business before that." An invisible weight lifted from Nate's shoulders. He'd never realized the enormity of the chip he'd carried all these years. "They would have loved this. It's inventive." He arched a brow. "Unique."

"It's bourgeois," Martha hissed. Her acrylic nail drove into his chest. "And don't you forget who controls the firm. Don't make me—"

"Don't you get tired of the threats, Aunt Martha?"

Her surprised eyes popped wide.

"If this business makes you so unhappy, why don't you give it up?" He leaned near. "Turn the control over to me. Let me live. Let the firm live."

Loud voices rang out from the other side of the party. Nate squinted to see what was going on. Bunny stood in the midst of a heated discussion between a man and a woman. A long-nosed dog cowered behind Bunny's back. This couldn't be good.

"If you ever speak to me like that—"

"I'll talk to you later, Aunt Martha. Have a drink. That always soothes your nerves."

He stepped away before she could utter another syllable.

* * *

Martha stood flabbergasted, watching Nate walk away. *Let me live. Let the firm live.*

That would be the easy way out, wouldn't it? She could walk away from the responsibilities that had weighed so heavy for so long. She'd done nothing but worry about the boys since their parents died. During the past year, she'd done nothing but wonder if stress would take the same toll on Nate as it had on her dear Arthur. Maybe she'd wash her hands of the entire situation. Move to Florida. Hell, maybe she'd seriously take up her pen and inks again.

She eyed Nate's face as he watched Bunny with rapt attention. He was the image of his father at the same age. Ready to rebel. Ready to self-destruct.

No. She couldn't walk away now. She'd shoved her dreams down for years and could do so a while longer. The day Nate and Jeremy's parents had died, she'd vowed never to let the boys make the same mistakes. She'd be damned if she'd start now.

Bunny had grown tired of waiting for a break in the verbal sparring. "What about the breathing?" she interjected. "Have you been practicing your breathing?"

Mitsi and Timothy Goodloe turned on her as if they were rabid. The noise of their argument had stopped every conversation in the room. Bunny had scrambled to diffuse the situation as soon as she'd spotted their negative body language. Somehow she was sure quarreling guests were not listed in Nate's decorum handbook.

"Breathing?" Mitsi spoke so forcefully she spat.

"We've moved way beyond breathing," Timothy bit out.

Okay. So much for upper-class refinement. Poindexter pressed against the back of Bunny's knees, hiding as much of his lanky body as possible.

"Do you see the effect your negative energy is having on Poindexter? How do you think this will affect his performance this weekend?" She planted one hand on the dog's head, the other on her hip. "Hmm?"

The Goodloes fell silent, considering her words with tense expressions.

"You need to remember why you're here, and you need to stop worrying about who slept with whom, or who didn't sleep with whom, or who's going to sleep with whom. Focus on Poindexter."

Timothy's mouth gaped open. Mitsi frowned. "Miss Love is right," she said, her voice soft for a change. "This is Poindexter's weekend and all we've done is argue."

"Loudly," Bunny added. "So loudly I heard you from the other side of the room."

Timothy winced. "Do you think anyone else heard?"

"Yes." Bunny smiled inwardly. It was amazing how much blue bloods worried about appearance. "I suggest you take a few cleansing breaths, drink some wine, apologize to Poindexter and enjoy the rest of your evening."

The Goodloes fell silent.

Bunny scrutinized their expressions. "Questions?"

They shook their heads.

"All right. Let's breathe, shall we?"

"Mind if I join you folks?" Jimmy's gravely voice rang out from behind Bunny.

Mitzi looked at her feet while Timothy shook his head.

"Of course not," Bunny chirped. "We were just discussing the power of yin breathing."

"So I heard." Jimmy stepped close to the Goodloes, so close Mitsi stepped backward, obviously startled by his sudden, gruff appearance. "Have you considered yang breathing?"

Was he questioning her abilities? Bunny's pulse quickened. "I'm trying to calm them, not energize them."

Jimmy ran a hand over his beard. "You know you

can't go wrong with your yang breathing in domestic situations. Soothes the soul and sparks passion."

Mitsi stiffened. "I'd hardly call this a domestic sit—"

"Now I'm not trying to be a buttinski," Jimmy interrupted. "I only want to determine whether you're utilizing the best tools available." He held his hands in the air like a symphony conductor. "Let's try something, shall we?"

The Goodloes stood slack-jawed, obviously not experienced in handling meddling biker breathing experts. Bunny held her tongue, deciding to let Jimmy get his words of wisdom out of his system.

"Let's stick with the slow inhale," Jimmy instructed. "But let's try four short puffs through the mouth for the exhale."

Try as she might, Bunny couldn't stay quiet. "I don't think that's what Mr. and Mrs. Goodloe need."

Jimmy held up one hand to cut her off. She narrowed her gaze, biting back what she really thought. Talk about cramping someone's energy field. Where were Chablis and Chardonnay when she needed a good distraction?

"And in."

Mitsi and Timothy cut their eyes to Bunny. She shrugged and nodded. They inhaled slowly, as she had taught them.

"And out." Excitement tinged Jimmy's words. At least the man interfered passionately. "Puff. Puff. Puff. Puff."

He led them through the exercise three times.

Bunny pressed a hand to her mouth to keep from laughing. She dropped it in astonishment when wide smiles spread across both Mitsi's and Timothy's faces.

"Well?" Jimmy urged.

"Amazing," Mitsi cooed. "Better than a seaweed wrap."

Timothy nodded. "I hate to say it, Miss Love, but this

method eased every muscle instantly." He beamed. "Yet I'm totally energized."

Bunny plastered on a fake smile. "Great," she chirped. "I'll leave you both in Jimmy's capable hands, then. Remember. The watchword is decorum."

She knew where she wasn't wanted. Hmph. Yang breathing to end an argument. Of all the ridiculous ideas she'd ever heard, this was the worst. *Amateur.*

She pivoted on one high heel, slamming right into the broad expanse of Nate's chest.

"The watchword is decorum?"

Chapter 22

Nate wrapped one arm around her waist to steady her, grinning. "The watchword is decorum?" he repeated, his tone teasing and light.

"When in Rome." The heat of a blush fired in her cheeks.

"Nice party, by the way."

Bunny longed to plant a kiss on his lips, but pushed away, putting some distance between their bodies. "Where've you been?"

"Got held up at the office." He tipped his head toward the entrance. "Then Aunt Martha blindsided me."

Bunny grimaced. "I saw her talking to the Monroes. What do you think Thurston said?"

"That you have no experience." He gave a slight shrug. "Although, I don't think he mentioned catching me in your building this morning."

Bunny's heart slapped against her ribcage. "He saw you?"

Nate nodded.

"Cripes."

"That's putting it mildly."

"What about Martha? What did she say?" Fear gripped Bunny's heart. If she lost her job now, her mortgage application would fall through with the speed of light.

"She'll get over it." Nate glanced around the crowded

room. "I was wondering what you had on under that ruffle."

His words kick started her libido. *Zing*. She planted her hands on her hips and grinned. "I guess there's only one way to find out."

One of the caterer's assistants approached them, her features twisted into a worried mess. "Miss Love?"

"Yes." Bunny squinted, not wanting to hear whatever it was that had caused the girl's facial expression.

"There's been an incident involving a Great Dane and a tray of bacon-wrapped scallops."

Bunny and her libido stifled a sigh. "Duty calls."

Nate was still shaking his head as she walked away.

Nate and Bunny's body language ratcheted Martha's fears to the next level. Too close and too familiar. Frustration simmered in her veins.

"That's another thing I forgot to ask you." Thurston Monroe appeared at her side, a partially empty martini glass in his hand. He followed her gaze. Bunny stepped out of view as Nate stood staring at her departing backside.

Thurston shook the olive from the bottom of his glass. "Is it McNulty policy for Nathan to make early morning house calls to his staff?" His silver brows met in a vee. "Or do you think they were up all night planning parties?"

The meddlesome man stepped away before Martha could respond. She felt as though she'd been slapped. Had Nathan spent the night with Beatrice Love? Impossible. Unthinkable. *Unacceptable*.

He'd agreed to marry Melanie, damn it. She'd raised him to know better than to sleep with some free-spirited New Age spouting sprite. What had happened to his control?

Miss Love had to go, and she had to go now. The

heat of Martha's anger singed her cheeks. She loved Nate too much to watch him suffer his father's fate. She could only hope that someday his heart would recover, and he'd understand.

Nate watched proudly as Bunny effortlessly worked the room. She'd repositioned the appetizers higher than every pooch in attendance and now mingled like a pro. Hiring her had been anything but a mistake. She fit—in his company and his life.

He leaned against a support column, brushing away the filmy material Bunny had insisted on. Something about softening the negative energy of the edges. He chuckled. She might be a fruitcake, but she sure was a sexy fruitcake.

Bunny's laugh rang out above the crowd, strong and vital. Nate longed to have her all to himself. He didn't want to share her with a bunch of canines and their owners. He wanted to touch her. Make love to her. Over and over, and over again.

His body responded and he realized he had to focus. And not on Bunny's shapely curves. Control, Nate. *Control.* Tonight he needed tunnel vision. The target—a successful Worthington Cup. He'd drop dead before he let Aunt Martha turn the firm over to Armand. Delivering a world-class weekend would ensure that didn't happen.

"I've been trying to find you all day." Melanie's voice interrupted his thoughts. Her curve-hugging, eyeball-popping cobalt-blue dress shattered them.

"Wow." He mentally chastised himself. *Way to be nonchalant, McNulty.*

Melanie's features warmed into a dazzling smile. "It's not too much?" A shadow of doubt flickered across her smile and he caught himself.

"I'm just not used to seeing you like this." He rocked

back on his heels, a chuckle slipping from his lips. "Hell, Mel. That's some dress."

A worried furrow pinched the skin between her brows.

He squeezed her hand. "You're a knockout."

Melanie beamed. "It's the new me."

Nate allowed himself a measured gaze. Stunning. Something had changed, though, and it wasn't just the dress. Melanie had a new energy. Dare he use that term? Lord, Bunny really had rubbed off on him, but it was true. Melanie oozed life.

"You're alive," Nate murmured.

Melanie placed her palm on Nate's chest. Warmth seeped through the jacket of his suit.

"I feel alive." She glanced around the room. "I owe it to Bunny."

"Bunny?" Nate's voice cracked. A puzzled look washed across Melanie's features. Guilt rippled straight from her touch to Nate's cheating groin. He fought the urge to close his eyes and moan. How could he have slept with Bunny before he came clean with Melanie? She deserved better.

"I'm leaving," she said softly.

"The party?"

"The state."

"What?" Her words jolted him back into focus.

"I hope you'll find a way to understand." She paused, pulling herself taller, straighter. "I've decided to explore my options."

"I'm a little confused." *Confused*? Between her scrap of a dress and the new alter ego, his brain hurt.

"You and I both know we were getting married because our families wanted us to."

So far, so good. Nate nodded.

"So you agree?" Her crystal clear blue eyes widened expectantly. "You're not upset about this?"

He shook his head. *Stunned.* But not upset. Maybe some things were meant to be. In the case of a marriage between him and Melanie, some things weren't. Nate felt lighter suddenly, as though a weight had been hoisted from his back.

"Come on." He held out his arm. "Let's go toast the new you."

Bunny watched the pair from behind the punch bowl. Nate and Melanie seemed cozy. *Too* cozy. She tamped down her jealousy. She'd feel a whole lot better if she could hear what they were saying. She measured the distance from the plant corner to where they stood. *Perfect.*

"Bunny, darling."

Kitty. Bunny flinched. Who'd eaten, peed on, or trampled what now? Chablis and Chardonnay stood on either side of Kitty's ankles, little evil noses sniffing for trouble.

"It's time for my remarks," Kitty said. "You'll watch the girls?"

Yeah. Like that had gone well previously. "I don't—"

"Armand always watched the girls during my remarks." Kitty arched one brow expectantly.

"*Fine.*" Bunny shot a warning look at *the girls.* They snarled in return. Not a good start. "Where are their leashes?"

"Oh." Kitty waved a hand in the air as she walked away. "They graduated summa cum laude from the obedience academy. They don't need leashes."

"That's what you think," Bunny muttered under her breath.

She scrutinized the dynamic duo. They stared back. "Ladies, we're headed for the plant corner. Can you handle that?"

She stepped casually across the room, angling closer to where Nate stood deep in conversation with Melanie. Bunny realized her jealousy was ridiculous, but, come on. Even in her dreams, she couldn't make sequins bounce like Melanie did.

Chablis and Chardonnay trotted happily at her heels. Maybe Kitty was right about the leashes after all.

She shuffled behind a large potted fern, hoping her basic black would blend into the greenery. "Psst." The poodles' fuzzy heads snapped in her direction. She jerked her chin and the two fur balls came running. "Do whatever you want," she whispered. "Just stay close and stay quiet. Aunt Bunny has some eavesdropping to do."

Two pairs of shiny black, beady eyes blinked attentively. At least she hoped it was attentively.

Bunny stepped deeper into the grouping of pots, stubbing her toe on a heavy ceramic container. She bit back a yelp just as Nate's words reached her.

"I never noticed what vivid blue eyes you have, Mel."

His silky smooth voice was unmistakable. *Mel*? Since when did Mr. Prim and Proper call anyone Mel?

"How's my energy?" Melanie's usually gentle voice sounded downright sexy.

"Sizzling." Nate laughed, rich and full.

Bunny twisted up her face so severely it hurt. *Sizzling*? This did not sound like a kiss-off conversation. More like a kiss *on*.

Nausea clawed its way up Bunny's esophagus. Maybe Nate had never intended to break things off with Melanie. After all, he'd never actually said as much. Had he? Bunny assumed his passionate lovemaking signaled the imminent demise of the McNulty-Brittingham merger, but perhaps she'd been nothing more than a momentary diversion.

No. She didn't really believe that. Did she?

Someone—or *something*—let out a blood-curdling scream.

Bunny searched the area around her feet, but Chablis and Chardonnay were nowhere in sight. "Damn it," she mumbled. "Demon dogs."

She unfurled herself from behind the greenery and froze, her worst fears realized. Chardonnay had launched a flank attack on a Saint Bernard. Holy cow. Chablis already hung, fang deep, from the massive dog's kicking paw. These poodles had serious size issues.

She scrambled to the scene just as Chablis flew through the air. She landed on the hard floor with a muffled cry. Bunny winced, but the fur ball shook it off, unscathed, racing back for a counterattack.

"Heel!" Bunny screamed.

Too late. The Saint Bernard had decided he wasn't taking any more abuse. He shook his massive body, sending both poodles scampering for cover. The giant's less than dainty physique clipped a candelabrum, sending two freesia tapers tumbling to the floor.

That would have been bad enough, but one candle rolled, still burning, straight for a decorated column. Bunny watched in stunned amazement as the ivory tulle burst into a ribbon of orange flame, licking its way up the pillar.

Dogs and party guests scrambled, shrieks and barks filling the air. Chablis and Chardonnay dashed for the plant corner. Jimmy Monroe ripped the burning tulle from the pillar, stomping the stubborn flames beneath his biker boots.

Bunny did what any practical event planner would do. She upended a giant martini water station, sending a torrent of water across the tiled floor. The inferno sputtered out, sending up one last plume of angry smoke.

"Is it out?" She uttered the words in one fearful breath.

Jimmy nodded. "Too much yang. Amateur mistake."

Bunny bit her lip. Everyone was a critic.

She cast a quick glance around the room. The guests had scattered. Nate stood where he had been, one arm wrapped protectively around Melanie's shoulders. Bunny's stomach clenched with dread.

Martha McNulty stood open-mouthed, all color blanched from her cheeks. Thurston Monroe smugly shook his head, no doubt planning the next tenant for Bunny's apartment. Kitty Worthington lay flat-out on-stage. Tilly gave Bunny the thumbs-up in between her attempts to revive Kitty with cheek pats. Bert leaned against the stage, head hanging, shoulders shaking.

A faint siren wailed in the distance, growing steadily closer. A loan canine guest launched a mournful howl. A second dog joined him, then a third, and a fourth.

Bunny's intuition screamed *job change*. And it wasn't talking promotion.

Chapter 23

Thirty minutes later, the fire chief nodded in Nate's direction. "All clear here."

"Sorry for the inconvenience, Chief." Nate shot an anxious glance to where Bunny stood. Her eyes flashed nervously as he caught her attention. She looked away, her expression pained and frightened.

He stood huddled with Aunt Martha who wanted Bunny's head on a platter. For once, he agreed. The chaotic menace might have a firm grasp on his heart, but she'd probably cost the firm any future Worthington Cups and certainly any referrals.

A local news reporter interviewed several guests in a far corner of the hall, the camera bathing them in bright light.

"Nathan McNulty," Aunt Martha snapped. "Look at me."

As soon as he did, he wished he hadn't. The fury in his aunt's eyes was like nothing he'd ever seen.

"This evening has been an abomination," she hissed. "If you don't fire her, I will."

He bristled. No one fired his staff. No one. "I'll handle it."

This time Bunny's antics had gone too far. Accident or not, each piece of the evening's puzzle traced back to her efforts at positive chi. Her creative efforts had resulted in the evening's fiery conclusion.

Confusion tugged Nate's heart down to his stomach. Could he fire Bunny? She had become the bright light pulling him out of his gray existence. She had also, however, become the Grim Reaper, pulling him into the abyss of failed event planning.

Bunny might be the yang to his yin, but her chaos had destroyed his carefully orchestrated control.

His traitorous stomach tightened and twisted. Furious as he was, he couldn't stop thinking about Bunny's slipper-covered feet wrapped around his waist, or the way it had felt to be inside her. When she was near, control went out the window.

"Nathan! You'd better be fantasizing about ways to fire her."

He swallowed, snapping himself out of his libido-induced trance. He nodded, resigned to the knowledge that his first mistake had been hiring Bunny for something as important as The Worthington Cup. His second had been falling for her.

"Fire her, or Armand Miller will be your boss by Monday."

Ice seeped through his veins. "Over my dead body."

"Then act like a McNulty."

Nate watched Bunny smooth the front of her dress. His eyes locked instantly on her damned ruffle and all strength seeped from his muscles. This entire situation was his fault. He'd broken a cardinal rule, mixing business with pleasure. *Lack of control.* He'd shown nothing but since Bunny entered his world.

"I'll do it now." He set his features, hoping the doubt rattling around inside his brain didn't shine through.

Bert stepped into his path halfway across the floor, his expression tense, his eyes pleading. "Don't do this. This wasn't her fault."

Not her fault? Anger bubbled from somewhere deep inside Nate. "Whose fault was it? The poodles? Granted, they're demonic, but they're dogs. Dogs Bunny failed to watch."

Bert grabbed his arm. "Is this your decision? Or Martha's?"

Nate didn't appreciate his friend's tone. "No one tells me how to run this firm. That includes Aunt Martha, Bunny and *you*." He shook his arm free of Bert's grip.

Color rose in Bert's cheeks. Nate stepped around him, more determined than ever firing Bunny was his only choice. The survival of his father's firm had to come before the needs of his heart. *It had to.*

Bunny stood waiting, her expression tremulous. She'd shoved her tangled hair behind her ears, achieving nothing more than drawing attention to the complete lack of color in her face. She touched Nate's arm. "Can you forgive me?"

He lost himself momentarily in the depths of her frightened eyes. He wanted to throttle her. He wanted to console her. His emotions tugged and pulled, maneuvering for position. Duty. Bunny. Control. Chaos. Expectations. Love.

"You're fired." *And I think I'm in love with you.*

Tears shimmered in her eyes. "F . . . fired?"

Be strong. She'll forgive you eventually. Think about the company. "Does this surprise you, or do you set fire to most cocktail parties you attend?"

His harsh words caused her shoulders to slump, as if he'd sucked the air from her body. Bunny stammered wordlessly. Red splotches blossomed in her cheeks. "I thought . . . I thought."

"What?" He dug deep, focusing on the firm. *Do it for McNulty,* his inner voice chanted. "Sleeping with the boss doesn't make you immune from responsibility."

Her mouth gaped open, hurt registering instantly on her face. He stiffened, moving a step backward to distance himself from the pain he'd inflicted.

Bunny's turquoise eyes went huge. "How dare you?"

She clasped her hands in front of her stomach. Her voice shook. Her shoulders trembled. "I'm sorry I believed you capable of caring about anyone or anything other than your precious company."

Now was his chance. His chance to tell her how alive he felt for the first time since his parents died. He looked past Bunny to where Martha stood a few feet away, scowling, daggers shooting from her eyes into the back of Bunny's tousled head.

It wouldn't work. It would *never* work. There was no room in his orderly world for a life force as vital as Bunny's. He'd tried a taste of her chaos and had gotten burned. Literally. Pain twisted in his chest. "I'm sorry you feel that way."

"I'm sorry you don't feel anything at all." Sadness washed across her features.

Something inside Nate broke. This was how things had to be. He couldn't handle the way he felt—the way he needed her—whenever she was near. *Coward.*

"You're a robot, Nate. A cold, unfeeling robot. Life is passing you by while you hide inside your gray cocoon."

She held her chin high, pulling herself taller, straighter. She turned, walking away from him. Out of his life. *Stop her*, a voice deep inside him screamed. *Don't let her go!*

Aunt Martha's steel blue gaze sliced him clean through. Damn her. Damn Bunny. Damn them both for making him choose.

Bunny stopped, looking back over her shoulder. "I'm going to make sure the caterers have everything they need before I leave. I'll stop by tomorrow morning to clean out my cubicle."

"Office," Nate mumbled, wondering how long the dull ache in his heart would last.

* * *

Bunny raced for the kitchen, nausea clawing at her throat. The strength she'd mustered for Nate's benefit shattered, and she staggered, fumbling against the cold wall of the passageway.

Jeremy approached, carrying two beers. "Bunny." He lightly touched his fingers to her shoulder. "I was coming to find you. You okay?"

She stared at him, unable to think or do anything more. How could she be okay? She'd lost it all. Her job. Her apartment. *Nate.*

How could she have been so wrong? He'd changed. Hadn't he? She'd seen the emotions. Yet he'd fired her, coldly, heartlessly. She'd thought him different from every other man in her past. But he wasn't. Her heart ached, twisting in her chest. It was better to find out now. Better to know before he'd sucked her life force dry. Her vision darkened and she slumped against the wall.

Jeremy's arms locked strong and sure around her waist, beer sloshing from the glass bottles. "Whoa, what's going on?"

She opened her eyes to meet his soft blue gaze. He squinted, lines of concern trailing to his temples. "Fired."

Disbelief washed across his poster-boy features. "Nate fired you?"

She nodded.

Anger flashed through his gaze. "That idiot."

Her throat tightened. She had to get outside. Now. "Take me home."

Jeremy turned toward the main room, one arm securely tightened around her waist.

"No," she choked out, sudden tears blurring her vision. "Not that way."

He frowned then focused at something over her shoulder. "We can go out the back. It's just as easy."

Bunny nodded, biting hard into her lip to keep from crying.

"You need to do anything here before we leave?"

"Caterers have instructions," she whispered. "It's okay."

But it wouldn't be okay. It couldn't. She squeezed her eyes shut as they headed down the hall toward the back door. She was fleeing like a coward. She should hold her head high and act as though she didn't care. That would show him.

The evening's fiasco *had* been her fault. *All her fault.* She'd tried to force her world onto his. And she'd failed. Miserably.

Maybe it was good the night ended as it did, forcing Nate's true colors into the open. Instead of defending or forgiving her, he'd let her go. He'd chosen cold expectation over warm emotion. And he had looked as though firing her hadn't fazed him in the least.

Her heart twisted, breaking deep inside her chest.

Jeremy shot her a worried look as he pushed open the heavy exit door. Bunny stepped into a dark alleyway, the night air cool against the moisture on her cheeks.

"This way." Jeremy took her hand, leading her toward a city parking lot. She followed in a trance-like state, willing her feet to move. She needed to be away from Nate. Away from Martha. Away from everything having to do with McNulty Events.

She'd been a fool to think he'd choose loving her over his career. After all, she had no connections to offer. No status. No rich client base. *Nothing.* To Nate, she'd been the off-the-wall new hire bringing temporary excitement into his bland life. Nothing more.

As Jeremy opened the passenger door, she fought a sob, trying to ignore the hollow ache spreading through her bones. She sank into the leather seat, finally letting the tears fall. Who cared what Nate's brother thought? Who cared what any of them thought? She wanted only to get home—where she could nurse her broken heart in private.

Tomorrow she'd figure out how to salvage what was left of her life.

Nate swallowed down the lump growing in his throat. *My God.* What had he just done? *And why?* For a company? A job? He'd let Bunny walk out of his life because of expectation. He didn't deserve her. He never had.

"Well done." Aunt Martha's clipped tone stung. "For once you've done the McNulty name proud."

"I'm not so sure," he muttered.

She grabbed his arm, her fingers tensing into his skin. "Stop that damned muttering. Act like a man."

Her steely gaze sent ice racing through his veins. *Act like a man?* He'd acted like anything but tonight. He'd acted like Aunt Martha's puppet, marching to the tune of her damned rules and wants. "You want me to act like a man?"

Her gaze widened. "Please."

"Then let go of my arm and get out of my way."

The flush in her cheeks faded. "I don't like your tone."

"And I don't like yours." He shook her hand from his arm. "I'm tired of your rules. I am a man. Let me live my life."

"With who? That flake?"

Nate's fists clenched at his side, anger rolling in his gut. "That *flake* is the best thing that ever happened to me." He plowed a hand through his hair. "And I just let you pressure me into chasing her out of my life." He shook his head, squeezing his eyes shut. "What the hell is wrong with me?"

"Think of the firm. She's ruined all you've worked for."

His mind raced. Had she? "I never even gave her a second chance," he stammered. "People make mistakes."

"*Not* McNultys."

"Damn it, Aunt Martha." He leaned so close she

backed away, fear flickering in her eyes. "Don't you get tired of being a McNulty? I do. Jeremy did. Look at him." He gestured wildly. "He lives to defy you, yet you hold him on a pedestal." Nate slapped his chest. "I break my ass for you, doing whatever you want, and you give me nothing but shit."

Her features puckered. "Don't you swear at me."

"Why not?" He paced in a large circle, his anger winding tighter and tighter inside him, coiling like a spring. "Because I'm a McNulty?"

Tears swam in her eyes, something Nate had only seen when his uncle died. "Jeremy's nothing like your father. You are. I worry you'll suffer the same fate."

Nate came to a stop, pounding his fists against his chest, anguish overtaking his every sense. He pointed to the hallway through which Bunny had fled. "Why? Because I love her?"

His aunt gasped, staggering under the force of his words. "What about Melanie?"

"We don't love each other. We never have. Do you hear me? I *love* Bunny." He shoved both hands into his hair.

"You need to calm down, Nathan. This will all seem less important in the morning."

"*No.*" The coiled spring inside him snapped. Adrenaline surged through his body, tingling to his extremities. He'd had it with the McNulty rules. "I'm going after her." He turned, jogging away, toward the exit, before Aunt Martha could stop him.

"You'll end up like your father," she yelled.

Nate paused, a vision of his mother and father flashing across his mind. Happy. In love. He turned slowly back to face his aunt. She stood, hands clasped, pleading with him.

"I'd rather die happy than continue to live half-dead."

She paled, taking a step backward.

"Did I hit a nerve?" Nate stared at her intently. "Maybe you're tired of living half-dead, too."

He spun away, racing after Bunny, hoping there'd be some way to undo all the senseless pain he'd just inflicted on the woman he loved.

Martha stood in place as though Nate's words had poured concrete around her feet. His anguish had been palpable, causing her own insides to ache.

Was she tired of living half-dead? *Yes.* She'd lived half-dead since the day his father and mother had died. Since the day fate had extinguished their bright lights. She and Arthur had never recovered from the sudden, unbelievable loss.

Tears threatened and she blinked them back. Mc-Nultys did not cry. Damn it. Certainly not in public. She glanced around the now mostly empty room.

Was she tired of being a McNulty? *Yes.* The pressure had been even more unbearable since Arthur had died, willing the firm to her. The admission made her sag, as though all of the anger she'd bottled up inside had held her stiff and straight.

What if Nate did love Bunny? She had no right to interfere. She'd devoted her life to keeping him safe, but he was obviously unhappy. *Unfulfilled.* Perhaps she should have tried harder to teach him how to live.

A lone tear slipped down her cheek. She let it fall. She was tired of being a McNulty, but it was all she knew. It was all Nate had known, too, but look at him now. Passionate. Sure of his actions. Racing off to chase the dream of true love.

Martha sniffed back a sob. *My God.* Perhaps she'd been wrong about Bunny Love. The woman obviously had no skills as an event planner, but she might just be able to teach Nate what Martha never had. With her help, he might learn to embrace a life beyond status and control. A life lived with passion.

Maybe the time had come for Martha to step out of the way. The boy had made the best point of all. It was better to die happy than to live half-dead. And she should know.

Nate let the exit door slam shut, slapping his palm against the wall. "Damn it."

"Problem, buddy?" A male voice sounded close and gruff. A burly, bearded man stared at him, rubbing his chin. "Looking for Bunny?"

Nate narrowed his gaze questioningly.

The man shrugged, extending a hand. "Jimmy Monroe."

"Nate McNulty." He let out an exasperated breath. "Did you happen to see her leave?"

Jimmy pressed his lips together, frowning. "With some blond guy. Kinda looked like that Brad Pitt fellow."

Jeremy. Nate groaned. When the hell hadn't his brother been in the right place at the right time?

"You going after her?"

Nate considered the man incredulously.

As if reading his mind, Jimmy spoke. "I'm here showing my dog. Met Bunny yesterday. Her poodle pissed on my bike." He shook his gray head. "She looked mighty sad on her way out tonight. You responsible for that?"

Nate nodded, squeezing his eyes shut for a beat.

"You should go after her. Come on. I'll give you a ride."

Nate met the stranger's gaze. Who was this guy? "I've got my car, but thanks."

"Bike'll get you there a whole lot quicker."

"Bike?" Nate's pulse quickened.

"Harley."

Nate didn't hesitate. "You're on." As he watched, the

man's gaze locked on something then softened. Nate turned to follow his view. Melanie stood a few feet away, eyes shining with moisture.

"I didn't mean to eavesdrop." Her soft voice trembled. "I wanted . . ." She sucked in a jagged breath, obviously fighting fresh tears. "I wanted to say goodbye, Nate."

Nate's gut twisted. "Oh God, Mel—" Had she heard everything? About Bunny?

She shook her head, waving her hand dismissively. "It's okay. Really." A tear tumbled over her lower lid.

Nate closed the distance in one stride, pulling her into his arms. She tensed then eased against him.

"I never meant to hurt you," Nate whispered against her soft hair. "Never."

She pulled away, looking up at him through tear-filled blue eyes. "We weren't getting married anyway, Nate."

"I didn't mean for you to find out like—"

"*No.*"

Melanie interrupted before Nate could finish his sentence, the ferocity of her tone startling him. He broke the embrace, taking a backward step.

"We were both unhappy." She swiped at her moist cheeks. "This is all for the best. It's fate."

Nate struggled to find his voice. "Why did we both go along with the engagement if neither of us wanted it?"

"Because we were expected to." A weak smile played at the corners of her mouth. "I'm tired of doing what they expect us to do. Aren't you?"

He nodded.

She took a deep breath, straightening. New tears glistened in her eyes. "Go chase your dream." She pushed against his chest. "Before it's too late."

"I'm sor—"

She pressed a finger to his lips, trapping the word inside. "Just go."

Jimmy Monroe stood to one side, holding a helmet

beneath his arm. He tipped his head sympathetically toward Melanie then looked at Nate. "Ready? Bike's around back."

Nate nodded.

He looked back as they hurried for the street exit. Melanie stood in the soft light of the hallway, her bright blue dress accentuating the beauty he hadn't fully noticed before tonight.

Deciding to chase her dream had filled her with light. Bright, vital life.

He turned back toward the street. Jimmy sat on the cycle, waiting. Nate climbed behind him, locking his arms around the man's midsection.

As they took off into the city night, Nate realized he was chasing his dream—Bunny.

He'd never felt more alive. Or more terrified.

Chapter 24

Jeremy gave Bunny a pensive look. "Sure you don't want me to stay?"

She closed her eyes, leaning against the doorjamb. The last thing she needed was a McNulty in her apartment. She shook her head. "I'm okay, but thanks. I appreciate the ride home."

"Won't be the same without you around, Bunny."

She forced a weak smile. Pain sliced through her heart. No more McNulty Events. No more Nate. No more bunny slippers wrapped around his waist. "I'll be fine," she lied.

She pushed the door closed, but pulled it open a crack when she realized Jeremy hadn't walked away. He stood frowning, his features tight with worry, his intense gaze locked on Bunny. "Nate only knows how to play it safe. What happened tonight—"

"He's a big boy," Bunny interrupted. "What happened tonight proves he never planned to change."

"You don't know that." Jeremy rubbed a hand through his hair.

Bunny's throat tightened at the familiar gesture. "I've never been more sure of anything." Her heart ached. She wondered whether this was as bad as the pain would be, or if it would grow worse as each day passed. *Without Nate.*

"Give him a little time, Bunny."

To do what? Break her heart again? She concentrated on not crying. "You should go now." She closed the door, leaning her forehead against the cool wood.

She listened as Jeremy's footsteps faded, letting a tear slip down her cheek. A second followed, then a third and fourth, until the torrent of unshed tears fell freely. She sank to the floor, pulling her knees tight to her chest.

Give him a little time, Bunny.

She trembled, the ache in her heart deepening, growing. How did you give time to a man who had chosen a job over your heart?

A noise sounded from the second bedroom and Bunny stiffened. *Alexandra.* The last thing she needed was to have her mother find her in this state. She dragged a hand across her damp eyes and looked down the hall.

Her mother stared back, her face more serious than Bunny had ever seen it. She approached, sinking to the floor next to Bunny and pulling her into her arms.

"My baby," Alexandra cooed. "Tell Momma what's wrong."

Momma. Bunny's tears flowed anew, a trickle of warmth replacing the chill in her heart. Alexandra's gentle fingers stroked several stray hairs from her cheek, and Bunny relaxed into her mother's touch, savoring the comfort.

"It's all over." Bunny forced the words through her sobs. "He fired me."

Alexandra sank back onto her heels, scrutinizing Bunny with her pale, violet gaze. She shook her head. "Maybe he made a mistake."

Nate's angry words flashed through Bunny's mind. "I don't think so. He thinks I'm a creative menace."

"Well, honey"—her mother gently lifted Bunny's chin with her fingers—"I've called you worse on many occasions."

The tease brought a smile to Bunny's lips. "He and I are too different, Momma."

The term of endearment obviously caught Alexandra off guard. She tensed momentarily then smiled. "My, that sounds nice." She took Bunny's hands in both of hers, her gaze pinning her daughter. "Opposites attract, dear. Just look at your sister, Vicki. Look at your father and me."

Bunny shook her head. "You and Daddy have just spent the past five weeks apart and Vicki wouldn't know creativity if it bit her in the—"

Her mother cut her off with a disapproving glare.

"She married the hair transplant king, for crying out loud," Bunny muttered.

"Hair transplant king to the stars," Alexandra corrected, referring to the family's recent move to Los Angeles. "Now, that's creative."

The two shared a conspiratorial giggle, then settled into silence once more.

"Nate McNulty doesn't have a creative bone in his body." Bunny sniffed. "It's over."

"You might be surprised." Alexandra patted Bunny's knee. "I saw the way that young man looked at you the other night. Don't give up on him just yet." She pushed herself up to stand. "Just look at your father. He's come up with an entire line of golf greeting cards."

Incredulity washed through Bunny. "Daddy?"

"Daddy." Her mother turned to head back to her bedroom. "We're leaving for Florida tonight. You can paint your walls any color you like after I'm gone."

Bunny sighed, taking in the expanse of eggshell that ran from the living room into the kitchen. Somehow the bland color summed up exactly how she felt. Flat, lifeless and heartbroken.

* * *

Nate held on for dear life as Jimmy's motorcycle careened down Twelfth Street.

"Lean into the corner," Jimmy yelled.

Nate followed the man's lead, shifting his weight as they turned onto Locust. The familiar sensation sent a rush of adrenaline through his limbs. A sudden vision of riding with his father flashed through his mind. *Lean with me,* his father had yelled. *Lean with me.*

Tears stung at Nate's eyes. He blinked them away. Must be the night air slipping around the goggles Jimmy had lent him.

Those long-forgotten afternoons had been heady ones—filled with thrills and laughter. He and Jeremy had taken turns riding, while their mother had watched, clapping—thrilled to see her boys chasing life.

Their happy family had been shattered not long after, on a hot, humid August afternoon. Nate's parents had gone out on the bike, but they'd never come home. A violent late summer thunderstorm had ripped their world apart. Nate could still remember the state trooper's voice—the way he enunciated the words—as if Nate and Jeremy wouldn't understand. *Multiple vehicle accident. Multiple fatalities.*

He had since learned to live safely. Lord knew Aunt Martha had drummed it into his head over and over again. But tonight when he watched Bunny walk away, he realized he didn't want to live safely anymore. Not if it meant living without Bunny.

"Next right," he yelled in Jimmy's ear.

The man nodded, smoothly navigating the corner.

Bunny's building rose in the middle of the block. Nate's chest tightened at the sight of Jeremy stepping out of the entry door. Nate pointed and Jimmy slowed the bike to a stop. Jeremy stood, fists on hips, as Nate climbed off the bike.

"Reliving your youth?" His brother's features belied

his attempt at levity, a grim expression overshadowing his words.

Nate pulled off the helmet. "I came for Bunny."

Jeremy arched a brow as he shook his head. "I don't think you're on her list of favorite people right now."

Nate stepped to the entryway and pressed the buzzer for Bunny's apartment. Dead air responded. He pressed the button a second time. Still nothing. "Did you see her go in?" He turned to his brother.

"I walked her up."

"Was she very upset?"

Jeremy laughed. "Was she upset? You fired her." He stepped close. "What the hell were you thinking? Or were you doing what you were told to do?"

Nate swallowed down his anger. "I made a mistake."

Genuine concern blazed in Jeremy's eyes. "When are you going to start living your life instead of Aunt Martha's?"

"Right now."

"Good luck." Jeremy shook his head. "You're going to need it. You hurt her bad." He jerked a thumb toward Bunny's building. "Reminds me of Mom. You ever think that?"

On a daily basis. "Sometimes."

Jeremy looked down at the sidewalk then straight into Nate's eyes. "You'd be a lucky man to find the kind of love Mom gave Dad."

Nate let the words sink into his soul. "I know."

Jeremy gripped his arm. "Then fight for her."

"I have to get back," Jimmy yelled. "You okay?"

Nate nodded. "Thanks."

Jeremy dropped his hand from Nate's arm and walked to his car, the headlights flashing as he depressed his key fob. "She's one in a million. Don't blow it."

Nate watched the two drive off. His perfect brother in his European sedan. Jimmy Monroe straddling his

Harley. Nate shook his head. Life had become anything but boring since Bunny had arrived on the scene.

He pressed the buzzer again, this time holding it down for several long seconds. Silence.

"Damn it, Bunny. Give me a chance." Nate leaned his forehead against the brick. "You've got to let me explain."

Then he did something he hadn't done since his parents died. He prayed. If there was a God, He surely couldn't intend for Nate to live his life without Bunny.

He pressed the buzzer again.

The intercom squawked in response. "*Go away.*"

Hope surged through his chest. "I'm sorry. I don't know how I could have done what I just did. Please. Let me talk to you."

Another squawk. A sniff. His heart caught.

"Leave me alone. I never want to see you again."

"Give me a second chance."

"Like you gave me?" Her words sliced through him. "You had your chance. Go away."

"Bunny." Silence. "Bunny!"

Someone grasped Nate's shoulder. "You blew it, buddy."

The cold reality of Bert's words stunned him. "I know."

A wild-looking brunette jumped in Nate's face, jabbing a pale blue nail into his chest. "You've loved her since the moment she walked into your life, but she scares you, so you do this? You *suit.*"

He steeled himself defensively. "Who the hell are you?"

"This is Tilly," Bert said. "My friend."

"Friend?" The pixie spun on Bert.

Bert winced. "Can we argue semantics later? I thought our current focus was Bunny."

His words worked. The sprite resumed her attack on Nate. "She makes you feel." Another jab to his chest. "Right here. Admit it."

"Yes." Nate backed away from her finger, searching Bert's face for support. "I can't deny that."

"Then how could you fire her?" Tilly's green eyes were huge and wild.

"I made a mistake." Nate sank to the step, lowering his face to his hands. "I screwed up."

"Understatement of the century." Bert shook his blond head. "You just ruined the best thing in your life."

Nate looked at the locked entry door. "She told me to go away."

"And this surprises you?" Tilly snapped.

Bunny wouldn't shut him out completely, would she? She wasn't capable of such a heartless act. His heart sank. Like the one he'd pulled tonight. The weight of his loss settled heavily around his shoulders.

Bert and Tilly eyed him, waiting for a response.

"Please, help me."

Tilly's head snapped in a gesture of disgust. "You don't deserve it." She pushed him out of her way and inserted her key in the door. "And you don't deserve her."

"I'll come with you." Nate clambered to his feet, standing behind her. She spun around, fists planted on hips.

"No way. The Condo Board would kick me out on my psychic ass if I let you in."

"Why? I'd be coming in as your guest."

"Think again, control boy."

"Control boy?"

"Yeah, you think you can control everything around you." She gestured wildly. Nate stepped clear. "Here's a news flash. It's all about karma, my friend, and right now, your karma needs a lot of help."

"Then tell me what to do." Nate's pulse quickened. "Whatever it takes, I'll do it."

Tilly tapped her fingertips against her chin, scrutinizing him. She tipped her head first to one side, then the other, making a tsking noise with her mouth. She wrinkled her nose.

"What?" Nate gripped her elbows. "Tell me."

Her nose wrinkle turned into a full facial scrunch. "You're not ready."

"I *am* ready." He paused for a beat. "I'm ready for anything that will win her back."

Tilly shook her head. "If you were ready, you wouldn't *need* to win her back."

Bert slapped him on the back. "Go home, Nate."

"Why won't you help me?" Nate scowled.

Bert's features fell slack, defeated. "The truth? Right now I don't like you a whole lot, but I'll talk to her." He pursed his lips before he continued, as if measuring his thoughts. "I'm not sure you deserve it."

Need simmered in Nate's gut. Desperate need. "Please."

Tilly pulled open the front door. Bert gave Nate's shoulder a slap as he stepped past, reaching for the door. Tilly moved close to Nate, standing on her tiptoes to whisper in his ear, "Embrace the chaos."

Nate eyed her disbelievingly. "If the past month of my life is any measure, I've embraced more than my share."

Tilly pursed her lips, shaking her head. "You think too much." She pinned Nate with her green gaze. He shivered. "And you worry about what other people think." Another jab to his chest. "Stop thinking and start feeling."

He stood alone on the sidewalk, looking up at Bunny's building for a long time after they went inside. His head hurt, his stomach churned and his heart ached. If he felt anything else, he'd need a doctor.

He walked toward the Parkway, letting Tilly's words rattle through his brain. *Embrace the chaos.* She was right. If he'd done that, he might have laughed at tonight's events.

Okay, he would never have laughed. But he might have been a bit more forgiving.

"My dog!" an elderly male voice rang out. "Please. Grab my dog."

An orange fur ball shot past Nate's feet, followed by a medium-sized gray dog. Toenails scraped against the sidewalk as the pair dashed toward the intersection. Startled, Nate dropped to his knees and whistled. The dog stopped, turning his head. An orange cat made a quick zig, disappearing down an alley.

"Come." Nate held out a hand. "I won't hurt you."

The short-haired dog approached cautiously, dragging his leash. He sniffed Nate's hand then gave his fingertips a slurp. Nate chuckled, capturing the leash in his free hand.

"Thought I'd lost him for good." A frail gentleman stood just behind Nate. "You've got to stop chasing that cat, Henry."

The dog cocked his head, wagging his tail sheepishly.

Nate handed the man the leash. The dog danced happily around his owner's feet. Nate couldn't help but smile at the obvious affection.

The elderly man stooped, patting the dog's head, but eyeing Nate. "He's a scamp, but I'd be lost without him."

"I can see that. He's a beauty."

"Schnauzer," the man said. "His momma was a champ." The man turned the handle of the leash, inspecting it. "Slipped right out of my hand."

"I'm just glad I could help." Nate smiled. At least he'd done one thing right tonight.

The man measured Nate with a watery gaze. "Ever have a dog?"

Nate shook his head.

"Damn shame," he said softly. "Nothing better than unconditional love."

The words struck home, ratcheting up the ache in Nate's heart. *Unconditional love.*

The man and his dog turned to leave. "Thanks again. Your quick thinking saved him."

"Oh, I didn't think . . . at all." Nate straightened, watching the pair walk away.

He'd done just as Tilly suggested. He hadn't thought. He'd felt and acted on pure gut instinct. If he hadn't been such a coward, he would have done the same tonight at the party.

Nate could have chosen Bunny over McNulty Events. He could have chosen his love for her over the expectations of Aunt Martha. He *could* have risked his comfortable life and career for the chance at true happiness with the mop-topped menace.

He could have embraced the chaos. But he hadn't.

An idea percolated in the back of his mind—an out-of-character, inappropriate, chaotic idea. A grin tugged at the corners of his mouth.

Would it work? *Could* it? People would say he'd gone off the deep end.

Nate laughed out loud into the cool city night. For the first time in his life, he didn't care what people thought.

He only cared about a blue-eyed woman named Bunny who had thoroughly and completely stolen his heart.

Chapter 25

The next morning, Nate waited anxiously as Bert dragged himself into the conference room. Bert took a long swallow of convenience store coffee then grimaced.

"Rough night?" Nate asked.

"Not as rough as yours."

Nate bristled. "Did you talk to Bunny?"

Bert shook his head. "Not good."

Nate slapped the table. "That's okay. I have a plan."

Bert visibly paused. "Plan?"

Nate leaned forward, his pulse quickening. "Will you help?"

Bert pressed one hand to his mouth, staring at the conference room table for several long seconds.

Nate drummed his fingers impatiently.

"Why should I?" Bert asked.

"Because this will make everything right."

Bert's expression grew nervous, his eyes narrowing. "What kind of plan?"

Nate shook his head. "No." He jumped to his feet and paced the room—from the plants to the water garden and back again. "No more explaining, just doing."

Bert let out an exasperated breath. "Okay. So you heard what Tilly said. That's great." He stared at Nate. "But you can tell me."

"Not until you agree." Nate stood his ground.

"Okay. Then tell me what's up with Melanie."

"It's over."

"Really?" Bert rubbed a hand across his face. "I thought she wanted to—"

"She doesn't."

"And you—"

"Want to be with Bunny." Nate crossed his arms, his heart jackhammering in his chest. "For the rest of my life." He held his palms out, pleading with his friend. "Will you help me?"

"What about Aunt Martha? This firm?"

"Screw them."

Bert blinked. "*Screw them*? After all the years you've fought for this company?"

"I'm a changed man."

"Why didn't you tell us this last night?"

"Why didn't you let me in?"

"Touché." Bert's eyes narrowed, carefully studying Nate. "I'm sworn to secrecy, but she's quitting."

"Courier already delivered her letter." Nate gestured with his hand. "I don't care."

Bert blinked. "You don't care that she's leaving?"

Nate dragged a hand through his hair. "She can't leave if I don't accept the resignation. And if she'd talk to me, I'd tell her she's not fired."

Bert stepped close to Nate, pointing at his hair. "What happened to the twitch that went along with that rat's nest?"

The question stopped Nate short. "Hell." He thought back to the last time he'd had to hold his eyelid steady. He burst out laughing. "Hasn't happened since I first kissed Bunny."

A devilish smirk spread wide across Bert's face.

Nate balled his hands into fists. "Are you in, or out?"

A long silence beat between them.

"In."

Nate clapped his hands on Bert's shoulders. "I knew I could count on you."

Bunny rolled her eyes at the sound of Armand's voice on the phone. "How'd you get my home number?"

"Please," he snorted. "I can get any number I want."

She gagged silently then steadied herself. "What's up?"

"I understand you're in need of employment."

Damn. That was fast. Gossip spread at the speed of light in this city, but this was ridiculous. Be that as it may, she had zero intention of letting Armand know he was right. "I'm not sure where you get your information, but I don't know what you're talking about."

"Bunny, *babe.*" He drew the word into two syllables.

She squeezed her eyes shut. If she concentrated hard enough, maybe she could wish him into cartoon land.

"McNulty Events will belong to me soon," Armand continued. "You could be my star planner."

That got her attention—and not the star planner bologna. Been there. Done that. "What do you mean, McNulty Events will belong to you?"

"Martha's selling." He paused. Bunny could just imagine his expression. "To moi."

"I think you need a new informant, *babe,*" she mocked. "Martha's perfectly happy with Nate running the firm. The Worthington Cup sealed that deal."

"This weekend's events have made headlines, but not the kind Martha wants." He stretched his last word into a hiss.

Bunny flinched. Like she needed a reminder.

"It's only going to get worse."

A nervous shiver trailed down her spine. "Why do you say that?"

"I have my sources."

She frowned. For once Armand sounded as though

he knew what he was talking about. "What kind of sources?"

"Let's just say, the Cup's total failure is guaranteed."

Bunny's blood boiled. She might be suffering from a broken heart, but she'd worked too hard to let Mr. I Love Myself Miller mess up this event. "*What* . . . did . . . you . . . do?"

Armand's evil laugh chilled her straight through. "Call me when you're ready to get back to work."

The line clicked dead. She hung up and lowered her face to her palms. Think, Bunny. *Think.*

The only thing odd—well, odder than usual—that Armand had done had been picking up the dog leashes. Dread tickled her belly. He had been insistent on the leads since day one. Hadn't Nate questioned Armand's interest in purple leads? After all, Kitty had fired Armand over his criticism of the color.

She knew a clue lurked somewhere in that tangled mess of thoughts. She stared at her apartment's eggshell walls. The lack of color made her brain hurt. How could her mother have upended her energy flow like this?

Then it hit her like a ton of bricks.

The paint. The plants. The slippers. Just look at the chaos she'd foisted on Nate. And he'd let her. Okay, not completely without argument, but he'd compromised. He'd embraced her chaos, and she'd done anything but embrace his control. Hell, just look at the mess she'd made of the last forty-eight hours alone. From his car, to the party, to Chardonnay and Chablis prancing right off their purple leashes in their curtain attack.

Oh my.

The leads hadn't worked when she tried them on Chablis and Chardonnay. The dynamic duo had skipped right out of them.

What if Armand had ordered faulty leads on purpose? She glanced at the clock. Ten fifty-five. In one hour and five minutes the festivities would begin. One thousand pooches and their handlers would be demonstrating agility and obedience skills—on their new purple leashes.

Bunny's jaw dropped open. A vision of slimy Saslow, his half-chewed stogy and skin-tight warm-up jacket flashed through her mind. If you were in the market for sabotaged dog leads, he'd definitely be the guy to see.

She dashed for her closet. She had one hour to make it to the Convention Center if she wanted to stop the handlers from using the leads. She loved a bit of chaos, but this would be ridiculous. The time had come for control—and fast.

Tilly pushed open the front door just as Bunny made it to the hallway. "Can't talk now, Til," she hollered. "I need to get to the—"

"Convention Center," Tilly finished. "I know."

Bunny stopped in her tracks, scrutinizing her friend's face. "How did you know that?"

"I keep trying to tell you, I'm touched." She hoisted her arms in the air, grinning.

Bunny frowned.

"Bert called." Tilly closed the door and crossed to where Bunny stood. "Something's going to happen you need to see."

"He knows about the sabotaged leashes?"

Tilly's features scrunched into a confused mess. "No, he needs you to see the press conference." She blinked. "Sabotaged leashes? Boy, you event planners have it all. Glamour. Intrigue. Sabotage."

"Why do I need to be at the press conference?"

"You just do."

Bunny chased the question out of her mind. She didn't have time to think about it, and she planned on being there anyway.

She raced to her closet and yanked open the door. "I need to look as McNulty as possible." She cast a desperate glance at Tilly. "Help me. It's important."

Tilly wrinkled her nose. "I'm in charge of getting you there. If you want to be a suit, that's on you."

"It's time I meet him halfway, Tilly. Please."

One half hour later, Bunny gazed at the finished product in the mirror. The pin-striped gray suit accentuated her figure. She'd sleeked her wavy hair back behind her ears, smoothing it flat. Her ruby-red lips were her only un-McNulty accessory. After all, a girl deserved to have *some* fun while she was saving the day. She turned to face Tilly. "What do you think?"

Tilly nodded at the clock. "I think you're going to be late."

Bunny followed her glance. *Drat.* Eleven thirty-five. Even if she caught a cab, it would take longer than twenty-five minutes to get through midday traffic. Her heart sank. "I'll never make it."

"You've gotta skate." Tilly nodded knowingly.

"Hurrying won't help."

"No." Tilly shook her head. "You've got to skate, *literally*. It's the only way. Let's go."

Five minutes later, Bunny stood on the sidewalk, strapped into Tilly's Rollerblades. "This is insane." She looked down at her feet. "I've gone completely bonkers."

"Sometimes that's a good thing." Tilly slapped her on the back. "Go!"

Bunny took off like a shot, down the sidewalk toward Market Street. It might be too late to save her career with McNulty Events, but she'd be damned if she'd let Armand sabotage things for Nate. No matter what she'd been trying to tell herself since Nate's outburst, Bunny knew she loved him.

As far as she was concerned, skating through Center City, Philadelphia, on a chilly October day was a small price to pay for the man you loved—whether he loved you in return or not.

* * *

Nate waited impatiently backstage as Bert scanned the crowd. "Don't see her." He shot Nate an anxious look. "You've got to get started. Some of these reporters are doing live remotes for their noon broadcasts."

"I've left her fifteen messages." Frustration simmered in Nate's gut. How could she not be here?

"You counted?" Bert rolled his eyes incredulously. "Control boy."

Nate sighed. "At least she knows I want to talk to her."

"You *fired* her, remember? Give her some space." A furrow formed between his pale brows. "You okay?"

Sweat trickled down Nate's back. Heat sizzled in his cheeks. Was it nerves or actual room temperature causing his problem? "Hot in here?"

"No." Amusement mixed with the concern in Bert's eyes.

"I'm suffocating." Nate's nose suddenly tickled and he batted, helplessly, at his face.

"Stop that." Bert grabbed his arm. "You'll mess up your face." Bert looked at the floor, shaking his head. "I can't believe you're doing this." He slapped his knee then looked back at Nate. "I'm proud of you, though. Tell me, will this be a McNulty first?"

"And probably a McNulty last," Nate growled.

Kitty Worthington came through the door, today's safari suit a navy blue. "Sorry I'm late—" Her last word froze on her tongue. She gaped openly at Nate. "What . . . what?" She pointed a shaking finger in his direction.

Did he look that ridiculous? Yes, he guessed he did. *Good.* That's what he was going for. Ridiculous. Out of character. *Creative.* He took satisfaction in rendering Kitty speechless. The plan was working beautifully. Or it would be, if only Bunny would show up.

Kitty began stammering anew. "Why . . . why?"

"Publicity stunt." Bert gripped her elbow, guiding her toward the stage door. "Nate's going to make an opening announcement, then introduce you as master of ceremonies."

Kitty stared back at Nate, eyes wide as saucers, jaw hanging slack.

"Kitty." Bert gave the woman's arm a gentle shake. "Are you clear on the agenda?"

She snapped her mouth shut then pursed her lips. "This wasn't in the plans—"

"No," Bert interrupted. "But it's going to make every news broadcast. You'll see."

"Was it *her* idea?"

Nate winced. Kitty undoubtedly referred to Bunny.

"No." Bert steered Kitty into position, gesturing to Nate. "Nate feels this will restore the Cup's festive tone. You know how the media is. They'll see this and forget all about last night's . . . er . . . activities."

"Dreadful," Kitty murmured. "It's a wonder Chablis wasn't trampled by that Saint Bernard."

Nate bit back a laugh. Would have served the little fleabag right.

"Ready now, on three." Bert pointed to Nate. "One . . . two . . . and three."

Nate stepped onto the stage. Flashes illuminated as he crossed to the podium. A deafening silence fell over the crowd of reporters. A lone person snickered.

What in the hell was he doing? Bert was right. This was insane. He fought the urge to turn and run, forcing himself to walk to the podium. He gripped the microphone, pausing for a beat to calm his thumping pulse. He breathed in for a slow count of four, then out. The tension in his muscles eased, his clarity of purpose returned. Looking like a total idiot was a small price to pay if he could woo Bunny back into his life.

"Good afternoon, ladies and gentleman of the press. Today we celebrate our region's oldest dog show. You're in for a treat. Shall we begin?"

* * *

Bunny careened down the sidewalk, skates humming. "Coming through," she bellowed as a woman backed away from a sidewalk vendor. Too late. Bunny caught the woman's elbow, sending a soft pretzel flying out of her hands.

"Sorry." Normally she'd slow down to apologize and pay, but these were desperate times. If she didn't reach the Convention Center pronto, last night's fiasco would look like amateur hour compared to what might happen today.

Bunny took the turn down Twelfth Street holding her breath. The lunchtime crush of pedestrians assailed her from every direction.

"Lady, watch it!"

"Whoa!"

"Yo!"

Philadelphians might not be the most articulate bunch, but they got their points across. She slammed with a thud into the heavy glass doors of the Convention Center. The security guard looked up from her station, scowling, as Bunny skated in.

"No way, honey. Not in here." The guard waved her hands, clambering around the side of her desk.

Bunny slowed, but kept skating. "It's an emergency. I may already be too late to avert disaster." Her words rushed out in a multisyllabic slur.

The guard frowned, hurrying to match Bunny's stride. "Did you say disaster?"

"Yes."

"Well, no disaster is worth those skates leaving marks on this marble floor." The guard reached for Bunny's arm, but missed.

"What would you call one thousand out-of-control dogs and their pissed-off owners all run amok in your Convention Center? On your watch." Bunny's heart rapped against her ribs. This had to work. There was no time to stop. Not now.

"On *my* watch?" The guard slowed from a full-out run to a trot.

"Yes," Bunny answered over her shoulder.

"I'd call that a disaster." The guard's eyes widened, fear washing across her features. "Honey, you'd better skate like the wind."

"Thank you!" Bunny pushed as hard as she could, knowing she still had the length of two football fields to cover before she reached the arena. She could only hope Nate hadn't done anything stupid, like start the event early.

Nate realized this was the most stupid thing he'd ever done. Damn it to hell. Bunny wasn't even here to see him. All this for nothing. He wanted to prove himself capable of creative thought. Capable of not caring about the opinions of others. And she wasn't here. Of course, he *had* fired her.

He stood to the side as Kitty fielded typical press questions about agility trials, dog breeds, and the show's history. A local PBS reporter stood and introduced himself. "I want to know what the guy in the . . . suit . . . was thinking when he got dressed this morning."

Nate snapped to attention. Kitty watched him expectantly.

"Me, too," a second reporter barked out.

"Same," a third yelled.

Soon the shouts of reporters rang out over top of one another. Kitty tapped the microphone, calling for quiet. "Nate? Perhaps you'd like to address this issue."

Nate swallowed. Why *had* he dressed like this? He stepped toward the microphone, jumbled thoughts battling for position in his brain. What had he been *thinking*?

He'd thought about Bunny, hoping a crazy stunt would win her heart. He'd thought wearing this suit would prove what she meant to him. He'd hoped she'd realize how each chaotic thing she'd done had slowly brought him back to life—out of robot mode, as she and Jeremy both called it.

Suddenly, he knew exactly how to answer the reporter's question. He'd tell the truth.

Bunny skidded to a stop in the hallway just outside the arena. Reporters' voices boomed from inside. What the heck? Things sounded a bit out of control. What if she was too late?

"Nate?" Kitty said. "Perhaps you'd like to address this issue."

What issue? Dogs. Agility. Obedience. The day's events were nothing new.

"Actually, I'm glad you asked." Nate spoke slowly, though Bunny could barely decipher his muffled words. Wasn't he holding the microphone close enough? "You asked what I was thinking when I got dressed this morning. I was thinking about a woman named Bunny Love."

Bunny's breath caught. She tugged one skate off then the other. She pulled the backpack from her shoulder, all the while concentrating on Nate's muffled words.

"I fired her last night."

Bunny winced.

"Because an event she'd planned got a little out of hand."

"That's an understatement," someone called out. Laughter rippled from inside the room.

Okay. She rolled her eyes. She deserved that.

Bunny slipped her shoes from the backpack and stuck her feet into the pumps. She pulled open the door, sneaking into the backstage area. Bert stood facing the stage, unaware of her arrival.

"Can we open the curtain, please?" Nate called out.

Nate held the rest of his thoughts as the large purple staging curtain slid open, revealing hundreds of dogs and their owners, waiting patiently for the agility and obedience trials to begin.

Cameras clicked and videos whirred. Nate beamed at the order with which the arena had been arranged. Bunny had pulled it off. Everything was perfect. Controlled. Organized. He'd been a fool to doubt Bunny's ability.

He gestured to the large area. "There before you are the finest each breed has to offer. Today they will dazzle you with their skills, strength and brains." He refocused on the media representatives gathered before him. "Bunny Love organized today's proceedings. Let's recognize her now."

Nate clapped his hands, smiling as those in the media area and the main arena did the same. "If you found last night's Whine and Dine exciting, wait until you see what's in store for you today."

Applause rang out for a second time.

"If you'd indulge me, I'd like your help in sending a personal message to Miss Love."

The room fell silent. Nate's heart beat so loudly he was sure every microphone in the room transmitted its thumping. He opened his mouth to speak then snapped it shut.

"Nate," Kitty whispered. "Are you all right?"

He met her puzzled gaze then closed his eyes. He pictured Bunny's face, her vivid turquoise eyes and her creamy cheeks. He thought of her wild tangle of hair and smiled.

"Nate." Kitty's whisper grew louder.

He opened his eyes to meet the crowd's expectant stare. Bolstered by the vision of Bunny, he began again. "I was wrong to fire Bunny over what happened last night. She's taught me that sometimes a little chaos is what everyone needs." He laughed. "Believe me. She's shaken things up in my life. She's taught me that embracing crazy is the sanest thing a person can do."

He held his arms in the air and turned in a tight circle. "That's why I stand before you dressed as a Schnauzer. To ask her to forgive me for not standing up for creative chaos."

Bunny could barely believe her ears. *Nate? A Schnauzer? For her?* She fought the urge to shriek for joy, pressing closer and closer to the opening.

Bert pumped his fist in the air.

"What's going on?" Bunny whispered.

His eyes grew huge. "You made it. Did you hear him?"

Bunny watched as Nate shrugged, dressed as a huge furry Schnauzer. Laughter bubbled up from her belly. *Unbelievable.* Her Nate. Her heart pressed against her ribcage, threatening to burst from her chest. "Why a Schnauzer?"

Bert shook his head. "Said it was karma."

Karma? *Nate?* She laughed out loud, savoring the warm joy seeping through her veins.

Sudden loud yapping pulled all eyes from Nate. *Yikes.* Reality check. She'd completely forgotten her mission. "Bert, I think Armand sabotaged the leads."

"Who cares about leads?" Bert hoisted his hand toward her in a high five gesture.

She fought the urge to slap him. "Bert. Pay attention. Faulty leads. Dogs run amok. *Again.* We can celebrate Nate's transformation later."

Bert did a slow head turn, the color draining from

his face. He stepped onto the stage and pointed. "Those purple leads?"

Bunny followed his gaze—and gasped.

Nate willed his feet to move, but his body refused to cooperate. A gaggle of small dogs chased a furry object across the arena floor. Handlers followed, stumbling and tripping, not far behind. The dogs ran free, unencumbered by the leashes that hung limp from their handlers' wrists.

The leashes. *Armand.* That double-crossing event planner from hell. Nate should have known as soon as Bunny told him Armand had offered advice. How could he have been so stupid?

Flashes fired like strobe lights, reporters and camera crews clambering to immortalize the action. Nate pulled the microphone from its stand and ran to the edge of the stage. "Order. Can we have some order, please?"

He watched in horror as a second grouping of dogs broke free. They circled and nipped at the smaller dogs. It was like watching a dozen Lassies corralling sheep. Only these weren't sheep. These were prize-winning, purebred pedigrees, and his firm was going to take the heat—and the fall. He slumped. It was no use yelling. The place had gone to the dogs—literally.

What was it Jimmy had said? *When in doubt, little lady, whistle.* Bunny stepped to the edge of the stage, pressing her fingers to her lips. She blew hard, whistling with all of her might. Ears perked, claws skittered, and heads snapped. "Heel!" she screamed for good measure.

Within moments, every dog but one was in the hands of his or her handler. A wayward Shetland sheepdog had decided to try his paws on the agility course. Judging by the look on his handler's face, the Sheltie was headed for the doghouse.

Nate pulled off the fake Schnauzer head and stared at her, wide-eyed. His damp chestnut hair stood on end. The warmth inside the suit had turned his cheeks crimson. She thought she'd never seen a man—or dog—look so breathtaking. "Nice save." He blew out a breath.

"That's what we call controlled chaos in the feng shui biz." She winked.

Nate closed his eyes and laughed. He raised his gaze to meet hers. Bunny's heart stopped for a full second. *Whew.* The man's eyes exuded serious heat.

"This isn't at all what I had planned." He shook his head, stepping toward her.

"It never is." She shrugged.

His gaze raked over her from head to toe, then back, slowly. Bunny tingled in all the right places. Nothing like being appreciated by the man you loved. "This is a new look for you." He pointed to Bunny's pin-striped suit.

"When in Rome," she quipped. "You like?"

"Mm." He stepped even closer. The heat from his body seared the air between them. "I have to admit I like the just-tumbled-out-of-bed look better."

A hot flush raced up Bunny's neck. She walked toward him, closing the remaining space between them. "Speaking of new looks. Schnauzer?"

He pursed his lips. A devilish glint flashed in his eyes. Bunny's pulse roared into overdrive. "I thought it might help me." His furry shoulders rose for a moment then fell.

"Do what?"

"Convince you to forgive me."

She shook her head. "I deserved to get fired."

"No, you didn't."

He leaned close—so close Bunny could smell the musky scent of his shampoo.

"Last night was chaos." Her words slowed, her

thoughts overwhelmed by the seductive warmth radiating from Nate.

"Controlled chaos." He grinned. "Don't know where I'd be today without it."

Bunny stood silent, not wanting to ruin the moment by saying something stupid.

"Thank you." His brows arched, his handsome features easing into a brilliant smile.

"Thank *me*?" She'd brought this man nothing but mayhem, and he wanted to thank her?

Nate ran his thumb along her jaw, sending hot desire rippling through her.

"I thought I was fired," she whispered.

"Foolish words spoken in the heat of the moment. Crime of passion." He winked. "As they say."

"Passion?"

"Yes. All these new emotions, they're hard for the robot to process." He ran his fingers into her hair, pulling the sleek strands from behind her ears. Bunny's knees wobbled and she struggled to stay upright.

"The robot seems to be doing fine," she murmured.

"He's better now that you're here." Nate traced a finger along her jaw. "There is something you could help him with."

She looked up at him, slowly shaking her head. "What?"

"Love."

The word sent white-hot heat scorching to her heart.

"I love you." Nate lowered his voice. "Think you'd be available to help me explore the possibilities of creative energy?"

"Be the yang to your yin?"

Nate wrapped one arm around her waist, squeezing her close. "Took the words out of my mouth."

Bunny stretched on her tiptoes to plant a soft kiss on Nate's lips. *Zing.* Straight to her core. She sighed deeply. "I love you, Nate."

He waggled his brows, a brilliant smile lighting up his features. "Maybe you can help me out of this Schnauzer suit."

She pressed away from him, holding up a finger. "On one condition."

"Anything."

"Well," she teased. "It's obvious you know nothing about decorum. From now on, I'll have to be in charge of publicity."

"You got it." He winked. "You can be in charge of whatever you want."

Epilogue

Two Months Later

Bunny pulled the potted fern away from the wall. "She's blocking the flow of chi. Anyone can see that."

Nate frowned. Bert bit his lip to hide a grin.

"Don't you think we've gone overboard with the plants?" Nate's features softened, his eyes pleading. "I'm not sure it's a problem of position so much as a problem of number." He gestured to the small jungle in the corner of the conference room. "I think you're out of control."

Bunny clucked her tongue. "Negative energy, Nate."

He blinked. "A little control. That's all I'm asking for."

"No." Bunny crossed her arms and set her chin. Her chest swelled with love for the man, even though he was clueless in the art of feng shui. Oh well, everyone had their faults.

He pointed toward the door. "Maybe the hall would like some chi."

"They stay here." Bunny tapped her foot. "The conference room is perfect just as it is."

"But I—"

She shook her head. "You worry about clients. I'll worry about chi."

Nate turned to Bert. "Help me out here."

Bert's wide grin twisted into a smirk. "Sorry, buddy.

She's right." He slapped Nate on the shoulder. "The place looks great."

"Traitor," Nate grumbled. "I'll be in my office."

"Let me know how you like it." A flush warmed Bunny's cheeks.

Nate's gazed narrowed. "What have you done to my office?"

Bunny shrugged. "Just a few small plants. Your energy won't know what hit it," she teased. "Trust me."

"Trust me," Nate muttered as he stepped into the hall. "How many times has that phrase gotten me into trouble?" He pointed at Bunny, his features relaxing into a lopsided grin. "You've got new employee orientation in five minutes."

Bert chuckled as he followed Nate. "Nice work, Bunny. As usual."

"Thanks."

She adjusted the position of the fern once more, then stepped back to admire her work. A candle glowed on the credenza, infusing the room with the soft scent of vanilla. She closed her eyes, listening to the water trickling through the rock garden. Her muscles relaxed as she blew out a slow breath.

How things had changed.

After apologizing for her role in the leash fiasco, Martha McNulty had given Nate full control of the company. How could she not? The press from The Worthington Cup had sent the number of new accounts through the stratosphere. It wasn't easy to duplicate the news value of one thousand dogs run amok, but the staff did their best.

Besides, Martha no longer had time to worry about McNulty Events or Nate. She'd busied herself resuming her career as an artist, one local gallery show under her belt and more in the works. To top it all off, she'd agreed to design a line of cards for the Loves' burgeoning enterprise.

John had fully embraced the greeting card business, converting his study into an office for Alexandra. They'd painted it eggshell, of course. Bunny shuddered. Their greeting cards had been picked up by several boutiques in Philadelphia and Florida. At last report, John's golf designs were among the leading sellers.

The rest of The Worthington Cup had gone off without a hitch. The official Best in Show title had gone to Poindexter, much to the amazement of Mitsi and Timothy Goodloe, who were now in counseling with Jimmy Monroe. Turned out Jimmy held certification as a Life Coach in addition to being a feng shui expert.

The popular votes for show favorite had gone to Nate. Jeremy had posted a still shot on the Web site of the Schnauzer suit, and he'd won by a landslide. Seemed people were suckers for a happy ending. The trophy sat in a place of prominence in Nate's office—right next to his lucky bamboo.

As for Armand, well, he'd confessed to taking Martha's instructions a bit too far by sabotaging the show and letting a rabbit loose in the arena. Bunny rolled her eyes at the memory. Not even Mr. Smooth Miller could have gotten away with that one.

Thurston Monroe had been thrilled when Bunny moved out of her condo and into Nate's. He hadn't been happy, however, when she'd sublet to a street mime. According to Tilly, there had been more than a few nonverbal confrontations in the lobby.

As for Melanie, she'd happily followed her heart to Las Vegas. While breaking into the showgirl circuit had proven more difficult than anticipated, her last letter mentioned a new job as the host of a cable access cooking show. According to Nate, Melanie wouldn't know how to open a can of soup.

Ah well. Time would tell.

Bert popped his head into the room. "You ready?"

"Sure." Bunny followed him down the maroon hall

to a walk-in storage closet. Four new event planners stood waiting, all with one thing in common. They frowned.

"Good morning." Bunny gave the group her most welcoming smile and planted her fists on her hips. "My name is Beatrice McNulty, but you may call me Bunny." She stepped forward, shaking each employee's hand. "You must be wondering why we're starting your orientation in a closet."

She tipped her head toward a wall of shelves lined with singing hamsters, candles, small plants, Slinkies, and shoe boxes. "On these shelves you will find what we consider the most important perk here at McNulty." She pulled down a box and hugged it to her chest. "Creative freedom."

Bunny removed the lid and plucked one pink slipper from inside, button eyes gleaming, fluffy ears standing at attention.

One young man's jaw fell open. "Bunny sli—"

Bunny held up a hand. "I'm sure this is not what you're used to, but at this firm we believe in nurturing positive chi—creative energy."

Nate appeared in the doorway. Bunny caught his eye and winked.

"*Controlled* creative energy," she continued.

"After all"—Nate stepped into the room, grinning from ear to ear—"a little feng shui never hurt anyone."

About the Author

After a career spent spinning words for clients ranging from corporate CEOs to talking fruits and vegetables, Kathleen Long now finds great joy spinning a world of fictional characters, places, and plots. She shares her life with her husband, Dan, and their neurotic Sheltie, dividing her time between suburban Philadelphia and the New Jersey seashore. There she can often be found—hands on keyboard, bare toes in sand—lost in thought and time. After all, life doesn't get much better than that. Please visit Kathleen at www.kathleenlong.com.

Contemporary Romance By
Kasey Michaels